LADY ROSE AND MR. STUART

LADY ROSE AND MR. STUART

Real Whisky Has No "e" Series - Volume 1

John Legget Jones

Publisher's note: This is a work of fiction. Names, characters, places, and incidents either are the product of the author's imagination or are used fictitiously. Any resemblance to actual events, locales, or persons, living or dead, is entirely coincidental.

Author's note: Whisky in Scotland is spelled without the 'e'. That convention is used by the English and Scottish characters. Author's note: The riddle in Chapter 26 is not original. The author of the riddle is unknown.

Edited, formatted, and interior design by Kristen Corrects, Inc.
Cover art design by Laura Duffy - Laura Duffy Design
Cover pictures - Givaga/Shutterstock.com
Cover images used under license from Shutterstock.com
Photoshop work done by Justin Wells

First edition published 2017

ISBN-13: 9780997329650
ISBN-10: 0997329653

CHAPTER 1

1901 – ABERLOUR, SCOTLAND

———

ACCORDING TO LEGEND, GOD GAVE the Scots the task of making whisky so man could face his problems with a smile. They take this heavenly responsibility seriously and are fiercely proud of what they make. To the Scots, only *they* make real whisky and real whisky has no "e."

To help in this heavenly task, the Whisky Angel guides the Scots in making whisky and watches over them. Every hundred years or so, the angel will bless someone with the talent to create whisky irresistible to men and angels. People say the Whisky Angel kissed Colin Stuart at birth. The story had to be true because no one could make whisky better than Colin. Born in Aberlour, Scotland in 1875 to a family who had been making whisky for five generations, whisky was in his blood.

Making whisky is a respected profession in Scotland, and the master distiller is a revered man. Few men rise to this lofty position, but Colin Stuart did—becoming the youngest master distiller in Scottish history.

Colin worked for the GlenWilliams distillery located in the village of Aberlour, in the heart of the Scottish whisky Speyside region. The Williams family owned the seventy-five-year-old business. Lord Patrick Williams, Earl of Brittany, the beloved patriarch of the family cared deeply about his family's long tradition of making premium whisky and providing jobs for hundreds of people. His son, Lord Richard Williams, Viscount of Whiten, preferred the genteel atmosphere of London life. He didn't care about his family's tradition of making whisky or the welfare of the people at the distillery. He only cared for money and pleasure.

Colin started work at the distillery when he was twelve. On his first day, Lord Patrick recognized there was something special about him and so he began to watch over him. At fifteen, Lord Patrick sent Colin to Scotland's premier distillery school where he received formal training on how to make whisky. A skinny kid with a mop of brown hair had left for school, however, three years later, he returned as a tall, handsome young man with a quick smile and a confident, engaging manner. He did well at the distillery, got along with everyone, and moved up quickly. He became the assistant master distiller at twenty.

Lord Patrick retired to South Africa in 1895 and turned the business over to his twenty-five-year-old son, Richard. Days after his father left, Richard hired a master distiller to run the distillery and moved to London. He bought an expensive estate, hired a large staff, entertained often, and soon ran out of money. Richard started to squeeze as much as he could from the distillery to pay for his lavish London lifestyle.

Richard cut costs everywhere at the distillery. He reduced maintenance and bought cheaper, low quality ingredients. A premium whisky takes years to suitably age and it is expensive to do. Desperate for money, Richard forced his master distiller to doctor the whisky. The whisky look aged but didn't taste like it should. Customers soon decided Williams Whisky was no longer a premium whisky and wouldn't pay the higher price.

The business started to rapidly deteriorate and Colin knew the distillery's future was bleak. In the spring of 1900, feeling desperate, he sent Lord Patrick a letter urging him to return home. A month later, Lord Patrick made an unannounced visit and found an absentee owner, bad whisky, and run-down facilities. He acted decisively to turn things around. He couldn't fire his son, but he did fire the master distiller and replaced him with twenty-five-year-old Colin.

Lord Patrick reduced the money Richard took from the business, invested his own money, and repaired the distillery. He put Richard on a strict budget which prevented him from living in London, and forced him to return to Aberlour. Richard felt Colin, by writing to Lord Patrick, was responsible for depriving him of his cherished London lifestyle.

During Richard's five-year reign, Colin did things he felt were necessary to keep the business going: including secretly trading whisky to buy better ingredients. He tried to age the whisky longer by changing dates on the barrels and hiding whisky away from the distillery. These actions could have gotten him fired or even arrested. The guilt haunted him but he felt he had no other choice if the business were to survive.

Soon after Lord Patrick's return, Colin confessed he had hidden hundreds of barrels of whisky and had been secretly nurturing them. This hidden whisky allowed the company to return to the premium market. When Richard learned of this, he wanted Colin fired for disloyalty. However, Lord Patrick commended Colin publicly for his actions. The already strained relationship between Colin and Richard spiraled downward.

Colin wanted to change the whisky's name from Williams Whisky to GlenWilliams Whisky, because he felt Williams Whisky had developed the reputation of being cheap and of poor quality. Richard was adamant in protesting the change. Lord Patrick, Richard, and Colin argued about the change for weeks, but Lord Patrick finally agreed with Colin. Outraged because his father sided with a commoner, Richard didn't talk to him for weeks.

Under Colin's leadership, the business turned around. The whisky quality improved dramatically, sales increased, and profits soared. Richard couldn't enjoy the achievement because he was jealous of Colin's success. A bitter hatred began to brew.

CHAPTER 2

JUNE 2, 1906 – DUKE OF BACKSHIRE'S COUNTRY ESTATE, NORTH OF LONDON

———◆———

BARONESS ROSE CAVENDISH AND HER lady's maid, Edith Kelsey, arrived midafternoon for a party hosted by Lucas Mawbray, Duke of Backshire and first cousin of King Edward. The duke and duchess welcomed her warmly then she retired to her room to rest and prepare for dinner. Two hours after arriving, Lady Rose was sitting on a chaise lounge and had made little progress getting ready.

Edith stood next to her with a hairbrush. "My lady, dinner will be announced in thirty minutes; we must hurry."

"I don't want to go," Rose moaned in a quiet and tired voice as she laid back on the lounge.

"You haven't been sleeping well since the anniversary of Thomas' death last week. It has been four years now but it still seems like yesterday."

Covering her face with her hands, Rose sobbed, "I miss him so."

"I know you do," Edith patted Rose's arm to comfort her. "I'm so glad you have Mia."

Her sobs subsided. "Yes, I would be lost without her."

"She's so pretty. She looks so much like you."

Rose sniffled. "I'm blessed to have her. Other than my mother, I'm closer to her than anyone." She sighed. "I should have stayed home with her. I'm so tired of these endless parties. Tonight's dinner will be another in a long string of elegant yet boring affairs. I received an invitation because I'm a young, titled, and rich widow. I'm the blue-ribbon milk cow at the county fair—someone to be paraded around and auctioned off to the highest bidder."

"Madam, please don't think that way. You're absolutely beautiful and a prize for any man."

Rose shook her head. "I don't feel like a prize. Men don't want to marry a woman who has a child. They want me, my title and my money, but not Mia. Several men asked when I would be sending her to boarding school. They assumed I should be willing to give up my child to be with them."

"Madam, it's common to send children to boarding schools. You shouldn't be surprised an eligible gentleman would ask such a question."

"To me those men are absolute fools! Mia is a delightful little girl. They should get to know her, but no! Ship the child off to boarding school is their answer! You remember Lord Richard Williams?"

Edith nodded. "Yes, my cousin is his valet. I met him; he is quite a handsome man."

"He is handsome, but he asked me if I was planning to send Mia away." She scoffed. "I was interested in him until he asked me such an ignorant question." A distant gaze came over her face. "Somewhere there is a man who will appreciate us. A man like my Thomas will be hard to find."

"I remember you telling me about the letters Thomas wrote you. He wrote that your emerald green eyes were the color of the English meadows, your figure was the envy of every Greek goddess and your hair was the color of fine gold."

Rose looked up at her. "Yes, I loved his letters. He intrigued me from the first minute I met him at the Harvest Ball. There was no need for a long courtship. I fell in love with him quickly."

"I remember," Edith acknowledged. "I thought you were moving much too fast yet he was perfect for you."

"At dinner, the duke's single and titled son, Robert, will be there. He is absolutely the plainest man I have ever met. There isn't one remarkable thing about him."

"You shouldn't judge him solely by his looks."

Rose sat up and confessed, "This sounds awful, but I don't want to spend my life with a plain, unattractive man just to say I have a husband. There is something else about Robert. The man has never worked a day in his life. He has spent his entire life relaxing or hunting. He has recently returned from a safari. During dinner, all he will talk about is the hunting trip. I don't want to hear about it. Now, if the rhino or lion had a gun and could shoot back, *that* I would want to hear about."

Edith chuckled. "Madam, please keep an open mind. Maybe this trip changed him in some positive way."

"From what I hear, his father is tired of paying for his expensive hunting trips. He has told him to marry and move out. I'm here because he needs a wife."

Edith urged her, "We should hurry so you aren't late."

"Yes, I cannot miss another boring hunting story," Rose said sarcastically.

Edith brushed Rose's hair and helped her get ready for dinner. Meeting the social norms of the day, which was over-dressing for every occasion, Rose was wearing an expensive, champagne-colored Parisian evening gown complimented with a breathtaking yellow diamond necklace. Once she was ready, she was stunning. Rose was thirty but looked much younger.

Rose had no problem attracting men—her problem was finding one who interested her. The smooth, socially skilled, typical London gentleman didn't appeal to her. Her late husband, Baron Thomas Cavendish, was a businessman who worked for a living and barely tolerated the aristocrats who didn't. His family was in the shipping business and owned considerable farmland. Thomas' father insisted he work in the business, so each summer as he grew up, he worked for his father. He inherited the business and had successfully expanded it.

Thomas died tragically at thirty-five when his ship wrecked on the North African coast during a terrible storm. His estate passed to Rose, and with the money and property inherited from her father, she became a wealthy widow.

The dinner went exactly as Rose expected. Lady Mawbray had Rose sit across from her son. Robert bragged throughout the dinner about his recent hunting trip and the animals he shot. He spoke at length about the tiniest mundane details of the trip which no one cared about. Not once did he talk to Rose but he spoke at her often. The insufferable evening dragged on until a conversation about America caught her ear.

Lady Ruth Davis, a young woman from London sat next to her and announced when Robert paused in his long story, "I'll be leaving for America soon. After some time in New York, I'll take a train to Chicago. I'm looking forward to the trip."

Rose inquired, "Is there a reason you're traveling to Chicago?"

"Yes, there is an International Art Exposition being held there. Art from across the world will be on display."

"That sounds interesting!" exclaimed Rose.

"It's billed as the largest impressionist art exposition ever held. Rose, I think you would enjoy it. You should consider attending."

"I'll give it some thought." Rose thought this could be what she needed—a marvelous adventure to America.

The dinner droned on for another hour. Before they retired to the parlor for brandy and more hunting stories, Rose told Lady Mawbray she had a headache, which she did not. She retreated to the safety of her bedroom.

CHAPTER 3

JUNE 9, 1906 - LONDON

———◆———

SIX YEARS AFTER COLIN BECAME master distiller, Lord Patrick decided to enter their whisky into the Royal Distiller Association's Gold Medal contest. This annual contest determined the country's best single malt whisky. The coveted gold medal meant worldwide recognition for the winner. The Association, a powerful group, always had one member of the royal family on the board. George, Prince of Wales, had been on the board for the past four years and he always presented the gold medal.

Lord Patrick and Colin traveled to London the day before the ceremony and brought their whisky for judging. The awards banquet was in a ballroom at one of London's finest hotels, The Savoy, where Lord Patrick and Colin arrived at six o'clock. It was customary to sample the competitors' whiskies before the ceremony with each distiller having a table to display their products. As they were visiting each table and tasting the whiskies, they bumped into Richard.

Lord Patrick confessed, "Richard, I didn't know you were coming."

Richard aimed his comments at Colin. "We have spent a fortune improving a product I always thought was fine as it was. I wanted to see if our efforts were paying off."

Colin looked at him, puffed out his chest and defended his efforts, "I nursed this whisky for eight years. It's a superior whisky!"

Lord Patrick patted Colin on the back. "I agree and the judges will decide this whisky is truly magnificent."

"We'll see. We could have sold Colin's hidden whisky years ago, and already had the money in our pockets," Richard replied sarcastically.

Annoyed, Lord Patrick exclaimed, "Enough of that nonsense! Colin acted to save the business and I am glad he did. Your feelings about premium whisky is well known. I want us to be known for having the best product."

"I would rather be known for having the fattest wallet. I'll see you at dinner." Richard replied before walking away.

"He's like his mother," Lord Patrick whispered. "She was a perfect wife except she never went past a store without wanting to stop and buy something. No matter how much money I gave her, she always needed more. My boy will die a pauper unless you keep making our whisky. You must promise to keep making it for me."

Colin nodded. "I will, sir."

"I wish I had not sent him away to boarding school. He has never appreciated what it takes to work hard." Lord Patrick put his hand on Colin's shoulder. "I remember the day I saw you for the first time. You were in the barley room, crawling around the floor with a tin bucket. I asked what you were doing and you said you were getting the bugs and twigs out. You said only pure water and golden barley should be in our product. You knew what was important to make whisky."

Colin added, "I only knew what my father and grandfather told me. The distillery school, which you so generously paid for, taught me how to make the best whisky. Thank you again for sending me!"

Lord Patrick clapped him on the shoulder. "Think nothing of it. I'm the beneficiary of all your hard work."

They continued their tour sampling the whiskies and approached the McGraw Distillery table. Lord Patrick suggested, "Let's hurry past before Baron McGraw sees me."

It was too late; he was already walking up to them. The man in his late sixties sported long gray hair, a full gray beard, a large belly and wore a colorful kilt. He had clearly been sampling the whisky. He bellowed, "Lord Williams, good evening to you!" He ignored Colin.

"Good evening, Lord McGraw," replied Lord Patrick with scorn in his voice. He disliked Baron McGraw because he was a braggart and because his whisky had won the gold medal for the past five years.

The baron boasted, "You must sample this year's gold medal winning whisky. You have never had superior whisky. I'll get you a large glass so you can truly enjoy it."

Lord Patrick's face hardened. "I wouldn't drink that swill of yours if it was the last drop of whisky in England. I would rather drink two-week-old beer."

The baron mocked surprise and put his hand over his heart. "You hurt me sir, however, let me remind you Prince George has had McGraw whisky in his liquor cabinet for the past five years."

"Having it and drinking it are two different things. I heard he uses it as liniment for his horse's arthritis. I'm sure he has been waiting for our GlenWilliams Heritage Whisky. The prince will take it home with him tonight when we win the medal," boasted Lord Patrick.

"You sound mighty sure of yourself. My master distiller has been making our whisky for forty years." He pointed his stubby finger at Colin and with a tone of condemnation uttered, "Yours only recently started wearing long pants."

"Everyone knows the Whisky Angel kissed this young man and gave him his talent. His whisky is so divine we lose a barrel every night because the angels stop in to relish what is truly God's nectar."

The baron huffed, "What a lie that is! We will see how you do later tonight."

As they walked away, Lord Patrick whispered to Colin, "When we win tonight, I'll send a bottle to him with a note saying the man in the short pants wanted you to have this." They laughed and continued their tour of the tables.

After an hour of sampling, the mood in the room was festive. Several men had forgotten the rule to sample only a tiny amount of the whisky and were drunk.

The ceremony began after dinner with several minor awards. The GlenWilliams distillery won an award for one of its younger whisky brands. Colin, as the master distiller, accepted it.

The final award was the gold medal for the best single malt whisky. Ten distilleries were competing for it, however, most people expected the McGraw Distillery would win again. Colin was nervous, he wiped his sweaty palms on his pants. Winning the award would provide the distillery worldwide publicity and would validate all the hard work he had done.

Prince George stood at the podium to give the award. He smiled as the head judge handed him an envelope and the gold medal. "Ladies and gentlemen," the prince began, "as you know, the whisky industry is critical to our country's economy. It provides thousands of jobs and our products are famous around the world. Not to mention, drinking our whisky is the only thing that allows me to work with my father."

The crowd roared with laughter and applause.

"It's my absolute pleasure to announce this year's award winner. The best single malt whisky is…." He opened the envelope, smiled, and announced, "The GlenWilliams Heritage Whisky."

The crowd applauded. Lord Patrick winked and smiled at Colin. Colin started to rise to accept the award but Richard stood first. With his usual cockiness and over-the-top confidence, he strutted up to the prince.

Richard was every inch the English gentleman. He was thirty-five, slim, average height, handsome with curly black hair and blue eyes. His impeccable clothes and demeanor reflected his years of social grooming. He always knew what to do and say in every social situation. He acknowledged the prince graciously with a small bow. The prince reached out and they shook hands. Prince George put the gold medal around Richard's neck.

Richard turned to the crowd. "Thank you, Your Royal Highness and the Association, for this prestigious award. I have worked long and hard to make our whisky the best in the industry. I'm proud of this accomplishment."

The crowd stood and roared its applause. Colin stayed seated, silent and unmoving. It was no surprise to him that Richard would take all the credit.

The tradition was for the prince to taste the winning whisky. The crowd started moving about the room. Lord Patrick saw Colin was glum and still in his chair. He pulled Colin up and they approached Prince George and Richard.

"Prince George," Lord Patrick began, "may I introduce Colin, our master distiller. He is responsible for us winning the award."

The astonished prince opened his mouth to speak, however, Richard interrupted him. "Let's sample some of our award-winning whisky, shall we?"

He led the prince, Colin, and Lord Patrick to sample their whisky. Lord Patrick glowed with pride as they drank it.

After the prince and Richard left, Lord Patrick took Colin aside. "I'm sorry Richard accepted the award and took all the credit. It should have been you. The tradition is the master distiller accepts all awards."

"There's no need for an apology. He is an owner."

"Yes, but our success is because of you. You are only thirty-one years old and no one has ever won the gold medal so young. You are truly remarkable!"

"Thank you for your kind comment, but without your support and money, we wouldn't have been successful."

"Colin," Lord Patrick began, "I want to show you my appreciation. I spoke to Richard about this last week. You will receive ownership in the distillery. My solicitor finished the paperwork and we will sign it when we return home. Every year we are profitable, we will increase your share."

Surprised, Colin stared at Lord Patrick, "Thank you, you are so kind to me!"

"You deserve it. Now take a walk around the room as the best master distiller in Scotland and as an owner. There are a few people I need to talk to."

Colin couldn't stop smiling as he strolled around. Everyone congratulated him on the award.

A dignified man in his sixties with white hair and a big smile approached Colin. "Mr. Stuart, my name is Charles Jones. I want to congratulate you on your award."

"Thank you! It's a pleasure to meet you. Your accent is American is it not. What brings you here?"

"I own a distillery in America. I'm here to learn how to make better whiskey."

"Of course, Jones Distillery—I have heard of your whisky though I haven't tried it."

"I'll save you the trouble. My whiskey is rotgut compared to yours. Yours is the best I have ever tasted. You're an absolute artist!" Mr. Jones patted Colin on the shoulder.

Colin beamed.

"Let me get to why I wanted to talk to you." Mr. Jones took a step closer. "I need a master distiller and I came to England to find one. I know your history and accomplishments. I want to talk to you about coming to America."

"I'm flattered, but I'm perfectly happy at GlenWilliams. My family has worked there for five generations."

The man nodded. "I understand, it would be hard to make a change although people do it all the time."

"I could never see that happening," commented Colin.

"Never is a long time. I would bring you in as an equal partner."

Colin grinned. "You Americans are bold in your proposals, aren't you?"

"I need to make sure I get your attention. In addition, I would double whatever salary you're making now. I'm getting older and I don't have the skill or the energy to make my whiskey the way I want it to be. I need someone like you. You're my first choice and the gold medal confirms it."

Colin tilted his head. "How did you hear about me?"

"Everyone in the whiskey business knows you turned around the GlenWilliams distillery. Richard nearly ran the business into the ground but you saved it."

"It was Lord Patrick who made it happen."

Mr. Jones nodded. "He's an honorable man but you did it. Once Lord Patrick passes—and I hope that isn't for many years to come—his idiot son will bleed the business dry again. Unless you're a full partner, you won't be able to prevent it. I'm offering you a chance of a lifetime." He reached into his coat. "Here is my card and I am staying at the York. If I don't hear from you in a week, I'll go with my second choice."

"I'll consider your offer."

Mr. Jones was disappointed Colin didn't show much interest. He decided to try another approach. "Have you ever been to America?"

Colin shook his head.

"Here is your opportunity! I'll pay all your expenses to come and see us. You will travel first class and if you don't like what you find, you can back out."

Colin replied more optimistically, "I want to visit there and your offer is indeed generous. I'll consider it and let you know soon."

"I look forward to talking to you."

They shook hands and Colin watched him walk away. He thought about the opportunity and the evening's events. It had been quite a day and one he would never forget.

CHAPTER 4

June 11, 1906 – Aberlour, Scotland

————

Colin was having breakfast at his home and reading a London paper. He lived in the master's quarters, which was a fine, two-story stone house on the distillery grounds. He had three servants and a cook provided by the distillery. For a commoner, Colin had an enviable life.

An advertisement for a trip to an art exposition in Chicago, caught his eye. The trip included berths on the luxury liner *R.M.S. Lucania* to New York and train tickets to Chicago. What an adventure that would be! He hadn't taken any time off in years and he would love to go. Mr. Jones and his offer swirled in his head. He could see Jones Distillery and the art exposition. He decided he would talk to Lord Patrick about taking some time off.

Colin arrived at the distillery and at the office door, a workman wearing a black armband was putting up a black bunting. He saw Colin approach.

"Good morning to you, Mr. Stuart. It certainly is a sad, sad day for us."

"I'm sorry, what do you mean?"

"Lord Patrick died last night."

Colin felt what seemed like a lightning bolt pass through his body. "No!" He found a chair and sat.

The worker followed him and added, "We received a telegram from London this morning." The worker noted, "Mr. Stuart, you look ill. Should I get someone to help you?"

In a stunned voice, Colin answered weakly, "No, I'll be fine. Lord Patrick and I were together in London on Saturday. This is so sudden."

"I hope things don't change here now that he is gone."

Colin put his hands over his face and said softly, "So do I."

The funeral was three days later. Hundreds of people from across the country including members of the royal family attended.

After the funeral, Colin received a note from Richard requesting a meeting the next morning. Colin arrived at Richard's estate at nine o'clock sharp and the butler led him to Richard's library. Richard sat at his desk and didn't rise to receive him.

Richard offered him a cold stare. "With my father passing, there will be some changes. I'm replacing you as the master distiller. You may stay on as assistant master distiller at a lower salary. I expect you to continue to work as you are now until I find a replacement, which may take some time."

Colin was shocked. "Richard—"

"I'm now the Earl of Brittany," Richard interrupted. "You will address me as 'my lord' from now on."

Colin paused and took a deep breath to calm down. "My lord your father told me I would become an owner in the distillery."

Richard sneered, "Why would my father give ownership to you?"

"He told me he talked to you about it."

"He never mentioned a word to me."

"Please call his solicitor. Lord Patrick told me the legal papers were completed."

Richard exclaimed, "I will not! It's insulting to me that you think we would be partners in any business. You're a commoner! There is nothing distinctive about you other than my father, for some reason, liked you. If you want to keep your job, you will never again mention this to me or to anyone else. Maybe I'll allow you to be the master distiller again if you accept who is the boss. Do you understand me?"

Colin stayed silent.

"Did you hear me?" Richard demanded.

Colin stared at him and answered quietly, "Yes."

"You will move from the master's quarters to the bachelor's quarters. You must vacate immediately. Do you understand?"

Colin nodded.

Richard said, "Now to business, since we won the award, we received a lot of orders. I hear we cannot fill the orders for the Heritage Whisky, is that true?"

"Yes."

"I want you to open up barrels from other years and fill the orders."

"Sir, we can't do that."

"Why?"

"It will not look or taste the same."

"I don't care. Color it, blend it, do what you have to but fill the orders now!"

Colin stood there and couldn't believe it was happening again. He knew what Richard would do—he would starve the distillery of money as he did before, and Colin's life would be miserable again.

"Did you understand me?" asked Richard.

"Yes."

"I have nothing else. You're dismissed."

Colin's mind was spinning and he thought of the American's offer. "My lord, I have one other thing. I have distillery business in London and I will be gone for a few days."

"Make sure we fill the orders before you go."

"I will."

Colin left the estate, fuming as he marched to the office. He got to the distillery and instructed the foreman how to fill the orders. The foreman couldn't believe what he heard and angrily questioned Colin about it. Colin told him it was an order from Lord Richard. Realizing what was happening, the foreman reluctantly agreed to do it.

Colin left the office and rushed home. He got Mr. Jones' business card, packed a bag, and left for the train station.

At the station, he telegraphed Mr. Jones requesting a meeting and informing him he would be staying at the York. Colin took the first train to London, arriving late. Waiting for him at the hotel was a letter from Mr. Jones, confirming a breakfast meeting.

The next morning, Colin arrived for breakfast and Mr. Jones was already waiting there.

Mr. Jones smiled when he saw him and stood. "It's excellent to see you again."

"You too."

They shook hands.

"I'm sorry to hear of the passing of Lord Patrick. He was a fine man."

Colin nodded. "Yes, he was. I miss him already."

"I'm sure you do."

They sat next to each other. Mr. Jones began, "Have you made a decision?"

"I'm close, however, I need more information."

"Of course."

"Let me start with some basic questions," Colin began. "Where is your distillery?"

"Lake Geneva, Wisconsin, which is northwest of Chicago. It's a scenic and peaceful area. Many of the rich and famous of Chicago have summer homes there."

"Where do you live?"

"I own homes in Lake Geneva, Chicago, and New York City."

"Where would you want me to live?"

"There is a fine home and servants for you near the distillery in Lake Geneva."

For the next two hours, Colin and Mr. Jones talked. Mr. Jones candidly assessed his business. The distillery was profitable but not growing and the whiskey quality was poor. Colin would have full control to make whatever changes he deemed necessary. Colin also told Mr. Jones what happened to him. Shocked by Richard's stupidity, Mr. Jones said when the distillery failed in the future, Richard would have to take the blame. The conversation went well, Colin felt comfortable with the situation and he accepted Mr. Jones' offer.

On Monday morning, Colin and Mr. Jones met with a London solicitor who composed a contract. On Tuesday evening, they had dinner and signed the document. Colin agreed to travel with Mr. Jones to America immediately.

Mr. Jones had received an invitation to a charity event at the American Embassy on Saturday. He asked Colin to attend with him. They spent the rest of the week enjoying London together.

CHAPTER 5

JUNE 11, 1906 – COUNTESS WINSTON'S COUNTRY ESTATE, NORTH OF LONDON

———◆———

UPON RETURNING TO LONDON FROM Lord Mawbray's party, Rose started planning her trip to America. She booked a first-class passage for her, Mia, her lady's maid Edith, and Mia's governess Elizabeth on the *R.M.S. Lucania* as well as first-class hotels in New York and Chicago. She met with her business manager for the shipping company and the business manager for her properties to make sure they had everything they needed during her absence.

Rose sent a letter to her mother, Countess Louise Winston, about the trip when she first started planning it and asked if she would like to go. The countess replied she thought it was an excellent idea for Rose to get away for a while, but she declined the invitation. She asked Rose and Mia to visit her before the trip.

Countess Winston was a dignified, aristocratic, seventy-year-old widow with a sharp tongue and a keen mind. Her husband, Frederick Winston, Earl of Rossford, died several years prior. One of the largest landowners in England, she owned thousands of acres of some of the richest farmland. Rose was now her only child as her son, William, an officer in the British Army, died in action during the Sudan Campaign.

Rose and her mother were always close and grew closer since the deaths of Rose's father, her brother, and her husband. Rose leaned on her mother heavily after Thomas died. They confided everything to each other.

Mia loved her grandmummy's estate and she considered it a second home. The countess had a home in London, but she lived primarily on a large country estate west of London with horses, cows, sheep, and other domestic animals plus many dogs and cats. When Mia visited, she would get up early and explore the estate all day. The countess always had to send servants to find her for lunch and dinner.

Rose and Mia arrived at the country estate mid-morning. It was a clear, warm day, and Louise was in the garden having tea. She sat in a white lounge chair next to a table with a formal tea setting. Mia jumped from the carriage almost before it stopped and ran to the garden with Rose following.

Mia hugged her grandmother who observed, "Mia, you are growing like a weed yet you are prettier than the finest flower in my garden. Your green eyes and golden hair are very much like your mother's."

"Thank you, Grandmummy; you look so pretty. I love your yellow dress."

Rose now in hearing distance chimed in, "Good morning, Mother. I agree with Mia; it's lovely."

"Good morning to you my dear and thank you both! It's a glorious morning, isn't it?"

Rose replied, "It is. The flowers in your garden are bursting with color."

"I love this time of year. Please sit with me. Would you two like tea?"

"Yes please. We left rather early and I would love a cup."

Rose kissed her mother on her cheek then sat, but Mia remained standing and was fidgeting.

"Mummy, may I go to the stables, please?"

Frowning, Rose answered, "You should have tea with us like a proper young lady."

"Mummy, please, I don't want tea. I want to see the animals."

The countess interrupted, "Let her go. She won't be able to sit still until she sees all her animal friends."

Mia begged, "Mummy, please."

"Alright, but you must stay clean. No climbing fences or trees, no riding any animals, and stay away from the lake."

Mia said in an impatient tone, "Yes, Mummy."

Rose kissed her on the head and Mia took off running.

Louise commented, "You know she will be covered in filth when she comes back."

Rose sighed. "Yes, I packed her pretty clothes for later. I hope she doesn't get muddy. Remember when she fell into the lake?"

The countess chuckled. "Oh yes, I'll never forget it."

"She had green moss and mud all over her."

They laughed.

The countess smiled. "Every day she looks more like you."

"I know. Everyone tells me that. At times, she can be so mature and carry on adult conversations, but there are times when she still acts like the nine-year-old she is."

"You were the same. You were always much more mature than your friends."

Rose poured them tea.

"My dear, are you ready for your trip to America?"

"Yes. Are you sure you don't want to go with us?"

"No, I've been to America and I loved it. There's so much to see and do. I don't want you to have to drag your old mother around."

"I wish you would go. I enjoy traveling with you."

"You go and have a grand adventure." Louise added, "I'm sure Mia will enjoy it."

"I'm sure she will. She talks about it constantly."

"So how was the dinner with the Mawbrays?" Louise asked over her cup.

Rose raised her eyebrows and inquired, "How did you hear about the dinner? Have you been conspiring with Lady Mawbray?"

"I did speak to her."

"Mother, I told you I have no interest in her son."

"Why not?"

Disgusted, Rose shook her head and responded, "Robert Mawbray is plain, boring and has no interests other than hunting, drinking, and smoking cigars."

Louise's eyebrows rose. "He is a titled gentleman who will receive a large estate in the future. His estate, the land from Thomas, along with the land you received from your father and eventually my property, you will become the largest landowner in England."

"Father's generous gift and Thomas' estate have made me a rich woman. Money isn't an issue for me."

"In this world, land is the only sure thing. Ships sink, houses burn, paper money and coins lose value, but land is forever. More land means more security. If you marry Robert, you would be providing security for our family for generations to come."

"I could never see myself marrying him."

"Rose, you had your life's love. Marry next for title and security."

"I don't want to marry without love."

"Many women marry for title and security."

"I would rather be alone," stated Rose.

"You shouldn't judge Robert too quickly," her mother said. "You should get to know him better. I understand many women are interested in him."

Skeptical, Rose asked, "Who exactly?"

Louise stammered, "His mother didn't tell me the names but there are several."

"I find it hard to believe. I haven't heard a woman say one admirable thing about him other than he's titled and his father has land."

"To most women that is enough."

"Not for me."

Louise shook her head. "I think you're passing up an opportunity."

"I don't think so."

They spent the morning catching up and talking about the trip. At mid-day, Rose sent a servant to find Mia. As they expected, she returned as dirty as the animals she had petted, hugged, or rode. Rose and Mia stayed the night and returned home the next morning.

CHAPTER 6

June 16, 1906 – American Embassy in London

———————

Rose's final social event was a charity auction at the American Embassy in London. She arrived at the embassy alone and was stunning in a white Parisian evening gown. The American Ambassador, Harold Stratton, met her and they chatted until a man approached.

"Good evening, Ambassador Stratton," said the man.

"Mr. Jones, it's a pleasure to see you," Stratton replied.

"You as well. I hope I'm not intruding."

"Not at all," Stratton said graciously. "Please let me introduce you to Baroness Rose Cavendish."

Mr. Jones bowed to her. "It's a pleasure, madam."

"Lady Cavendish, this is Charles Jones."

Rose nodded and smiled. "I'm pleased to meet you."

"What an exquisite dress, if I'm not mistaken, it's from Paris," observed Mr. Jones.

"Thank you! You're correct, how do you know that?"

"My wife loves Parisian dresses."

Rose replied, "She has excellent taste."

"I have to admit she always dresses well."

Ambassador Stratton changed the subject. "Mr. Jones, I hope your trip here was successful."

"It was," replied Mr. Jones.

The ambassador asked, "Did you find the man you needed?"

"I did. He is here tonight. Let me find him. Please excuse me for a minute." Mr. Jones stepped away.

Ambassador Stratton commented, "Mr. Jones owns several businesses in America including a railroad, a bank, several mines, and a distillery. He came here looking for a man to run his distillery business. I have known Mr. Jones for years. He's an excellent businessman and a fine gentleman."

Mr. Jones returned with Colin. "Baroness Rose Cavendish and Ambassador Stratton, I would like you to meet my partner, Colin Stuart. Colin recently won the gold medal for the best malt whisky."

Colin bowed to Rose. "Lady Cavendish, it's a pleasure to meet you." He shook hands with Ambassador Stratton.

Rose nodded at the tall, fit, and strikingly handsome man. He had a warm smile with deep dimples, light brown hair, and blue eyes. Unlike most English gentlemen, he was clean shaven. He was wearing a new, well-tailored evening suit with highly polished black boots.

Ambassador Stratton asked, "Mr. Stuart, what distillery were you with?"

"I'm still with the GlenWilliams distillery, but I will be resigning on Monday."

Rose asked, "Isn't Lord Richard Williams the owner of GlenWilliams?"

"Yes, do you know him?" Colin asked.

"I do," she answered.

"Did you know his father?"

Rose nodded, "Yes, he was a kindhearted gentleman. I heard he died recently."

"He did, which is one reason why I became a partner with Mr. Jones."

"I wouldn't want to work with Lord Richard either," Lady Rose said. The men chuckled.

She blushed. "I'm sorry, that wasn't a polite thing to say. I can be too frank at times."

Colin stated, "The years I worked for him when his father was in South Africa were difficult. I don't want to work for him again."

"I take it Lord Richard will be surprised when you leave?" asked Rose.

"Yes."

Rose chuckled. "I would like to see his face when you tell him. He never likes to lose at anything."

Ambassador Stratton asked, "Mr. Jones, when will you be leaving for America?"

"Next Saturday."

Rose added, "I will be as well. Are you leaving from Liverpool on the *Lucania*?"

"Yes, Colin and I will be going," Mr. Jones said. "We will stay in New York for a few days then travel to Chicago."

"I'll also be going to Chicago," Rose replied, smiling.

"There is an International Art Exposition in Chicago. I believe it will be the largest display of impressionist works ever. Will you be attending?" asked Colin.

Rose blinked, surprised at the serendipity. "Yes."

"So will I. My favorite artist is Monet. I saw some of his paintings in Paris."

She stated, "I love Paris."

"I do too, the best time in my life was in Paris," added Colin.

She smiled thinking not only was the Scotsman handsome, but he also had a softer side. He resembled and reminded her of Thomas in many ways, especially with his light brown hair and blue eyes. She thought it was a shame he wasn't a titled gentleman.

"Gentlemen, you must excuse me there is someone I must speak to. It was a pleasure talking to you. Mr. Jones and Mr. Stuart, I look forward to seeing you during the voyage."

The ambassador and Mr. Jones bowed slightly. Colin saw them bow so he did belatedly. She strolled away and started chatting with a woman across the room.

Ambassador Stratton commented, "She is beautiful, don't you think?"

Mr. Jones replied, "Yes, she is."

Colin stayed quiet.

The ambassador and Mr. Jones stared at Colin with surprised faces. Mr. Jones asked, "Colin, you don't think she's beautiful?"

He answered, "Yes, but I have learned to try not to think about aristocratic women."

The ambassador scolded him, "You must stop thinking like that! You will be living in America where class distinction is not so prevalent like it is here."

"That will be hard for me," Colin admitted. "All my life, I've had to live with the upper class looking down their noses at me. When they're around, I'm always concerned about what I do or say. Is it really true all people are equal in America?"

The ambassador joked, "Yes all people in America are equal, however, money or a pistol can make some people more equal than others."

Ambassador Stratton and Mr. Jones laughed while Colin looked confused.

The ambassador saw that Colin didn't understand his joke. "In America, a woman like Lady Cavendish could marry an ordinary fellow. I know this is a fact because it happened to me."

"And to me," said Mr. Jones, smiling.

"That's good to know." Colin thought about Lady Cavendish, yet it was hard for him to see how a woman of her station could ever be interested in a commoner. He thought she was beautiful, but he didn't feel comfortable saying it.

CHAPTER 7

June 17, 1906 – Aberlour, Scotland

———

ON THE LONG TRAIN RIDE home, Colin thought about what he had to accomplish before leaving for America. The most important thing was to talk to his family about his decision. He dreaded telling them he was leaving.

Another task he needed to do was to talk to the McCarthys. Colin had married his childhood sweetheart, Kathleen McCarthy, when they were twenty-three after a two-year courtship. They had a large wedding, a delightful honeymoon in Paris and the future for them was bright. However, three years later Kathleen died during the birth of their daughter, who was stillborn. The loss of his family devastated Colin. Four years had passed yet he remembered her fading away from him like it happened yesterday. He loved her so.

Colin often visited his in-laws and he was especially fond of Mrs. McCarthy. Mr. and Mrs. McCarthy had hoped he might become interested in Kathleen's younger sister, Abigail. Kathleen and Abigail, though sisters, were markedly different not only in looks but in personality as well. Kathleen resembled her mother and had had dark black silky hair, a shapely figure, and was shy, quiet, and pretty. Abigail took after her father in looks and manner. Abigail was twenty-five, slender and had her father's thick red hair, which she wore long. She was emotional, bossy, manipulative, loved to gossip, and always had to be the center of attention.

Mr. McCarthy used every opportunity to try to get Abigail and Colin together. Colin saw Abigail often yet considered her only a friend. Abigail loved Colin and she had been bold in telling him so, but Colin wasn't ready for another relationship and told her so many times. However, the determined Abigail wasn't going to let him slip through her fingers easily.

Colin arrived home in midafternoon and had decided to see the McCarthy family first. Mr. McCarthy worked for the Royal Mail and was the postmaster in Aberlour. He owned a small home with a well-kept garden on the edge of the town. When Colin arrived, Mr. and Mrs. McCarthy and Abigail were having tea in the garden.

Colin shouted from the garden gate, "Hello to the owner of this fine estate. May I stop in?"

Mr. McCarthy responded, "You're always welcome!"

Abigail was wearing a white cotton dress and her long red hair cascaded down her back as she ran to the gate. She hugged him when he entered.

She smiled and oozed, "I was hoping to see you today."

"That is a charming dress. Is it new?"

She purred, "Yes, it is. Thank you for noticing." She pulled him close and they strolled arm-in-arm to the garden.

Colin said, "Mrs. McCarthy, it's a pleasure to see you."

Mrs. McCarthy remained seated and held out her hand. Colin took it and squeezed it gently with both hands.

"You as well," she replied.

"You look especially lovely today," said Colin.

"Thank you! You're such a charmer!"

"Mr. McCarthy, I hope you don't mind me intruding."

"You're part of our family and are always welcome. Please sit with us."

Abigail and Colin sat at the table.

Mrs. McCarthy asked, "Tea?"

"Yes, with cream please."

Mrs. McCarthy made his tea. She handed him a teacup and saucer.

Colin sipped the tea and then turned to Mr. McCarthy. "How was your trip to Edinburgh to see your brother? I hope he is doing better."

"The trip was fine and my brother is doing much better."

"When did you return?" asked Colin.

"We arrived home last night."

"You were gone for over a week, weren't you?"

Abigail whined, "Yes, eight days but it felt like a year. It was rainy and cold the entire time we were there. How was your trip to London?"

"It was exciting!"

Abigail bubbled, "I love London; there is so much to do there! In this sleepy hamlet, unless a cow gets out, there is never any excitement."

Everyone laughed.

"Did you do anything exciting?" Abigail asked.

"I went to a party at the American Embassy."

"That sounds fun! Was it?" inquired Abigail.

"It was! I met the American Ambassador."

Mr. McCarthy interjected, "I want travel to America, especially out west and meet a real cowboy."

Mrs. McCarthy boasted, "Matthew is an expert on the American west. He has read every dime western novel available."

Colin thought it was time to tell them his news. "Speaking of America, it is the reason why I stopped by. An American has offered me a partnership in a distillery. I accepted his offer and I will be moving to America soon."

Mrs. McCarthy gasped and dropped her teacup on her saucer. She caught it but some tea spilled to the ground. She tried to regain her composure.

Shocked, Abigail remarked, "Colin, I have never heard you talk of America before."

"Yes, this is something new. It's a great opportunity."

The McCarthys stared at each other, not believing what they heard.

Mrs. McCarthy asked, "When will you be going to America?"

"I leave from Liverpool on Saturday."

"Saturday? You leave Saturday!" Abigail exclaimed. Her usually ruddy cheeks had paled.

"Yes. I know this is sudden, but I'll never have this kind of opportunity here."

"What about me! Are you taking me?"

He had not anticipated this question because he never considered asking her to go with him. "Abigail, I'm here to tell you why I'm going."

Insistent on getting an answer, Abigail was blunt. "My question is simple: Are you taking me or not?"

Colin stumbled for a second as he thought about what to say. "I will be going alone."

Abigail stood, covered her face with her hands and rushed into the house crying.

Mrs. McCarthy murmured, "Please excuse me." She ran after Abigail.

After a silent moment between the men, Mr. McCarthy said, "As you can see, the women are shocked. Frankly, so am I. I don't want any more tea. I need whisky." He reached into his coat, pulled out a small flask, and took a long drink from it.

Mr. McCarthy let the whisky sink in for a few seconds. "Why are you leaving so suddenly?"

Colin told him the story of what happened with Richard and how he traveled to London to meet with the American. Mr. McCarthy sipped from the flask as they talked.

Angrily, Mr. McCarthy snapped, "That bastard Richard! I knew something like this would happen when Lord Patrick died. He almost ruined the distillery before but you managed to save it. Now he is chasing you away. It will be a sad day for everyone when you leave. I hope you know Mrs. McCarthy and I love you like a son."

"I do, sir."

"We hoped someday you and Abigail would marry."

"Sir, I loved Kathleen so much that the hole in my heart hasn't healed yet. I'm not sure if it ever will."

"Yes, I know." Mr. McCarthy nodded solemnly. "She loved you too. My granddaughter would be four years old now. My heart aches every day for them."

Colin agreed, "So does mine. I didn't mean to upset Abigail."

"She can be emotional at times. You do know she loves you."

Colin nodded. "Yes sir, I know. I have been careful not to hurt her."

"Yes, you have been a gentleman. She was hoping you would love her over time once the hurt of Kathleen passed."

"I know."

"Colin, you falling in love with Abigail will never happen if you're in America."

"I have to do this. There is no future for me here. I'll have no influence over Richard now that his father has died."

Mr. McCarthy leaned forward and put his hand on Colin's arm. "I understand why you want to go. To keep the relationship with Abigail going, maybe we could visit you there?"

"Ah, well…." Colin wiggled uncomfortably in his chair.

Mr. McCarthy squeezed his arm. "A visit from us will help you decide if you and Abigail are meant to be together. You owe us at least that."

Mr. McCarthy looked at him with a sad face and Colin gave in. "I guess once I'm settled a visit would be fine."

"It will be an expensive trip for a poor postmaster. Do you think you could help me with the expenses?" Mr. McCarthy squeezed Colin's arm again.

Colin hesitated. "Ah, well…."

Mr. McCarthy pulled on Colin's heartstrings. "Kathleen would have wanted you to stay in touch with us."

The sorrowful eyes of Mr. McCarthy caused Colin to give in again. "Maybe I could help you with the costs."

Mr. McCarthy clapped his hands together and exclaimed, "Colin, my boy, that is a generous offer! Mrs. McCarthy's health won't permit her to travel, but I have always wanted to go there. I'm sure this will help Abigail and Mrs. McCarthy feel better. Should I tell them about it?"

"Yes, of course."

"I'll explain to them why you're leaving and what our plan is. Can you stay for a while? I'm sure Abigail will want to talk to you."

"I'm sorry sir, but I cannot. I have to talk to my family; they don't know yet."

Mr. McCarthy nodded. "Before you leave for America, please plan to come here for a bon voyage dinner."

"I look forward to it. Please convey my apologies to Mrs. McCarthy and Abigail for ruining your tea."

"I will. This decision was difficult for you and I appreciate you speaking to us about it in person. You have also given me some hope there may be a future for you and Abigail."

"Sir, I don't know what the future holds. Please don't describe the trip as anything more than a visit between friends."

"I understand, but the emotions of a young woman are hard to control. I'll try to temper her expectations, but I'm sure she will want the trip to be much more."

They stood and shook hands. Colin left for his mother's farm, which was a short walk down the road. As he walked, he thought about the conversation with Mr. McCarthy and wondered if he had done the right thing when he agreed to the visit.

CHAPTER 8

———————

COLIN'S MOTHER LIVED IN THE farmhouse where she was born. Her family had farmed there for four generations. She was sixty-two but could pass for much younger. She was slender, attractive with silver hair and blue eyes. She had two children, Colin was the youngest and other son Paul ran the farm and lived in a small home on the property.

Every Sunday, Colin went to his mother's house for dinner. Paul and his family would also be there. Paul had a lovely wife, Amanda, and they had two daughters ages four and six. Colin and Paul were close. He always looked forward to being there especially around the holidays.

When Colin arrived, Paul was sitting on the front porch. Although, Paul was two years older, they looked quite similar and folks often thought they were twins. Paul shook hands with him and led him into the house. Colin hugged everyone and kissed his mother.

Colin and Paul settled into the parlor to have a drink. Colin told him about what happened with Richard.

Paul commented, "Richard has already shown he cannot lead the business. Now he is demoting you and bringing in some lackey he can push around. Why can't he leave things alone? The business is doing great." His forehead creased with anger.

"That is exactly what I can't understand. All he has to do is let me run the business and he can make a great deal of money without lifting a finger," added Colin.

"I wouldn't be able to return to my old job. I know even the assistant master distiller is an excellent position, however, I wouldn't be able to do it," stated Paul.

"That gets into what I wanted to talk to you about. An American gentleman by the name of Charles Jones has offered me a partnership in a distillery and I have accepted it."

Paul shook his head in disbelief. "You aren't serious?"

"Yes, I will be leaving for America shortly."

Paul blinked several times and tried to understand what was happening. "I know you're upset with Lord Richard, but this move to America seems drastic. Couldn't you go to another distillery here in Scotland? Within twenty miles of here, there are several distilleries. Any one of them would give you a job."

"I could find a job but not ownership. If I stay here, I would be another worker. I don't want to be looked down on by another aristocrat who never worked a day in his life."

"There you go again." Paul shook his head. "You have never accepted the fact we were born common people. Fate has already determined who we are."

"I don't want fate to rule my life. I want to be known for what I have accomplished."

"The aristocrats and nobility rule our world."

"They don't rule in America."

Paul chuckled. "You have always pushed against the entitled ones. You're so different from me. I accept things as they are but you don't. I have often wondered if the Whisky Angel's kiss also gave you more courage than most. You're always willing to take big risks. I remember when you were hiding the whisky in our barn. I worried constantly you would get caught."

"Remember when old man Roberts came over and asked questions about the whisky smell? You told him it was a new kind of feed you got from the distillery."

Paul grinned. "It worked. He believed it."

Colin laughed. "Looking back on it now, I would have had a tough time explaining to the authorities why all the Williams' whisky was in our barn. Once I moved it out, you got the idea for the dairy farm."

"Yes, I remember looking at that empty barn and asking myself what in the devil am I going to do with it."

"You made an outstanding decision going into the dairy business."

"I think so, it has worked out well." Paul paused. "When do you plan to tell Mother about your decision?"

"After dinner."

"You will need some time alone with her. I'll take the girls for a walk."

"I would like you to be here. I want her to know you support me on this. You do support me, don't you?" asked Colin.

Paul hesitated. "Reluctantly."

"I'm pleased you do. Also, I want to make it clear when the time comes, I want the farm to be passed to you."

"Colin, let's not discuss that again. I told you before I want us to be partners in the farm and the dairy."

"Paul, that's your dream, not mine. I'll be in America and you will be here. I want you to have the farm and take care of Mother. If I fail in America, you can hire me as the master distiller of your dairy."

They laughed heartily.

"Colin, I don't think you should talk about the farm with Mother tonight. She'll have enough to handle with you leaving."

"Yes, I suppose so."

Their mother entered the parlor. "Boys, dinner is ready."

They retired to the parlor after the meal. The kids were sitting on the floor reading while the adults were talking and sipping brandy. Paul and Amanda sat on a love seat. Colin was in a cushioned armchair and Mrs. Stuart sat in a rocking chair and knitted.

Colin looked at his mother. "I have some news to share."

He told what happened to him at the distillery.

Angry, his mother said, "Richard is an evil man. He is nothing like his father."

Amanda added, "I agree. I believe he walks with the devil."

"I also have some other news," Colin continued. "I have been offered ownership in a distillery in America. I have accepted it and I'll leave for America soon."

Amanda gasped. The kids stopped reading and listened. Mrs. Stuart stopped rocking and put down her knitting. She picked up her brandy and took a long drink. A few moments passed. Mrs. Stuart sat her glass down. The only noise was from the crackling fire in the fireplace. Everyone stared at Mrs. Stuart and waited for her reaction.

"Son, I have never known you to make a rash decision. I'm sure you must have thought this through and don't require your mother's advice. However, I have one question." Mrs. Stewart paused. "Are you doing this to spite Richard or is this opportunity something you really want?"

Colin leaned forward toward her. "Mother, this is a superb opportunity. I'll never again have the opportunity to own a distillery if I stay here."

She picked up her knitting and started to rock again. The tension in the room lifted.

Amanda asked, "Where will you be?"

"I'll be outside of Chicago in Lake Geneva, Wisconsin. I understand it's nice there."

Amanda said, "I don't know much about America. We have a world atlas." Her face brightened. "Let's look it up."

Amanda stepped to a wall of books and took an atlas. The family, without Mrs. Stuart, crowded around a table and searched for Lake Geneva. Everyone excitedly talked about Colin's adventure while Mrs. Stuart continued to rock and knit quietly.

An hour of discussion on his decision passed, and it was starting to get late. Everyone would have early mornings. Mrs. Stuart walked Colin to the door.

"Son, I have always feared this day would come. Many of our village boys have left for America never to return. Please come home to see me when you can." She wrapped her arms around him.

"I will."

"Please promise," she pleaded.

"I promise. Do I have your blessing?"

"Of course, you have my blessing."

She kissed him and hugged him long and hard. Tears were running down her face.

She pulled back and sniffled. "You know if your father was still alive, he would want to go with you." She wiped her tears away.

"I was thinking of him today and I wondered if he would approve."

"Of course he would. He loved making whisky but he never had the chance to be an owner. He would have made the same decision." She paused. "I want you to do so well that Richard will regret his decision."

Colin agreed. "That would be justice, wouldn't it?"

"It would. Now later this week, we will have a goodbye party for you."

"I look forward to it." He kissed her on the forehead.

As he walked home, he thought about his father. He was glad his mother talked about him. It gave him confidence that he made the right decision.

The final task Colin needed to accomplish was to resign and he knew exactly what he wanted to say to Richard.

CHAPTER 9

———◆———

COLIN ROSE EARLY AND PREPARED for his meeting with Richard. He rehearsed what he wanted to say while he wrote his resignation letter. After breakfast, he walked to the estate. At nine o'clock, he knocked on the door and the butler answered.

"Good morning, Mr. Stuart. I wasn't expecting you. Do you have a meeting with Lord Williams?"

"I don't, but I must meet with him. Could you please tell him I'm here?"

"He hasn't gotten up yet. I'm afraid rising at this early hour will upset him."

"Yes, I understand; tell him it's urgent."

"I'll talk to him. Please have a seat in the parlor. Would you prefer coffee or tea?"

"Coffee."

"I'll have it brought to you."

Colin sat in the parlor. A few minutes later, a maid brought him coffee. A properly ironed and neatly folded London paper was on the table. It was not appropriate for him to read Lord William's paper yet he picked it up anyway. Colin drank the coffee and read the paper.

Ten minutes went by. Colin had started his second cup of coffee when Richard strolled into the parlor. He was wearing a burgundy robe and white silk pajamas. Colin didn't lower the paper to look at him.

In a loud angry voice, Richard asked, "Are you reading my paper?"

Colin didn't lower the paper and replied, "Yes."

Richard shook his finger at Colin. "How dare you insult me! Put my paper down now! I hate anyone to touch my paper. Are you mad?"

Colin lowered the paper, slowly folded it, and put it on the table. He picked up his coffee, took a sip and savored it. "No, I haven't been drinking."

"Why are you here? It had better be important."

"I have something for you."

Colin reached into his coat pocket, took out his resignation letter, and handed it to Richard.

Richard opened it, read it and asked with contempt in his voice, "You're resigning? I don't believe you." He dropped the letter on his desk.

"I don't care if you believe me or not."

"I can't stop you from resigning, but you won't be able to find another job anywhere in Scotland. I'll damn make sure of that! I'll tell everyone you almost ruined the company by deliberately hiding whisky from me. No one will give you a job. You won't even be able to get the job you started with here, picking bugs from the barley floor."

Colin sipped his coffee and replied, "I already have a job and not only will I be the master distiller but I'll be a full partner."

Richard's eyes narrowed. "You're lying. It isn't possible for you to get a job so fast…and no one would offer you ownership. This is a ploy to get your old job back, isn't it?"

Colin sipped the coffee.

Richard shouted, "Answer me!"

"My last day is today."

Richard exclaimed, "Today! You cannot leave today. I have no one to replace you."

"I leave today."

Richard paused and thought for a few seconds. He took a few deep breaths while Colin sipped the coffee.

Richard smiled. "I can see you figured out my plan. I never intended to hire another master distiller. I thought you would beg me to give you your old job. I was wrong. I can see now you're a much smarter and bolder man than I thought. I give you credit for that."

Without a care in the world it seemed, Colin continued to sip the coffee.

"I'll make it up to you. I'll give you a twenty percent increase in your salary." Richard stood there proud of himself with his hands on his hips.

Colin looked up from the coffee. "My salary will be double what it is here."

"Doubled? I don't believe you. You're lying to me."

"My salary is doubled."

Richard sputtered, "I'll match it."

Colin didn't say anything.

Richard was anxious and felt the pressure to add to his offer. "I'll also provide one additional servant and he will be your butler."

Colin sipped the coffee.

Richard saw his offer wasn't enough. "This is my last offer. I'll consider giving you ownership next year if we win the gold medal award again." Richard smiled, confident he had made an excellent offer.

Colin finished the coffee and put the cup down. "Thank you for the coffee." Colin got up and walked toward the door.

Richard remarked, "You're bluffing. You aren't leaving. I have made you more than a generous offer."

Colin was about to leave.

Richard added, "Alright, alright, I'll give you ownership in the distillery now."

"Do you have the document your father talked about?"

"Yes, I have it. We can sign it now."

"Let me see it."

Richard went to his office, returned with a document and handed it to Colin. Colin read it carefully. The document was exactly as Lord Patrick promised. Colin smiled.

Richard saw Colin liked what he read. "Now you have read it. Let's sign it. We will have a dinner here tonight to celebrate."

Colin shook his head no. "I'm not interested." He crumpled the document into a ball, stepped to the fireplace, and tossed it in.

Richard was shocked and stared at the burning document. "Why aren't you interested? Isn't this what you have always dreamed about?"

"It has always been my dream to own a distillery. However, you lied to me about the document."

"It was business; there was nothing personal about it."

"It was personal to me."

"Colin, you have to get over these things in business."

"You lied. What will you lie to me about next?"

Richard lectured him. "You're taking the high moral ground on this, aren't you? Weren't you the one who hid things from me? You hid whisky from me."

"I did," Colin conceded, "but I had to."

"I feel the same way," Richard stated with confidence.

"It's not the same."

Richard claimed, "Of course it is."

"We will never agree on what I did, but I did it to protect the distillery. I don't think we could ever work together again."

"You'll forget about it," Richard assured him.

Colin shook his head. "No, I will always worry you will lie again. I need to move on with my life. I hoped this morning I would be able to see the document your father said he prepared. I was praying Lord Patrick had completed it. I didn't want to lose faith in him. The document confirmed everything I loved about your father and it also confirmed everything I despise about you!"

Colin walked to the door.

Richard shouted. "You're making a mistake! You will regret this for the rest of your life! You have until tomorrow at noon to accept my offer. No later!"

Colin didn't acknowledge him as he left. He walked home knowing he had made the right decision.

When Colin got home, he packed his belongings and sent most of his things to his mother's farm to store. He then packed his clothes and personal items for the voyage to America. Afterwards, he checked into a village inn for the rest of the week.

Over the next few days, he said goodbye to everyone. He had a farewell dinner with the McCarthys and another with his family. On Friday morning, he took a train to Liverpool. His family, the McCarthys, most of the townspeople, and all the workers in the distillery went to the station to see him off. Colin was grateful and pleased so many people came to support him.

CHAPTER 10

JUNE 23, 1906 – LIVERPOOL, ENGLAND

———◆———

ROSE, MIA, MIA'S GOVERNESS ELIZABETH, and Edith stayed in Liverpool the evening before their departure. Excited about the trip, they arrived at the dock an hour before it was time to leave. Their ship was the *R.M.S. Lucania*, one of the fastest and most luxurious passenger ships.

Carts, wagons, dockworkers, and passengers packed the dock. Nearly 2,000 passengers would be onboard along with 400 crew members. There would be roughly 600 first-class passengers while the rest would be the second- and third-class.

Rose checked with the dock clerk to make sure their luggage was on the ship. According to the clerk, eight trunks were in their stateroom and another eight were below. Rose and her party made their way to the staterooms. Rose and Mia had the largest stateroom on the ship. Their accommodations were elegant and truly first class. The stateroom had a parlor, two large bedrooms, a grand, white Italian marble bathroom, and two smaller bedrooms for the servants. Fine Persian rugs covered the floors, the furniture was a French Renaissance style, and exquisite mahogany adorned the walls.

Rose supervised Edith and Elizabeth as they unpacked the trunks. Excited, Mia ran back and forth from one porthole to the next trying to see what was happening on the dock. "Mummy, may Elizabeth and I go on deck?"

"No Mia, it is much too busy there with everyone loading. Once we are underway, you may go for a walk."

"It's so exciting! I can't see anything here. I'm sure Elizabeth will keep me safe. Please Mummy, may I go?"

"Elizabeth, would you mind taking Mia on deck? I'm sure she will drive us to distraction if she stays here."

"No madam, I wouldn't mind. I have never been on a ship before. I would also like to watch," replied Elizabeth.

"Thank you, Elizabeth. Mia, you may go on the deck for a while but don't get too tired."

"Thank you! Thank you!" exclaimed Mia. She ran to Elizabeth and took her hand.

Rose stepped to them and kneeled in front of Mia. She lectured, "Now Mia, before you leave, please listen to me. You must hold Elizabeth's hand always. You cannot leave the ship with anyone. I don't care if Queen Alexandra is here and asks you to take a walk with her on the dock. Once the ship leaves the dock it will not return. You would be all alone in Liverpool with no one to care for you. I would hate for the authorities to put you in an orphanage while we are in America."

Mia nodded. "Yes Mummy, I will not leave Elizabeth's side. May I go now?"

"Yes, you may."

Mia nearly dragged Elizabeth out the door. It was only a few steps to the deck that circled the first-class staterooms. They rushed to the port side rail and leaned over to watch the activity on the dock. Huge cranes lifted freight into the holds. Scores of men loaded boxes of food and other provisions. On the second- and third-class decks, people scurried aboard. People from across Europe were there, dressed in many distinctive styles and most carried suitcases or bags. A young girl in third class saw Mia above. She had long, black hair, light brown skin and was wearing a bright red dress. The girl smiled and waved at Mia. Mia smiled and waved back.

Elizabeth scolded her, "Mia you shouldn't do that. She is in third class. You don't want her to think she can visit you here. She or someone with her may be sick, or they could even be gypsies. You should only talk to people in first class."

Mia looked down and replied, "Yes, Elizabeth."

The ship's whistle blew. It was loud, and it startled Mia. She held her ears and stood close to Elizabeth. "Why do they blow the whistle?"

"I'm not sure," replied Elizabeth.

A young ship's officer was standing near and overheard her question. He commented, "That's the boarding whistle. It will sound two more times then we will depart."

The ship workers rushed to finish loading. Men were yelling, horns and bells were sounding. People, carts, and wagons still jammed the dock.

Mia and Elizabeth stood near the first-class gangway and watched all the activity around them.

A well-dressed woman boarded with a small, white poodle on a leash. Mia immediately left Elizabeth and went to the woman.

Mia kneeled by the dog. "You have a cute dog."

"Thank you, my dear."

"What's its name?"

"Her name is Daisy."

"I love dogs. May I pet her?"

"You may."

Mia petted it and said in a soothing tone, "Hello Daisy, you're so pretty."

The woman asked, "Do you have a dog?"

Mia looked up. "No, but I want one. I have asked my mother and she said I can have one when I'm a little older."

"Yes, you have to be responsible to own a dog. They need a lot of care."

The ship's whistle blew again. The frightened dog pulled away from the woman. The dog ran down the gangplank, dragging its leash.

The woman shouted, "Daisy! Stop this second! Daisy!"

Mia, without thinking, ran after the dog.

Elizabeth yelled, "Mia stop! Stop!"

Mia reached down and grabbed the leash near the end of the gangway but she couldn't hold on. She tripped, fell, and scraped her knee. She got up and started running after the dog again.

There was an open area between the gangway and the crowd, set off by rails. The dog ran under the rail and across the open area and so did Mia. The crowd was pressing against the rails to wave goodbye to people onboard. The dog couldn't run through the crowd. It turned and ran to the edge of the dock with Mia trailing close behind. On the outside of the dock, between the dock rail and the ship, were three narrow wooden planks that made a ledge designed to keep people from being too close to the constantly bobbing ship. The dog saw the wooden ledge and started to run down it. Mia squeezed under the rail and stepped on the ledge to chase after the dog.

Mia felt a hand on her shoulder stopping her and she turned around. A man commanded, "You go on board! I will get the dog." He picked her up and put her over the rail. He stepped over the rail, got on the wooden ledge, and chased after the dog. In a few seconds, she couldn't see Daisy or the man anymore. She returned to the gangway. Elizabeth and the woman were there.

Mia said with tears in her eyes, "I'm sorry, I couldn't catch her."

The woman sobbed, "Thank you for trying."

Mia tried to reassure her, "A man is chasing after her."

Tears began to roll down the woman's cheeks. "I don't know what to do without her. She is my baby."

Elizabeth put her hands on Mia's shoulders. "We should get on board."

Elizabeth, Mia, and the woman walked up the gangway to the crowded first-class deck and pushed their way to the rail. They couldn't see the dog or the man. The final whistle blew, workers released the ship's lines, and a tugboat pulled the ship away from the dock. They had given up hope when they heard a dog barking behind them.

A man approached Mia, carrying Daisy and he smiled. "Here's your dog. She seems to be fine, only a little scared."

"Oh, thank you! Thank you! She's not mine. She belongs to…." Mia turned to the woman. "I'm sorry, madam. I never learned your name."

"I'm Lady Florence Mitchell. The dog belongs to me." She stepped forward to take Daisy from the man's arms.

"Lady Mitchell, it's a pleasure to meet you." He handed the dog to her. "My name is Colin Stuart."

Lady Mitchell hugged Daisy and tears rolled down her cheeks. "Thank you so much Mr. Stuart! I would have been devastated if I lost my Daisy."

Colin replied, "I'm sure you would be."

Everyone petted and consoled the dog.

Elizabeth pleaded, "Lady Mitchell and Mr. Stuart, I beg you to not say anything to Mia's mother about this incident. She had given explicit directions to Mia not to leave the ship."

"What is her mother's name and yours?" asked Lady Mitchell.

"Her mother is Lady Rose Cavendish. This is Mia Cavendish. I am Mia's governess, Elizabeth Carpenter."

Colin smiled when he heard Lady Cavendish's name.

Lady Mitchell said, "I know Lady Cavendish well. Of course, I will keep this between us. Mia was a brave girl to try to help. She shouldn't be punished—nor should you, for trying to help."

"Thank you, madam!" Elizabeth turned to Colin. "Sir, may I ask you to keep this confidential?"

"Absolutely," replied Colin.

"You are a gentleman for helping me in this situation. Thank you!"

Colin nodded his head. "You're welcome. Now to this young lady who tried to help. You're a brave young lady. I think you must be Scottish."

"No sir, I'm English."

"You are?" Colin acted surprised.

"Yes sir."

"I must absolutely change my view on the bravery of English women because you're the bravest young lady I have ever met."

Mia was proud and puffed up her chest. "Thank you!"

"Now, I see you have been wounded in action. You have scratched your knee."

Mia's knee was bleeding.

Colin kneeled down. "Please sit here and let me examine your wound."

Mia sat on a deck chair. Colin reached into his pocket and removed a silk handkerchief. He and Elizabeth examined the knee. Colin pressed the handkerchief to her knee and cleaned the wound.

Colin concluded, "It doesn't look too ghastly. I doubt we will need to amputate the leg. Elizabeth, do you agree? Otherwise I have a knife in my pocket and I can remove her leg immediately."

Elizabeth smiled and added, "She has suffered far worse from chasing her cat."

Colin smiled at Mia. "You have a cat?"

"Yes, his name is King Richard."

Colin laughed. "Not King Richard the Lionheart?"

Mia said, "Yes, how did you know?"

"I'm a good guesser, plus I have two nieces so I know how young ladies think. Your knee has stopped bleeding. You should be fine now."

Elizabeth and Colin stood.

"Mr. Stuart, I'm in your debt! I hope you will accept an invitation to dinner later this week," said Lady Mitchell.

Colin replied, "I would be honored. Ladies and young lady, please excuse me; I need to get to my stateroom and make sure my luggage has arrived. I'll see you on the voyage." Colin walked away.

Lady Mitchell whispered to Elizabeth, "If I were thirty years younger, I would try my best to get to know him."

Elizabeth smiled. "Yes, he does seem to be a special man. Madam, please excuse me but I must get Mia to her stateroom."

"Of course, but before you go, I need to thank Mia." She put her hand on Mia's shoulder. "It took a lot of courage for you to help me. Mia, would you and your mother please be my guest for tea sometime on this trip?"

Mia curtsied. "It would be a pleasure."

"I'll send you an invitation...and I promise not to mention anything about your brave deed."

Mia smiled at her.

"Mia, we must get back," urged Elizabeth.

Elizabeth and Mia returned to the stateroom. As they walked, Elizabeth commented, "Your mother will want to know what happened to your knee. I'll tell your her you tripped and fell."

"Well, it's true! I did trip and fall."

"Mia also don't say anything about the dog or leaving the ship."

"Yes, I know, we'll both be in trouble if I do."

"Yes, we will be in big trouble," Elizabeth agreed.

As soon as the door swung open, Mia immediately blurted out, "I slipped on the deck and hurt my knee."

Rose blinked and her brow creased with concern. "How serious is it?"

Mia responded, "It's only a scrape. A kind gentleman helped me with it. He took a silk handkerchief and cleaned my knee. He is a thoughtful and kind man; don't you think, Elizabeth?"

"Yes, he is."

"You should point him out to me and I will properly thank him. Now, it has been a busy day! Let's rest for a while then we'll get dressed for dinner."

"Mummy, may I stay here tonight? I don't want to go to a fancy dinner."

"Darling, I don't blame you. Of course, you may stay here but unfortunately I'm expected to be there."

"Will you tell me all about it later?"

"I'll be late tonight, so tomorrow we'll talk."

CHAPTER 11

Dinner was at seven and Rose was to be a guest at the captain's table. At the cocktail reception before dinner, Rose stumbled upon Mr. Jones.

Mr. Jones bowed. "Lady Cavendish, it's a pleasure to see you again."

"You as well, Mr. Jones."

"I hope your accommodations are adequate."

"They are indeed; I'm very pleased."

Mr. Jones commented, "I understand from the captain we can expect rain for only one day of the trip but it shouldn't be terribly stormy."

She nodded. "I'm glad. I'm not sure if I would do well in rough seas."

"I'm not sure I would either." He chuckled.

"Mr. Jones, where is your master distiller? Did he make the trip?"

"Yes, he is in his stateroom."

"Hopefully, he's not ill."

"No, he's fine. I was with him most of the afternoon. We were talking business."

"Does he not like being on a ship?"

"No, he likes the ship, but he doesn't enjoy formal dinners. He's having a quiet dinner and working on a hobby of his. You may have heard he has already gained some notoriety in his brief time on the ship."

Her eyebrows rose. "How so?"

"Apparently, he saved a woman's dog on the dock today. The captain told me a woman's dog panicked because of the ship's whistle and ran down the gangway. The dog ran down the narrow wood planks between the dock and the ship. Colin jumped over the rail, ran down the narrow wooden planks, and swooped it up."

Rose gasped. "How exciting!"

"Lady Florence Mitchell owns the dog. She's the wife of a British diplomat."

"Yes, I know Lady Mitchell." She nodded, thinking. "Her dog is named Daisy, she is a small white poodle."

"He returned the dog to her and gallantly didn't mention how he caught her. She didn't know the true story until the captain told her. One of the crew witnessed the event. The captain said it was a brave thing to do. He or the dog could have easily fallen into the water and the ship could have crushed them. Lady Mitchell has told everyone about Colin rescuing the dog."

Rose exclaimed, "That's quite a story! Here you traveled all the way to England to find a master distiller and you could have lost him while he was chasing a dog."

Mr. Jones laughed. "I chastised him for that. However, he said he thought the dog belonged to a young girl who was chasing it from the first-class deck. He said he didn't want the young girl to be sad on the trip because she lost her dog."

"I see." Rose thought for a few seconds. "Lady Mitchell has no small children. Was the girl a niece traveling with her?"

Mr. Jones shook his head. "No, I understand she was with someone else."

"The girl was on the dock?"

"Yes, I understand the girl ran from first-class gangway to try to catch the dog. Apparently, she almost caught it but she fell."

"I see. She fell on the dock. Please tell Mr. Stuart I think what he did was admirable. Lady Mitchell would have been distraught the entire trip without her prized Daisy."

"I'll tell him."

"Also, please tell Mr. Stuart I hope he can attend dinner tomorrow evening," Rose added. "I want to hear from him firsthand about his adventure."

"I will. I'm sure he will be pleased to talk with you."

Rose walked away and searched for Lady Mitchell. She wanted to know more about the girl. She soon found Lady Mitchell with a small group of women.

Rose stated, "Lady Mitchell, it's a pleasure to see you."

Lady Mitchell lowered her drink. "You too, my dear; what brings you on this voyage to America?"

"I'm going to an art exposition in Chicago."

She gasped. "So are we! Our husbands are in Chicago on a trade mission and we will be meeting them there. I understand the art exposition will be grand."

"I have heard the same thing. I also heard you have an exciting story about Daisy."

Lady Mitchell tensed up a bit and was cautious, "How did you hear about Daisy?"

"Mr. Jones from America told me about it."

Lady Mitchell smiled and added, "Oh yes, a brave, handsome man saved my precious Daisy today. His name is Colin Stuart. I would be absolutely lost without Daisy."

"I'm sure you would. Please tell me what happened."

Lady Mitchell told the story but left out the part about the young girl. The story had grown some now and Mr. Stuart was now a cross between a Greek god and an angel.

"Let me ask you a question. Was there a young girl involved?" Rose inquired.

Lady Mitchell paused for a few seconds. "Rose, I promised not to tell anyone about her."

"I understand. Was the girl my Mia?"

She hesitated again. "Yes."

Rose frowned.

Lady Mitchell said, "I can tell you're upset. Please let me explain. We were on the deck chatting. The whistle blew and Daisy pulled away from me. Daisy ran down the gangway and Mia ran after her."

"I told her not to go on the dock."

"Yes, I know you did, but she was trying to save my dog. It shows she is a brave girl with a big heart."

"Yes, this isn't the first time she has demonstrated her bravery. She has rescued numerous cats, birds and once stopped carriage traffic to save some ducklings. I'm afraid one day she may be hurt in one of her rescue adventures."

"I understand your concern. For my sake, don't punish her or her governess," Lady Mitchell implored.

"I won't, but I'll talk to them about this."

"Please, do it with a heart that sees an exceptional child who cares for people and animals. You're fortunate to have her."

Rose smiled. "Yes, I am."

"I'll send an invitation to you both for tea. I hope you can make it."

"Of course we will."

Lady Mitchell asked, "Would you like to dine with us this evening?"

"Thank you, but I will be at the captain's table and I should head that way now. Thank you for telling me the entire story."

Rose started to turn away, but Lady Mitchell reached out and touched her arm. "Do you know Mr. Stuart?"

"Yes."

"I think he is a perfect gentleman."

"I'm not sure he is a gentleman. I believe he works in a distillery."

Lady Mitchell chuckled at her remark. "I know many men who call themselves gentlemen but aren't close. He is kind, intelligent, handsome, and brave. I also understand he is the best whisky maker in Scotland so he has an outstanding future. What else would a woman need in a man?"

Rose smiled. "I understand your view."

"No, I don't think you do. If I were single, as you are, I wouldn't care if he was a stable boy. I would want to get to know him. My husband and I were in France for several years on diplomatic assignment. I learned the married French women could have young men if they did it quietly."

"I've heard the same thing."

Lady Mitchell winked. "Unfortunately, we aren't in France."

Rose giggled. "I understand even better now what you mean. I look forward to your invitation."

Rose left for her table. The dinner was enjoyable and she heard again from the captain about Colin. The story had grown even larger.

CHAPTER 12

THE NEXT DAY, MIA WAS up early. The morning was clear and warm. After having breakfast, she wanted to walk around the deck, and she talked Elizabeth into going with her. As she strolled around the deck, she spoke to everyone. Several dogs were on walks with their owners and she stopped to pet each one. As they rounded the turn to the stern of the ship, Mia saw a man flying a kite. It was Mr. Stuart.

Colin saw them approaching. "Good morning Lady Cavendish and Miss Carpenter, how are you?"

Mia said, "We are both well."

"How is your knee this morning? I have my trusty knife in my pocket. Do I need to operate on it?"

Mia giggled. "My knee is fine. Thank you for asking. Where did you get the kite?"

"I made it."

"You made it?" asked Mia skeptically.

"Yes, the wind on a ship is strong so I made it extra sturdy. I have two more. Would you like to fly one?"

"Yes please."

"Elizabeth, could you take this one?"

She was hesitant. "I have never flown a kite before. I've only watched."

"I'll show you. It takes a lot of skill and if you aren't careful, the kite will lift you right off the boat. If that starts to happen, let go of the kite. I don't want to have to jump into the cold water to save you."

Elizabeth's eyes got wide and she shook her head. "I don't think I want to do this."

Colin replied, "I'm joking with you. It's easy to do. The kite is small so it won't lift you up. Let me show you. Now hold this control stick with both hands."

He handed it to her.

"Now if you pull this way the kite will turn to the left. Pull this way and the kite will go to the right."

In a couple of minutes, Elizabeth was handling it well and smiled. "This is fun."

Colin led Mia to a deck chair that had two kites on it. "Now Mia, you need to help me pick out a kite for you. This one is a box kite and this one is a dragon kite. The box kite is easy to fly and it goes high. The dragon kite flies fast and is harder to fly. Have you flown a kite before?"

"Yes, when I was little."

"Now let me think about it. I need to be careful because dragon kites have been known to eat little girls." He held up one of the kites. "This is a new dragon kite. I don't know if he is a good dragon or a bad dragon. Maybe we should start you with the box kite."

Mia's eyes got big. "What do you mean dragon kites eat little girls?"

"Dragon kites sometimes turn into real dragons. Have you never heard about dragons eating little girls?"

"No, my mummy and my governess never tell me dragon stories."

Colin said, "You must learn about dragons. All brave girls like you should know how to deal with a dragon in case in one of your adventures you come upon one."

"Could you tell me about them?"

He nodded slowly. "Aye, I could...but only with your mother's permission, otherwise she might feed me to the dragons or to the sharks."

"I'll ask her."

"Now let's get you started with the box kite. I'll get it up and then you can take over."

Colin took the kite and got it into the wind. The kite took off and gained altitude. He handed the control stick to Mia. The box kite moved slower so she handled it easily. Mia was soon flying the kite like an expert.

"Elizabeth, do you like it?" asked Colin.

"This is fun! I'm surprised how much it pulls on your hands. You really have to hold on."

"Yes, you do. If this was a large kite with this wind it would pull you right off the ship."

"That sounds scary."

Colin said, "It is, but it's fun."

He watched Mia and directed her. "Give her some more line. Let's see how far she'll go."

Mia let out more line and soon the kite was a small speck in the sky.

"Ladies, you're doing fine. I'll get the dragon kite ready." Colin sat on the deck chair and prepared the dragon kite.

Rose was on the deck looking for Mia and Elizabeth when she rounded the corner and saw them. She walked up. "I wondered where you two were. Are you having fun?"

"We are!" they replied.

Rose asked, "Where did you get the kites?"

Mia replied, "Mr. Stuart made them."

"Mr. Stuart?"

From behind her she heard, "Good morning, Lady Cavendish."

She turned and smiled. "Good morning to you."

He stood to greet her.

"Mia and Elizabeth are enjoying your kites."

"They are. Mia learned quickly."

"Her father took her kite flying years ago, I wonder if she even remembers it."

"She does. She mentioned she had flown before."

"She was so small then."

Colin motioned toward the chair. "Please sit and you can watch for a while."

"I think I will." She sat next to him and watched the kites. "You made the kites?"

"I did. It's a hobby of mine. I love making kites. My brother always teases me about building and flying kites like a child, but it's relaxing to me. When I was in distillery school, there was a young man from Japan who was my roommate. We were lonely and homesick. We became friends and he taught me to make Japanese kites and origami."

"What is origami?"

"Let me show you."

He reached into his pocket and pulled out a folded sheet of paper. "Please close your eyes and don't open them until I say you can."

Rose closed her eyes. Colin carefully folded the paper and fashioned a swan.

"Now hold out your hand."

He put the swan in her hand.

"You can open your eyes now."

Rose gasped. "Oh, what a charming swan! How did you make it so fast?"

"The swan was already in the paper. A fairy must have put it there. I only shaped the paper around it."

"The swan is in the paper?" Rose questioned.

"Yes, and if you put this on a lake, it will float like a swan."

"Since this is paper, won't it sink?"

"No, this paper has a unique coating which doesn't absorb water easily. It will float until it turns into a beautiful swan."

Rose smiled. "You mean a real swan?"

"Yes," he replied.

She looked at him skeptically. "Mr. Stuart, I have heard Scottish men are known to spin yarns. You're quite a storyteller."

"How do you know it is only a story?"

"I know men."

Colin grinned. "You don't know me."

"You're right, but most men I know can spin a yarn or two."

He pointed to the origami swan. "You keep it and we will put it on a lake in America. You'll see."

"Yes, we will see. Does every piece of paper have something in it?"

"No, sometimes a piece of paper is only a piece of paper. I have to listen to the paper."

Rose chuckled. "You listen to the paper? What does paper say?"

"When I first picked up that paper, I thought I heard the distinct call of a swan. I held it up to my ear and I could hear a swan calling for me to let it out."

Rose cocked her head to the side and smiled. "Mr. Stuart, did you sample your whisky a little too much this morning?"

Colin laughed. "You'll see what I'm telling you is true."

"We will see, but your yarn seems far-fetched."

"You'll see," he said.

Elizabeth shouted, "Mr. Stuart, my arms are getting tired. Can you take this back?"

"Of course," he replied. He said to Rose, "Please excuse me."

Colin went to the rai and took the kite. "Mia, please try this one. I think you'll like how it flies."

They exchanged kites. Mia was soon squealing as the kite darted to the left and right. Elizabeth and Rose watched from the deck chairs.

Elizabeth whispered, "I hope you don't mind us flying kites."

"Not at all. Mia seems to be enjoying it."

"She is and I did too."

Colin reeled in the box kite. He set it on a deck chair. "Lady Cavendish, would you like to fly a kite?"

"No thank you!"

"Are you afraid someone might see you having fun?" he teased her.

"Maybe," she answered, "but it's time to get inside before Mia gets too tired."

"Of course, I'll be here each morning if the weather is decent."

Rose called, "Mia, we need to go inside and get dressed for lunch."

Mia responded, "I haven't had the chance to see if the dragon is going to try to eat me yet!"

"What?" asked Lady Rose with a surprised look on her face.

Mia explained, "Mr. Stuart has a dragon kite. He said sometimes dragon kites turn into real dragons and dragons have eaten little girls before. The kite is new and he doesn't know if it's a good dragon or a bad dragon."

Rose turned to Colin with a concerned face. "Mr. Stuart, you told my Mia about dragons?"

Colin smiled. "As you know, we Scots have a few stories."

"I have learned that." She turned to her daughter. "Mia, Mr. Stuart will be here tomorrow morning and you can come back."

"Yes Mummy."

Colin took control of the kite from her.

"Mr. Stuart, thank you so much!" Mia said.

"You're welcome! I'll be here every morning we have fair weather and we can check on that dragon."

"If Mia has nightmares tonight, tomorrow you will answer to me," Lady Rose teased as she wagged her finger at him.

"Yes, madam. Ladies, please have a good day."

Rose, Mia, and Elizabeth walked to the stateroom.

As they walked, Mia saw the origami item. "Mummy, what are you carrying?"

"It's a swan."

"Where did you get it?"

"Mr. Stuart made it for me."

Elizabeth smiled and commented, "My, he is a handy man, isn't he?"

Rose smiled and winked. "Yes, he is."

They returned to the stateroom and Rose set the swan on a table.

Edith inquired, "My lady, where did the swan come from?"

"A gentleman made it for me."

"Who is this gentleman?"

"His name is Colin Stuart. He is a commoner who makes whisky. I met him recently at an event at the American Embassy, he is a fine, likable fellow."

Puzzled, Edith wondered what was going on because Rose had never spoke about a commoner before in such a way. Edith asked, "Why would you talk to a commoner who makes whisky?"

Rose replied, "It's a long story we can talk about later. Please help me dress for lunch."

Edith decided she would find out more about this man.

CHAPTER 13

———◆———

COLIN RETURNED TO HIS STATEROOM and found an invitation from Lady Mitchell for dinner. He debated about going because he didn't enjoy formal dinners. Not wanting to embarrass his new partner, he wrote a note accepting the invitation and had a porter deliver it.

Colin waited as long as he could to go to dinner. He knew cocktails started at six-thirty with dinner promptly at seven-thirty. He arrived a couple of minutes before dinner began. Lady Mitchell saw him approaching.

"Mr. Stuart, I'm so pleased you accepted my invitation." She held out her hand to him.

He took her hand and bowed. "I've been looking forward to seeing you again."

"So have I. You'll be sitting next to me."

She led him to their seats like she was showing off a prize. Lady Mitchell stopped at the head of the table. Colin stood to her left. Directly across from him was Rose. Ten people were standing around the white clothed, rectangular table.

Lady Mitchell smiled. "Mr. Stuart, you know Lady Cavendish, don't you?"

Rose nodded to him.

"I've had the pleasure of talking to this beautiful lady on two occasions."

Rose blushed and said, "I see you have brought your Scottish charm."

Colin smiled.

Lady Mitchell said in a loud voice to everyone at the table, "This is Mr. Colin Stuart. He is the hero who saved my precious Daisy."

The people around the table clapped. Embarrassed and red faced, Colin nodded to them.

Lady Mitchell motioned to the people at the table. "Please, everyone, let's all sit."

A lively conversation started. As people talked, Colin couldn't take his eyes off Rose. Elegant and strikingly beautiful, she was wearing a soft blue evening gown with a magnificent diamond necklace and matching diamond earrings. Her hair was up and adorned with a delicate diamond tiara. Rose noticed Mr. Stuart looked at her frequently. She tried not to look at him often because a lady shouldn't do that.

Dinner started and Colin was feeling uncomfortable. In front of him were a confusing array of forks, spoons, and knives. He wasn't sure when to use each one. He had been to dinners before with Lord Patrick, but he never seen this much silverware.

The first course was soup. Colin picked up a spoon and he felt a slight kick under the table from Lady Mitchell. He looked at her and she was discreetly pointing to a different spoon. His face reddened, he put down the spoon and picked up the correct one. He finished the soup and found the woman next to him was staring at him.

The woman observed with a smile, "Mr. Stuart, you must have been hungry. I have never seen soup go so fast."

Embarrassed, Colin said, "It was excellent soup."

Colin was a quick learner and wouldn't pick up a spoon or fork without checking to see what everyone else was using.

While waiting for the next course, Lady Mitchell told everyone at the table how Colin had saved her Daisy. Colin listened to the story and noted how much it had grown. He smiled and thought to himself that not only do the Scots expand their stories but so do the English. He didn't know aristocratic women told such yarns.

When she finished her story, the people at the table applauded. Colin looked down and was embarrassed.

Rose asked, "Lady Mitchell, I have something to add to the story if you don't mind."

Colin raised his head to listen.

"Please my dear, add anything you wish."

"Lady Mitchell didn't mention that a young girl chased the dog down the gangway and to the dock. The captain told me the young girl was about to run on the wooden ledge between the dock and the ship. If she had fallen, she could have drowned. Mr. Stuart stopped her, told her he would get the dog, and instructed her to go to the ship. He scooped the girl up and put her out of harm's way. Mr. Stuart then chased after the dog on the scary planks. Mr. Stuart, is that correct?"

Colin didn't say anything. He had promised to keep the story confidential.

Rose added, "Mr. Stuart is a humble man. The girl he helped was my daughter Mia."

The people at the table gasped audibly and applauded.

Rose held her glass of wine in a toast. "Mr. Stuart, I'm in debt to you."

Colin nodded, picked up his glass and everyone did as well. After the toast, the people at the table started asking him questions. Colin answered patiently and hoped the questions about the overblown dog story would soon end.

Rose thought the way he handled the situation was impressive. He answered the questions in a humble manner. She knew many men who would have bragged about their role and would have talked at length about it. Colin didn't want any attention or acclaim for what he did.

Once excitement about the dog story passed, the conversations started at the table as Lady Mitchell, Rose and Colin got to know each other. Lady Mitchell asked where he was born, about his family and how he had gotten into the whisky business. After he told his story, Rose admired how far he had gotten on his own efforts.

Finally, Lady Mitchell asked the question Rose had been waiting to hear: Was he married? He replied his wife had died. He told the story of his engagement, his honeymoon in Paris, and how his wife died during childbirth and that his daughter was stillborn. As he spoke of his wife, Rose saw the depth of the love he had for her. She felt the same way about Thomas. She had never heard a man express his love for a woman in such an endearing and sweet way.

She found herself starting to like Colin, but she kept reminding herself he was a commoner. So many things about Colin showed he was one. She saw the mistake he made at dinner with the silverware and how Lady Mitchell helped him through it. Also at times, he used the King's English incorrectly. Colin wasn't a polished English gentleman but she felt he was a loving, intelligent, and thoughtful man.

After dinner, Rose hoped Colin would ask her to dance but he didn't. Soon after the orchestra started, he left. Disappointed he left and with no compelling reason to stay, she stepped outside on the deck to walk to her stateroom. It was a clear night and the stars were bright and sparking. Colin stood at the rail looking out on the water.

She teased him, "Mr. Stuart, are you thinking about jumping in?"

He laughed and replied, "No, I'm enjoying the evening stars. With no moon or city lights, you can see so many."

Rose stood next to him at the rail. "Yes, they are breathtaking, aren't they?"

"Yes, they are."

"You left right after dinner. Is there something wrong? Don't you like to dance?"

He sighed. "The conversation about my wife during dinner made me think of her. I didn't want to dance because I haven't danced with another woman since her death. I wanted to leave and be alone."

"If you need to be alone, I understand. I'll leave."

"No, please don't leave. I'm better now. I enjoy talking to you."

Rose smiled. "I enjoy talking to you too."

"I learned from Mr. Jones you lost your husband."

"I did, so I know what you mean when you say your heart still hurts."

"I never expected my wife would die so young. I was in complete shock for months."

"So was I."

"I still wake up at night and reach for her."

She nodded knowingly. "I do the same."

There was a long, sad pause. Colin decided to change the subject. "You're so lucky to have Mia. She's a wonderful girl."

"Thank you!" Rose smiled. "I think so too."

"Did Mia and Elizabeth get in trouble?"

"I was upset at first, but I decided to let it go. I didn't talk to them about it."

"I'm glad."

He saw Rose shiver a bit. "It's a little chilly, would you like my coat?"

She hesitated for a second. "Yes, please. That is thoughtful of you."

He removed his jacket and wrapped it around her.

"That is much better, thank you. You're making a substantial change moving so far away from family and friends. Are you nervous about it?"

"Not really," he answered. "I'm excited about the opportunity. Do you know anything about whisky?"

She chuckled. "Only that I drink it on occasion."

"May I tell you something about it?"

She nodded. "Yes, please."

Colin told her the history of Scottish whisky and how it's made. As he talked, he waved his arms and used his hands to express what he was saying. Soon they were sitting in deck chairs at the stern of the ship where there was no wind and it was warmer. His story of how to make whisky was interesting to her. Making whisky was more complicated than she thought. She loved the story about the Whisky Angel kissing him.

Colin checked his pocket watch. "I have been talking for an hour. I'm so sorry about boring you with all my stories."

"They aren't boring. I enjoyed it. I often go to formal dinners and never learn anything. I now know how to make whisky. I'm sure I could walk into any Scottish distillery and impress them with my knowledge. I could even ask for a job."

Colin smiled. "I would hire you in a minute."

"Could I be a master distiller?"

Colin mocked surprise. "Are you trying to take my job? Let's start you as an assistant first."

"I accept. After the art exposition, I'll come to your distillery and apply for a position."

Colin held out his hand. "That is a deal."

She shook his hand.

She sighed. "I should be getting in. Mia will be up early and she will expect to know all about tonight."

"You should skip the whisky part."

"I don't think so. Once she knows you told me about making whisky, she will want to know all about it. You should know she likes you."

"I'm glad. I like her too."

Rose stood and so did Colin.

"Lady Rose, I hope I'll see you tomorrow."

"I hope so too."

"May I have a dance with you tomorrow evening?" asked Colin in a hopeful voice.

She nodded. "I would enjoy that."

"Till tomorrow then." Colin offered a slight bow. Rose gave him his coat and returned to her stateroom.

Colin stayed out looking at the stars. To the west, he could see clouds and lightning. The predicted storm was coming.

CHAPTER 14

THE NEXT MORNING, IT WAS raining hard and the sea was rough. After breakfast, Colin was sitting in the dining room completely engrossed in his origami hobby.

Rose, Mia, and Elizabeth stayed in the stateroom. The movement of the ship rocking and moving on the ocean waves had made them seasick. Edith was feeling fine and decided to go for a walk.

Edith entered the dining room and saw a man sitting at a large table. Spread out across the table was paper in assorted sizes and colors. She noticed an origami swan; it looked like the one Lady Rose had on the mantel in her room. She concluded this was the man Lady Rose, Mia, and Elizabeth met. A woman was talking to him as she walked up.

The woman asked, "Can you make a flower?"

Colin replied, "Of course."

Colin picked up a pink sheet of paper. He expertly fashioned a delicate pink rose and handed it to her.

The woman said, "This is delightful, thank you!"

"You're welcome!"

The woman walked away. Edith stepped up to the table. "Good morning. What are you doing?"

"Good morning to you. I'm practicing origami. It's a hobby of mine."

Edith sneered, "You look like a child playing with paper."

Colin ignored her tone. "That's exactly what I'm doing."

"Why would a grown man want to play with paper?" she asked in a sarcastic tone.

Colin tried to ignore her tone but it was harder this time. He looked at her closely. She was in her late-thirties, a rather plain looking woman with short black hair, pale skin, a boyish figure, and an unsmiling, gloomy countenance. "Origami is an art form that has been practiced for hundreds of years in Asia."

"No matter what fancy name you call it, you're simply playing with paper."

"Let me ask you a question. Do you knit?" asked Colin.

"No."

"Do you paint?"

"No."

"Do you garden?"

"No."

"Do you have any hobbies?"

"No."

"How do you spend your free time?"

She arched an eyebrow. "I read."

"Reading is relaxing to you, is it not?"

"Yes."

"This is relaxing to me."

She dismissed him by saying, "Seems to me to be a colossal waste of time."

Her answer perplexed him and he concluded she was an odd sort of person. "Let me make you something. What would you like?"

"Why would I want anything?"

He answered, "Because it's fun. I'll surprise you with something."

Edith stood there with her hands crossed. Colin turned his back, fashioned an item for her and handed it to her.

She stared at it. "What is it?"

"Something whimsical."

She examined it and said reluctantly, "Thank you."

"You're welcome." He chuckled because she didn't recognize what it was.

She inquired, "Are you Colin Stuart?"

"I am. I apologize for not introducing myself."

"Yes, I was surprised you didn't. A gentleman would have."

A little taken back, Colin now knew he definitely made her the right item for her. It perfectly matched her personality.

He spread his arms wide, bowed nearly to the floor, and over-dramatized all his movements. He said with as much sarcasm as he could muster, "My lady, I beg your forgiveness for my grievous and un-gentlemanly conduct." He remained bent over.

Edith didn't recognize his sarcasm and said snobbishly, "I forgive you."

Still looking at the floor, he asked, "May I have the honor of your name?"

"I am Miss Edith Kelsey."

He rose.

She said with an air of condemnation, "I understand you make alcohol."

Colin replied with pride, "Yes, I'm a master distiller. I made the finest whisky in Scotland."

"You sound proud of that."

"Why wouldn't I be?" Colin replied, irritation now creeping into his voice.

"The Bible has many cautions about wine and strong drink. Proverbs chapter twenty, verse one says, 'Strong drink is a brawler.' In my experience, that verse is true."

Colin countered, "I have served many priests, preachers, and holy men my whisky. Not one of them ever complained. I believe in my heart God approves of what I do."

"I can tell from your accent that you're a Scot." She looked down her nose at him.

"I am," he replied with pride.

"I have found Scotland is a backward land. I prefer London."

Colin nodded. "I can tell you're a proper and well-mannered lady." The sarcasm was thick in his voice.

"Yes, I am. I need to be on my way."

Colin was glad she was leaving and he said, "It was an absolute pleasure to meet you."

Edith left carrying her origami piece and returned to the stateroom. She entered and Lady Rose, Elizabeth, and Mia were sitting in the parlor. Edith asked, "Is everyone feeling better?"

"Yes, much better," Rose said. "The ship has begun to settle down." Color had returned to her cheeks.

"Yes, the storm has passed and the waves are much smaller," replied Edith.

Mia commented, "With the weather getting better, maybe Mr. Stuart will be flying kites later."

"Mr. Stuart is in the dining room playing with his paper. He made me something." She held out her hand and showed her item. She sneered, "I don't know what it is."

Mia examined it for a second then exclaimed, "It's a dragon!"

Edith's eyebrows rose high on her forehead and she questioned, "It is?"

"Yes," Mia answered. "Can't you see the wings? It's a fine dragon, too."

Edith's face crumpled into a scowl. "He made the woman in front of me a dainty rose yet he made me a dragon!"

Elizabeth and Mia giggled. They weren't surprised Colin made her a dragon instead of a flower. Edith tossed the dragon into the trash.

Mia jumped up and took it out. "May I have it?"

Edith replied sourly, "If you want it, you can have it."

"Thank you!" Mia begged her mother, "May I go and see Mr. Stuart?"

Edith barked, "You shouldn't spend any time with that Scotsman!"

"Edith, it's not your place to tell Mia that!" Rose sharply replied.

Edith coiled back. "I'm sorry for intruding, however, in my opinion, he isn't a gentleman. He was rude and didn't show me proper respect."

Rose rebutted, "That's not the Mr. Stuart I know. I have found him to be sweet and considerate."

Edith stared at Rose, opening and closing her mouth, not believing what she had heard.

"Mia," Rose said, "you may go to see Mr. Stuart. Elizabeth will go with you if she is feeling up to it."

Elizabeth volunteered, "I'm feeling much better, madam, and I would like to go,"

"Thank you, Mummy! Could you please keep my dragon for me?"

Rose stared at Edith. "I'll cherish it." Edith turned away from her.

Mia handed the dragon to Rose then asked, "Elizabeth, are you ready?"

"I am. Let's go."

After the door closed, Edith stepped over to Rose. "Madam, are you developing feelings for the Scot?"

Rose forcefully responded, "How is that any of your business?"

Surprised, Edith said, "Madam, I'm only making sure you don't get hurt in some way."

Rose tilted her head. "And how am I getting hurt?"

"The Scotsman is handsome and he knows how to talk to a woman. He isn't from your station and it's obvious he is trying to move up in this world."

She sighed. "Edith, why are you worrying about this?"

"I always worry about everything that might affect you. I only want what is best for you."

The conversation was getting on Rose's nerves. "I know you do, but I'll decide who I'm interested in, it is certainly not your place to do so."

Edith pursed her lips. "Yes, my lady. If you don't need anything, I'll retire to my room for a while."

Rose replied without looking at her. "I'm fine, thank you."

Edith retired to her room, angry with Mr. Stuart and disappointed with Lady Rose for chastising her in front of Mia and Elizabeth. She wondered why Lady Rose couldn't see through Colin's façade.

—◆—

CHAPTER 15

MIA AND ELIZABETH ARRIVED AT the dining room and Colin was still there. He saw them as they walked across the room.

"Good morning, ladies, how are you on this stormy day?"

"We are feeling better. It was rough earlier today," Mia said.

"Yes, it was," agreed Colin.

"What are you making today?" asked Elizabeth.

"I have made all kinds of things including a dragon."

"Yes, I saw one." Mia grinned.

"How did you see my dragon? Did it come to life? Is it now running about the ship? My dragons have been known to do that."

Mia giggled. "No silly, Edith brought it to our stateroom."

Colin cringed, wrinkled his nose, and was afraid to ask, but he did: "Is she traveling with you?"

"Yes, she is my mother's lady's maid."

Colin hung his head and shook it slowly. "Just my luck. Was Edith upset with me?"

Elizabeth snickered. "Oh yes! She wondered why another woman got a rose but she got a dragon. I think I know why you gave it to her."

"Me too," said Mia.

They laughed as Colin frowned.

"Edith strikes me as a different sort of person. Is she?"

"Oh yes!" said Mia.

Elizabeth shot Mia a look. "Mia, you shouldn't say that!"

"Well she is," retorted Mia.

"Did she complain to Lady Rose about me?"

Mia said, "Well, Mother…"

Elizabeth interrupted her. "Let's move away from the topic of drag-ons and Edith. Can you teach us to make some things?"

"Of course, I can," he replied. "We will start with the basics. It's best to start with a square piece of paper. Mia, is this sheet of paper square?" Colin held up a sheet of paper.

"No, it's a rectangle."

"You're so smart. You're correct! It's difficult to use a rectangular piece of paper when you first start. Now both of you take a sheet of square paper and follow what I do."

Colin started to show them how to make a few items. The girls had an enjoyable morning and lunched with Colin. At three o'clock, Elizabeth said they had to return to their rooms and Mia did so reluctantly.

After dropping Mia off in her room, Elizabeth went to her room. Shortly, there was a knock on her door. Elizabeth opened it and there was Edith. Elizabeth sighed because she didn't want to see her; she and Edith didn't get along. Elizabeth was twenty-five, pretty, cheerful, outgo-ing, and took her job as governess in a serious and responsible manner. Edith often acted superior to Elizabeth and tried to manage her affairs, which irritated Elizabeth.

Edith stepped in without an invitation and closed the door behind her. "You have been gone a long time. Where have you been?"

"Mia and I were learning origami."

Edith gasped. "Not with that Scot!"

Elizabeth nodded.

"What do you and Lady Rose see in him?"

Elizabeth replied. "He is kind, brave, intelligent, loves children, and is rather handsome."

Edith retorted, "He is a low-class Scot who makes liquor."

"Making whisky is an honorable profession."

Edith shook her head. "He is fooling you with his charm. He wants something."

"I don't think so," rebutted Elizabeth.

"If you like him that's fine, but Lady Rose cannot," stated Edith.

Elizabeth put her hands on her hips. "Why not?"

"He isn't in her class. It would be demeaning for us if she got involved with him." Elizabeth didn't reply, but Edith continued on. "If our matron marries a lower-class man, it lowers our station."

Confused, Elizabeth didn't know what to say. "I don't understand; why does it affect us?"

"It *does* affect us. I provide an honorable service, but my friends will look down on me if she married him."

Elizabeth scoffed, "Aren't you getting ahead of yourself a bit? They have only recently met."

"I have seen this before. She fell in love last time quickly. I can tell by the way she talks about him that she fancies him. Since Thomas died, she has never spoken of another man. Now she and Mia talk about him constantly." Edith's tone had changed to pleading. "You have to help me with this."

Elizabeth stepped back. "Help you with what?"

"You must help Mia see this isn't the right thing for her mother or for her."

"What exactly do you want me to do?"

"You must tell Mia that Mr. Stuart isn't the right type of person for Lady Rose."

Elizabeth's shook her head and her eyebrows furrowed. "No! My job isn't to push my ideas on Mia. I'm to educate and guide her to be a proper lady not to tell her who she is to love."

"You're wrong! You have to shape her opinions!"

Elizabeth's eyebrows rose. "I agree and I do. However, the only reason you want this done is so you will not lose status. I think that's wrong!"

"I helped you get this position. You owe me! You have to support me!"

Elizabeth said defiantly, "I will not!"

Edith glared at her. "My job is taking care of my lady. I have dedicated my life to taking care of her. I'll do anything I can to make sure she is happy. There is nothing wrong with me shaping her opinion on a subject."

"You shouldn't try to guide Lady Rose's heart. She could hate you in the future for it."

"She will respect me if I'm right," Edith countered.

"How will you judge if you're right?"

Edith stood in a defiant stance. "Being interested in a Scot who has no title and no wealth is wrong! It is as simple as that."

Elizabeth shook her head. "I don't want to discuss this anymore."

"You can't ignore this."

"Yes, I can. If you would please excuse me, I need to rest for a while."

Edith left the room, incensed over Elizabeth's reaction. She decided even without Elizabeth's help she was going to undermine the budding relationship between Lady Rose and Mr. Stuart.

CHAPTER 16

LADY MITCHELL WANTED TO MAKE sure Rose and Colin spent as much time together as possible, so she sent out invitations to them for dinner. Colin received the invitation and immediately met with Mr. Jones to learn more about proper table etiquette. Afterward, he was more comfortable and prepared on what to expect.

The dinner was enjoyable for Rose and Colin and they talked continuously. After dinner, the orchestra started playing. Colin had thought about this moment all day. He turned to ask Rose to dance, but the first officer was already at her elbow. Irritated because he had been too slow and missed the opportunity, Colin watched as they moved across the dance floor,

The first dance had hardly ended when Colin marched up to them. He asked anxiously, "Lady Cavendish, may I have the next dance?"

She smiled and nodded. "Yes, you may."

As they waltzed, Colin's dancing impressed Rose. The first officer was stiff and formal, but Colin was smooth and gracefully moved her across the floor. Colin was quiet, concentrating so as not to make a mistake, although he was smiling the entire time.

As soon as the dance ended, the first officer appeared. "Lady Cavendish, may I have the next dance?"

Colin was crestfallen; again, he had not acted fast enough.

She replied to the first officer after seeing Colin's hurt expression. "I'm sorry, but I have promised Mr. Stuart the next several dances."

The first officer's expression didn't change. He bowed stiffly and moved away. Colin smiled and his confidence soared. The first officer, along with the rest of the dinner party guests, seemed to fade into the background.

It was almost midnight when the orchestra finished, the crowd had thinned considerably. Rose and Colin had been dancing and talking most of the evening.

"May I take you for a walk?"

Rose smiled and nodded. "Yes, I was hoping you would ask."

Arm in arm, they left the ballroom. They strolled outside where many couples were standing along the rail looking at the ocean and quietly talking. They found a secluded spot and stopped.

He turned to her. "I hope I didn't wear you out tonight."

"No, I had a fantastic time, although my feet are sore from all that waltzing." She chuckled. "You're a superb dancer."

"Only because I had a beautiful and talented dancing partner."

Rose blushed. "Thank you! You're always so sweet. You are staying in New York for a few days, aren't you?"

Colin's face fell. "Unfortunately, no, my plans have changed. I had hoped I could chaperone you and Mia around the city."

"You want Mia to go?" asked Rose, pleasantly surprised.

"Of course," Colin answered. "She is adorable. I enjoy being with her."

"That's nice of you to say." Rose looked at him out of the corner of her eye. "I hope you mean it?"

"Why wouldn't I? She is smart, friendly, adventuresome, and pretty like her mother."

"Mr. Stuart—"

Colin interjected, "Would you mind calling me Colin?"

"Only if you call me Rose."

"I will."

"Colin," she began again, "many men I know think of a child, like Mia, as a burden."

"A burden?" Colin looked perplexed. "She's a gift, not a burden."

"I've had men directly ask me when I would be sending her to boarding school."

Colin said, "Those men have never been around children. Children are gifts to us. They are like fruit trees that need nourishing and care. If raised properly, they will give a lifetime of fruit and joy. I don't believe boarding schools provide the tender care a child requires. I hope I'm not offending you. Did you attend a boarding school?"

Rose gasped. "Heavens no! My mother had a governess and several teachers for me at home. She always wanted me close to her."

"I feel the same way. I was thinking about my schedule change, since we can't see each other in New York, how about Chicago?"

"I would love to."

"Maybe you, Mia, and I could go together to the art exposition."

She smiled. "I would enjoy that."

"Perfect! I will settle in my new position and contact you. Where will you be staying?"

"At the Chicago Grand Hotel."

"I'll contact you there. I'm so delighted knowing we will see each other again."

"So am I."

There was a slight pause. Colin wanted to kiss her. Everything inside him was telling him to, but he didn't want to offend her with a potential faux pas. A few awkward seconds passed.

"Mia enjoyed learning origami today," Rose said, ending the moment. "She can't stop talking about it. All she talks about is origami, kites, and you."

Colin smiled. "I have taught others, but she has learned faster than anyone else. She has an artist's touch."

"Yes, she does. She loves to draw. Her drawing class is her favorite."

Colin glanced at his watch. "It's getting late," he said. "I should get you to your room."

They leisurely walked to her stateroom.

At the door, he said tenderly, "I have had a marvelous evening. Thank you for spending it with me."

"It has been a while since I had such an enjoyable time."

He reached out and took her hand and kissed it.

He bowed. "Till tomorrow."

CHAPTER 17

COLIN WAS UP EARLY THE next morning. This would be his last opportunity to fly kites before they reached America.

In her stateroom, Mia paced back and forth. She had gotten dressed, had breakfast, and waited impatiently to ask permission to go on deck. Her mother was now awake and having breakfast in the parlor.

"Mummy, may I go outside? It's a nice morning and I'm sure Mr. Stuart will be flying his kites."

"Have Elizabeth go with you."

"Elizabeth doesn't feel well this morning. May I please go alone?"

"I'll have Edith go with you."

Mia wrinkled her nose; she knew Edith didn't like Mr. Stuart and she was so strict. "I'll be fine. I won't go anywhere else, I promise."

"Let me have breakfast and I'll go with you."

"Mummy, that will take too long," Mia said. "Please let me go, please."

Her mother sighed. "Alright, you can go. I'll come and check on you soon."

"Thank you!" Mia ran from the room to the first-class deck at the ship's stern. She saw Mr. Stuart at the rail with a kite. A few feet away she stopped and tried to calm down like a lady would. She caught her breath.

"Good morning, Mr. Stuart."

"Good morning to you, Miss Lady Cavendish. How are you on this fine day?"

"I'm well, thank you. I see you're flying the box kite."

"Yes, she is steady and reliable. I have something special for you today."

"You do?"

"Yes, let me pull this old girl in and we can talk about it." Colin reeled in the kite and they sat on deck chairs.

"Do you know the story of the Scottish girl and the butterfly?"

"No I don't." Mia sat up straighter, interested. "Is it a true story?"

"My grandmother told it to me so I'm sure it's a true story," Colin said. "There once was a Scottish girl named Emily. Emily loved her grandmother and her grandmother's garden. Every spring she helped her grandmother in the garden, so she always anxiously waited for springtime. As soon as the weather warmed up a bit, she and her grandmother would prepare the garden and plant the seeds. Emily would check often to see if the plants were growing. She would watch in awe each year as the garden grew. Later, as the flowers blossomed, she would help her grandmother pick them. Her grandmother's house always smelled of flowers and freshly made bread."

Mia was listening intently.

"Emily had a quiet place in the corner of the garden where she would sit on a bench and watch the butterflies. If she was still, the butterflies would land on her. She would hold out her hand and butterflies would land on it. Sometimes a dozen or more would rest on her. Her grandmother said it was because she was so sweet and kind."

"Emily turned ten in late summer and that winter she became ill. The town doctor treated her but Emily didn't get better. Her mother took her to a large city hospital, however, she only got worse. The doctors said they couldn't do anything for her. Her mother brought her to her grandmother's home, where they cared for her and prayed every day for Emily to get well. Spring came and her grandmother planted the garden without Emily's help because she was too ill."

Mia had a tearful look on her face.

"The flowers were starting to bloom and the butterflies were in the garden. Emily had gotten worse with each passing day. She was only a breath away from death. Her grandmother was afraid she was about to die and she wanted Emily to be in her garden when it happened. Her grandmother bundled her up and took her to the garden bench. She propped Emily up with pillows and blankets. Emily seemed happy there in the warm sun and the fresh air."

Mia sniffled and was trying to hold back the tears.

"Emily's grandmother was quietly tending the garden nearby and she saw a butterfly she had never seen before land on Emily's bench," Colin went on. "The blue butterfly was the most colorful one her grandmother had ever seen. Emily saw it too and slowly, with great effort, she reached out to it. The butterfly landed on her hand. Emily smiled for the first time in ages. Her grandmother watched as the butterfly stayed on her hand as Emily drew her hand to her chest. The butterfly rested there for a long time. Emily seemed to gather a little strength from the butterfly's visit. Her grandmother took her into the house after the butterfly left."

Mia started to smile and tears ran down her cheek.

"The next day, Emily's grandmother wrapped her up again and brought her to the garden bench. Soon the butterfly returned. Like the day before, Emily reached out her hand and the butterfly landed on it. This time Emily talked to the butterfly; it was amazing because she hadn't had the strength to speak in weeks. The butterfly stayed again for a long time. Each day after that, her grandmother did the same thing. Slowly, Emily's strength began to return and the butterfly came every day until the end of the season."

Mia, between small sobs, asked, "Was Emily well again?"

"Yes, Emily recovered completely. The next summer, several blue butterflies arrived and they always came to Emily's bench. The following summer, more came and more came every year after that. The butterflies soon spread across Scotland and became Scotland's most prized butterfly. Emily grew up and later married in the garden. Her children learned to garden with her the same way she learned to garden with her grandmother."

"Oh...." Mia sniffled.

"Now some people say the butterflies came to Scotland because there was a change in the African trade winds," Colin said. "Others say a botanist brought the butterfly in. However, my grandmother believed an angel sent the butterfly to the garden so Emily would regain her will to live. What do you think caused the butterfly to be there?"

Mia said with tears flowing again, "I think an angel sent the butterfly."

"I do too."

Mia wiped her eyes. "I love that story."

"Yes, the Emily story is loved by the Scots. Now every year there is a festival in Edinburgh to celebrate all our Scottish butterflies. People at the festival fill the sky with butterfly kites of all sizes. There is a trophy for the person who has the best butterfly kite and I have won it twice." He paused. "Now I have something for you." He reached behind their deck chairs and fetched a box. He handed it to her. "This is for you."

She pulled the lid off the rectangular box and pulled out a kite, shaped like a butterfly and painted in bright colors.

Mia gasped. "Mr. Stuart, it's amazing! Thank you!" She hugged him.

"Would you like to fly it?"

"It's too pretty to fly. What if I damage it?"

"We can fix it or we will build a prettier one."

He assembled the kite and had it flying in a few minutes. He handed the controls to Mia. Against the sky, a colorful butterfly flying from the ship was a spectacular sight. Soon people crowded around watching. People on the second and third class decks watched too. He showed her how to make it turn and dive. The crowd applauded at the display.

Rose and Edith were on the deck looking for Mia when they saw the crowd. They got closer and could see Mia flying the colorful kite.

Edith clucked her tongue. "Look at the spectacle Mr. Stuart is causing, and your daughter is right in the middle of it."

Rose, who was watching the butterfly kite, frowned as she glanced back at Edith. "What's wrong with her flying a kite?"

"We English don't call attention to ourselves. The kite is flamboyant and audacious. Look at the crowd cheering her on!" she complained.

Sternly, Rose replied, "Maybe you should go to the stateroom if this bothers you."

Surprised with her tone, Edith asked, "Madam, are you dismissing me?"

Rose replied sharply, "Yes."

Edith turned in a huff, and left for her stateroom.

Rose watched Mia fly the kite. She noticed how Colin worked with Mia. He was patient and was teaching her, not doing it for her. Mia was enjoying herself sending the kite back and forth with occasional dives. Suddenly, the kite dove toward the water and the crowd gasped. Colin calmly told her what to do and she did it. The kite recovered and gained altitude. The crowd cheered her. A few minutes later Mia said something to Colin and she handed the controls to him.

The people near Mia patted her on the back and congratulated her on how well she flew the kite. Mia saw her mother and walked through the crowd to her. "Did you see me flying the kite?"

"Yes, and you did so skillfully."

"I had to give it to Mr. Stuart because my arms got tired. He made it for me."

"I'm not surprised; he seems to be a handy man."

"Can you see it's a butterfly kite?"

"Oh yes."

"Have you ever heard the story of the Scottish girl and the butterfly?"

Rose shook her head.

"Mr. Stuart told me the story. Let me tell you."

She took her mother's hand and they stepped to the deck chairs. They sat and Mia told her the story.

Mia wiped tears away from her mother's face and hers as she told the story.

Rose said, "What a lovely story!"

"Mr. Stuart said every year there is a festival in Edinburgh to celebrate all the Scottish butterflies. People at the festival fly butterfly kites. There is a trophy for the person who has the best butterfly kite and Mr. Stuart has won it twice."

"My," Rose said, surprised. "He's won it twice!"

"Yes. He is fun to be with. I like him."

"I think he likes you too."

Mia offered, "Mummy, it's fine with me if you like Mr. Stuart."

"What do you mean?"

"It has been a long time since Father died. You were sad for so long after he died. You seem happy when you talk about Mr. Stuart."

Rose thought about her comments. "I do like him."

"I never wanted you to go to dinner parties because I knew men would be there. I didn't want you to be with anyone else other than Father. Now I know there are nice men like Mr. Stuart."

Rose took Mia's hands and squeezed them. "Mia, you never told me that before."

"I know. I always felt it but never said it."

"Thank you for sharing that. I love you."

"I love you too."

Mr. Stuart returned, carrying her kite. "Rose, how are you this morning?"

She smiled and replied warmly, "I'm well, thank you."

"Did you see Mia fly her kite?"

"I did."

Colin said proudly, "She is doing excellently. She's absolutely the best student I ever had."

"Thank you for building the kite for her." Rose reached out and touched his arm tenderly.

He looked at her hand on his arm and looked into her eyes. "I enjoyed making it for her. Ladies, I beg your forgiveness because I must leave for a luncheon appointment with Mr. Jones. Mia, here is your kite. It comes with a lifetime of free repairs."

"Thank you, Mr. Stuart."

Rose said, "I hope to see you at dinner tonight. I received an invitation to dinner from Mrs. Whitten. I understand you did too."

"I haven't seen her invitation yet," Colin said. "It may have arrived this morning. I hope to see you as well. Mia, I enjoyed flying with you."

"Thank you, Mr. Stuart, for everything," said Mia.

"You're welcome. Ladies, until next time." He tipped his hat, picked up his box kite, and left.

CHAPTER 18

———◆———

"WHAT ARE THE FIRST STEPS you will take when you arrive at the distillery?" Mr. Jones sipped on a drink as he stared across the lunch table at Colin, awaiting his reply.

"It's all about the whisky," Colin began. "I'll start with the way it's made. I'll then meet the people and understand their roles. As soon as I can, I want to understand who buys our whisky and what we can do to sell more."

"Excellent; you are doing exactly what I would do. I expected to go with you to the distillery but I received a telegram this morning and I need to travel to Washington. I'm sorry; I must leave you alone for a bit. I'll be there as soon as I can. I'll have someone meet you in Chicago and take you to the distillery. Is that acceptable?"

"Yes."

Mr. Jones nodded. "The person who will meet you in Chicago is the accountant for the distillery, Mr. Babcock." He paused for a second, trying to find the right words. "Colin, I have been completely honest with you regarding every detail of the distillery except for one."

Colin raised his eyebrows but said nothing.

"The plant foreman, Shawn O'Brien, is a hard-working Irishman with an awful temper. He may not like you being there."

"Does he know I'm coming?"

"Yes."

"Does he know I'm your partner?"

"Yes."

"Does he know I'll be his boss?"

"Yes."

Colin gave a brief nod. "I've faced this before."

"You must be prepared for a rough time. He has an awful temper," advised Mr. Jones.

"You said that twice. If he has such a bad temper, shouldn't he be fired?"

"That's the difficult part—he's my sister's nephew."

"I see." Colin nodded. "He is family."

"Yes, my sister would never forgive me if he was fired."

"Is this man Goliath or something?"

"No, he is only an Irishman."

"I can handle it."

Mr. Jones smiled and commented, "I'm impressed you aren't worried or upset."

Colin leaned backed. "I've had to deal with hardnosed distillery workers since I began in this business. I know what to do."

"Good," Mr. Jones said. "Now there's another sensitive topic I want to talk to you about."

Colin gave a nod. "What is it?"

"You and Lady Rose are the talk of the ship."

Colin's eyebrows rose. "We are?"

"Oh yes, on every voyage a romance sprouts, and apparently, you two are this trip's romance."

"I didn't know we had created such a stir."

"You have. I only bring this up because our partnership is new. How serious is this?"

"I've gotten to know her and I like her," Colin answered right away.

"I can understand that; she is a beautiful lady."

Colin's cheeks reddened. "She certainly is."

"Did you know she is one of the richest women in England?"

"No."

Surprised, Mr. Jones stated, "Colin, I find that hard to believe!"

"It's true. I didn't know anything about her money. I don't care about her money."

Mr. Jones chuckled. "My lad, that is certainly commendable, but I can tell you without a doubt she is wealthy."

"What's your point?"

"A wealthy woman is interested in you. Most men would stop everything they were doing to marry a woman like her."

Colin shrugged his shoulders. "Not me. I want to make my own mark on the world, not through marriage to a rich woman."

Mr. Jones stared at him and gauged what he said. "I believe you, but here's the dilemma I have. I want you to marry whoever you want; however, I don't want you to return to England."

"I have no interest in that if I can be successful in America. I want to be successful on my own. Haven't I made it clear enough?"

"Yes, you have." Mr. Jones put his hands up. "Now please understand, I don't want to meddle in your life, I only want the distillery to be successful."

Colin nodded. "I understand completely."

"It's clear Lady Rose likes you, so how do I say this…"

Colin broke in, "You want me to slow things down."

Mr. Jones nodded. "That would be prudent. Let the distillery be your prime goal for a while. Stay involved with her, but take your time. People are saying they have never seen a titled woman get her head turned so completely by a commoner."

"Are people really saying that? Or are you exaggerating?"

"Not at all; several people have said that to me."

"I planned to have dinner with her tonight. There's probably an invitation from Mrs. Whitten waiting in my stateroom. What should I do?"

"I think you should stay away for a bit. Decline it, saying you're feeling poorly or a business issue has come up that needs your attention."

"We have already made plans to meet in Chicago later," Colin said. "Should I follow through on those?"

"Yes, of course you should. Maybe she is the one for you, however, take some time to decide."

"I agree. I want the business to be successful too."

"I'm sorry about having to talk to you about this," Mr. Jones offered. "I'll never butt into your personal business again as long as you don't run home to England with a rich woman."

Colin assured him, "I won't."

CHAPTER 19

———◆———

ROSE LOOKED FORWARD TO DINNER and was glad she had saved her best evening gown. She took extra care to make sure her hair and dress were perfect.

Mia came into her room as she finished getting ready. "Mummy, you look beautiful!"

"Thank you, dear."

"I love that dress and your necklace is dazzling. There must be something special happening tonight. Can you tell me what it is?" Mia asked and giggled.

"You, monkey, you're always so nosey. You always have to know what's going on, don't you?"

"I do. Otherwise what is there to talk about?"

Rose chuckled. "Well, if you must know, I'm looking forward to seeing and dancing with Mr. Stuart."

"Oh, that's so romantic."

"Mia, it's not romantic, it's simply something fun that I'm looking forward to."

"No, Mother, I'm old enough to understand romance."

Rose smiled. "I guess you are. There's no fooling you anymore, is there?"

"No, I'm almost ten and I'm not a baby anymore."

"I guess you aren't." Rose paused. "Elizabeth isn't feeling well, so you're to stay in the stateroom and read."

"Yes, Mummy, I know. Will you tell me everything that happens tonight?"

"I will tell you most of what happens."

"I see," Mia pondered. "So, you won't tell me about any of the romantic things?"

"Mia, you're only nine."

Mia put her hands on her hips and declared, "I'm almost ten."

Rose smiled and agreed, "Yes you are. Now I must go. I can't be too late."

"Yes, a lady must not be too prompt or too late," Mia recited.

"You are correct. Always have the man anticipate your arrival."

"I know. That way he appreciates you more."

Rose marveled, "You know so much more about men and relationships than I did when I was your age."

They walked to the door and Rose kissed her.

"Please don't kiss any frogs!" said Mia.

Rose chuckled. "Sometimes you have to kiss a few frogs to find a prince."

"I already know who the prince is."

"Mia! You're such a bad girl!" Rose laughed. "Now Edith will check in on you. Tell her if you need anything."

"I will. Mummy, have a good time!"

"I'm sure I will."

After her mother left, Mia sat on the couch. She picked up a book and started to read, but her eyes glazed over and she started to daydream about the dinner and the dance afterward. It seemed so romantic; she would love to see it. She thought about all the people dressed in their best. She decided she had to see for herself.

She thought about how she could do it. She remembered there were windows in the dining room. She thought she could sneak down and peek in for a few minutes. After Edith checked on her, she could leave and return before Edith checked on her again. Mia decided her plan could work so she patiently waited for Edith.

Ten minutes passed. The door adjoining their room with the room next door opened and Edith stepped in.

"Mia, are you doing well?"

"Yes, I am."

"Do you need anything?"

Mia shook her head and said sweetly, "I'm fine."

"I'll check on you again. If you need something you can ring the bell."

"I will, thank you."

Edith pulled the door closed. Mia sprung up and put her ear against Edith's door. Everything was quiet.

Mia crept to the stateroom's main door and quietly opened it. She snuck down the hall and on to the deck, then she ran to the dining room and peeked in. She couldn't see her mother. She moved around to several windows. Finally, after the fifth window, she saw her mother from behind. The table had ten chairs and only nine people were there. The chair across from her mother was empty. Mr. Stuart wasn't there.

She was away from her room now for a few minutes and couldn't stay to see if he showed up. She hurried to her room and quietly entered.

She paced the floor and wondered what could have happened to him. Didn't he get his invitation? Was he ill? Did he forget? Maybe Mr. Stuart was simply late. Her mother would be heartbroken if he didn't attend. All these questions swirled in her head. The first thing she should do was to check and see if he was there now.

Edith's door started to open. Mia quickly sat on the couch.

"Your mother said you could have milk and biscuits. Are you hungry?"

Mia wanted them but later. She had to figure out what happened to Mr. Stuart. "I'm fine for now."

Edith closed the door. Mia tiptoed to the door and listened. The room was quiet. Again, Mia hurried out and rushed to the dining room window. She peeked in to see if Mr. Stuart was there—but he wasn't. She returned to her room and quietly entered.

She paced the floor, worrying about what to do. Mr. Stuart wasn't there. Maybe he was ill and needed help. She knew his room was on the other end of first class and down one level. It would take quite a while to get there and return. She decided Edith must stay in her room for a longer period. An idea came to her. She knocked on Edith's door.

When Edith answered, Mia asked, "May I have the milk and biscuits now?"

"Of course; I thought you would get hungry soon."

Edith retrieved the milk from the icebox and poured a glass. She put three biscuits on a plate, which she placed along with the milk on the parlor table.

"Ring the bell when you're finished and I'll put the dishes away."

Mia smiled because now she could predict when Edith would return. Mia said, "Thank you, I will."

Edith left and so did Mia. She ran to the dining room window to check to see if Mr. Stuart was there. He was not. She sprinted down the corridor and down one level to his room. She knocked on the door, out of breath. In a few seconds, he opened it.

"Isn't this a pleasant surprise! Miss Lady Cavendish, how may I help you?"

"Mr. Stuart," she panted, "I wanted to make sure you were well. You were expected at dinner."

"I had some pressing business that needed attention."

Mia hung her head. "Oh, I see. I'm sorry to bother you." She started to walk away.

"Mia, wait a minute. Who was expecting me at dinner?"

Mia said, "I shouldn't say."

"Is it your mother?"

Mia turned, smiled, and admitted, "Yes, she is hoping you would be there."

"Did she tell you that?"

"Yes, she dressed especially for you."

Colin stood in the doorway and thought about what to do. He'd promised Mr. Jones he would take it slowly with Rose.

Mia urged him, "You should go. She is dressed in her finest gown and is absolutely beautiful."

Colin tried to explain, "Mia, this is complicated—"

Mia put her hands on her hips and interrupted him, "No it's not. Grownups make things too complicated. She likes you. I think you like her. Tomorrow we will be in New York and you may not see each other again. You should see her tonight. She wants you to be there."

Colin smiled, stepped over and hugged her. "You're right, we do make things too complicated. I'll get dressed and be there as soon as I can."

"Please don't tell anyone I was here. I'll get into trouble."

"I won't. Thank you for coming."

"You're welcome." Mia turned and ran to her stateroom. She quietly entered and tiptoed to the table where the milk and biscuits were. She gobbled the biscuits, drank the milk, and wiped her mouth with her sleeve. She sat on the couch for a few moments to catch her breath before she rang the bell.

Edith heard the bell, walked in, and stopped in front of Mia. "You look flushed. Are you feeling ill?" She felt Mia's forehead. "You're perspiring some. You may be coming down with something. I'll send for your mother."

Mia gasped. "No, no don't do that! I'm feeling fine. It's a little warm in here."

"Are you sure?"

"Yes, I'm fine. Thank you for asking. I'm going to get ready and go to bed."

"Your clothes are laid out for you. I'll clean up here."

Edith put away the dishes and left.

Mia wondered if she should risk one more trip. She had been lucky so far. Normally when she went to bed, only her mother would check in on her. She decided to sneak out one more time.

Colin dressed and rushed to the dining room. He apologized to everyone at the table for being late. Rose was smiling at him as he sat.

"I was wondering what was so important that you couldn't make our last dinner," Rose said with one eyebrow arched.

"There's a story to tell you about that. Maybe during our first dance, I can tell you."

"I look forward to it."

He was glad he decided to come. He looked around the room and didn't see Mr. Jones. He sighed in relief. After dinner, Colin escorted Rose to the dance floor.

"Colin, you said there was a story you wanted to tell me."

"Oh yes, I was in my stateroom working and a little angel came to me."

Rose smiled. "A little angel came to your stateroom?"

"Yes, she was the prettiest angel I have ever seen."

Rose laughed. "You have seen other angels?"

"Yes, I have. I'm an angel expert."

"I have learned you're an expert on many things." Rose smiled.

"You're correct," Colin said good naturedly, "but let me get back to my angel. The little angel said I must come to dinner. She said there was nothing more important for me to do than to come tonight. She said if I came I would see a beautiful woman in a gorgeous dress."

Rose smiled knowingly. "Did you see the woman?"

"Not yet, I'm still looking for her."

Rose laughed and shook her head. "Colin, that was a nice story until the end. You must create a new ending or find a new dance partner."

He took her hands in his. "Let me try the story again. The little angel said I must come to dinner. She said if I came I would see a beautiful woman in a gorgeous dress. I came here and I saw you. You simply took my breath away...and also, I believe, my heart."

Rose gasped. "That is the nicest thing anyone has ever said to me. I hope you mean it."

"I do. Every word of it. By the way, the angel was *almost* right about you. She should have said I would see the most beautiful woman I have ever seen...because you are."

"Oh Colin, you're going to make me cry." She squeezed his hands.

The orchestra started. Colin asked, "May I have the first dance?"

"You can have every dance."

They began the dance. Outside the window was Mia, watching them. They looked so happy together. She listened to the music and danced in her mind. She stayed until the song finished then hurried to her room. She changed clothes, got into bed, and said her prayers. Thinking about her mother again, she decided to go to her mother's bed. Her plan was to stay awake until her mother got back and she tried, but she was soon asleep.

CHAPTER 20

———◆———

THE ORCHESTRA PLAYED THE LAST dance then everyone started to leave. Colin had an important decision to make. Last evening, he walked Rose to her room and kissed her hand. Tonight, he wanted to kiss her, but he wondered if it was too soon. Considering his conversation with Mr. Jones, he thought maybe he should wait.

He and Rose strolled from the ballroom outside to the deck. It was cool so he removed his coat and put it around her. They stopped at the rail as many other couples had done. It was a starless night with the moon occasionally peeking out from behind the clouds.

Colin said, "Tomorrow, I leave for Chicago. There will be a taxi waiting for me and will take me to a train. I'm sorry we cannot see New York together."

"So am I," Rose said.

"How long will you be there?"

She answered, "Two weeks then we travel to Chicago."

"I promise to contact you in Chicago and we will make arrangements to go to the exposition."

"I'm looking forward to that." She smiled at him. "Now tell me what business kept you from dinner this evening?"

Colin turned to her. "Honestly, it wasn't business. I hesitate to tell you what it was."

"Why?"

"I...." He paused to find the right words. "I was worried that maybe I have been rushing things with you and maybe I should slow down some."

"Why would you think that?"

"Rose," he began, "you're a titled woman as well as a beautiful and intelligent woman. I'm a simple man with no title and not much money but I have truly great prospects. I have no right to think there can be a future for us even though I want there to be."

She nodded. "I have thought some of the same things."

Colin had a disappointed look. "You have? What a shame!"

"Please don't take my comment the wrong way. I mean I've thought about it, however, I haven't allowed it to affect how I feel."

"It's a shame something like social class should keep a person from doing what they want to do. That's one reason why I'm going to America—there are no social classes there. Everyone is equal."

"I have heard people say that." She questioned, "But are people really equal?"

He shrugged. "I'm told that, and I hope so. I want to be known for what I do, not how I was born."

"It's hard for me to know how you feel because I was born with a title."

"I should have known better. I know how I'm supposed to act with you. Maybe it's because I'm going to America that I feel I'm free to act differently. I'm sorry if I've stepped out of line by letting my emotions for you and Mia get out of control."

"You've done nothing wrong," Rose said, her eyebrows furrowed with emotion. "You have been kind, gentle and brave. I've allowed you to get to know me and I've enjoyed it. However, I would be remiss if I did not tell you I worry about the fact we are from two different worlds."

"Your world has always shunned me. I'm not welcome there even today with the success I have had. Does it bother you that I'm not titled and wasn't born into the aristocracy?"

Rose hesitated. "At first it did," she admitted, "but now I know you better, I don't think as much about it. People remind me you're from a different class, but I ignore them. I do what I want to do."

"What about your family? What will they say?"

"There is only my mother, and frankly she will have a problem with me even talking to you."

Colin hung his head. "Maybe I should focus on being successful in my new business and stop being a bother to you."

Rose's voice was stern. "Colin Stuart, you aren't a bother! You keep being the gentleman you have been and I'll deal with anyone who says anything wrong about you. You will find I'm a strong, independent woman who lets her own heart guide her."

Colin smiled. "My lady, I think I have received the first of what I believe will be many lectures regarding my behavior."

Rose admitted, "I do get on my soapbox and lecture often."

"I love the fact you're willing to state your view on a subject."

"I'm glad you do," she chuckled, "because I state them often."

Colin confessed, "I'm not skilled in all the things a gentleman should do. When I leave you at your door tonight, I want to kiss you, but a London gentleman probably wouldn't do that so early in a relationship."

"Colin, I don't want a typical London gentleman in my life. A London gentleman is boring, stuffy, pretentious, and more concerned about what others think than what his wife thinks. I want a man who is a gentleman but is also kind, gentle, passionate, unconventional, and willing to work hard for what he wants. He—"

Colin stepped close, cutting her off, gently cupped her face and kissed her. It was a long, passionate, and romantic kiss.

Her heart was racing like it hadn't since Thomas. She pulled back from the kiss. "I guess you won't have to think about what you will do at the door, will you?" she quipped.

He smiled. "Oh yes, I will."

"Now Colin, I was just saying I was looking for a gentleman," she chided.

"Yes, but you also said you wanted someone who is passionate and unconventional."

She chuckled. "I can see already I made a mistake in telling you that."

"Yes, you did."

He kissed her again. After a long kiss, she pulled back. "You're stealing my heart right here on the deck of this ship."

"I'm trying my best to do so."

She looked around. "Let's go to my stateroom. There are too many people here."

They walked to her room and stopped at the door. This time he reached around her and pulled her close. He again kissed her deeply as she put her arms around him. After the kiss, they held each other. She felt his body against her, lean and strong.

She reluctantly pulled back because it was so late. "Colin, thank you for a breath-taking evening. I can't remember when I have had a better time."

"I'll try to look for you tomorrow. I'm told that arrival day is chaotic so I may not see you, but I will see you in Chicago soon."

"Yes, I'll be anxiously waiting to see you."

Rose opened the door and he stood in the hall. She fought the urge to ask him in.

"Goodnight," she said.

He paused because he wanted to go in but he said, "Goodnight."

She closed the door.

Edith was sitting on the couch waiting for her. She stood as Rose walked in. "My lady, how was your evening?"

Rose knew not to say anything to Edith about the wonderful time she had with Colin. "It was fine."

"I checked on Mia and she decided for some reason to get into your bed."

"I know why. She wants to hear about the evening. She said earlier she would wait up for me."

"She is sound asleep."

Edith helped her change out of her formal dress attire. In a few minutes, Edith left and Rose eased into bed.

Mia woke and sat up. She rubbed her eyes, still half asleep. "You're back."

"Yes dear."

"How was the evening?"

"It was perfect."

"Was Colin there?"

"Yes, but he was late. I thought he wasn't coming, however, like a white knight, he showed up. My evening then became a fairy tale."

"Oh, that sounds so romantic." Mia smiled.

"Colin said a little angel insisted he should come to dinner. The angel said if he came, he would see a beautiful woman in a gorgeous dress."

Mia giggled. "Oh, that's such a sweet thing for him to say. So, a little angel came to him?"

"Yes, he always has the best stories."

Mia smiled and wondered what her mother would say if she knew the real story. "I have to ask you. Did you kiss a frog tonight?"

Rose smiled. "A lady never tells about her kisses."

"Mummy, you said kisses...so there was more than one kiss?"

Rose blushed. "Let me say this: Colin isn't a frog."

"Mummy, I noticed you call him Colin."

"Yes, he asked me to."

"What does he call you?"

"You sure are nosey, aren't you?"

"I am. I got that from Grandmother and you," Mia retorted. "What does he call you?"

"Rose."

"Oh," she said. "This has been a grand night for us."

"Why has it been grand for you?"

Mia smiled. "Because if you're happy, it's a good night for me too."

"That is so sweet of you. We need to get our rest because tomorrow will be a busy day."

She nodded. "Goodnight, Mummy."

"Goodnight, dear."

Mia snuggled up to her and soon was fast asleep. Rose wrote in her diary about the evening. She said she had found a prince that night.

CHAPTER 21

JUNE 27, 1906 – ARRIVAL IN NEW YORK

———◆———

THE NEXT MORNING, COLIN WAS up early to pack and then had a meeting with Mr. Jones. He hoped to see Rose and Mia before he left. The ship docked at noon and soon after there was a knock on the door. A porter was there with a driver to take him to the train station.

The driver said, "Sir, we must hurry; we don't have much time to get to the station. Mr. Jones owns the railroad; however, the train will still leave on time."

"I'll meet you on the dock," Colin replied. "I have to make a quick stop."

"We will load the luggage and I'll be waiting in stall nine," instructed the driver.

Colin ran to Rose's stateroom. He knocked on the door and Edith answered.

"Mr. Stuart," she said coldly. "How may I help you?"

"I would like to talk to Lady Cavendish."

"Madam isn't ready for visitors yet."

"Is Miss Lady Cavendish available?"

"No."

"I see. May I leave a note?"

Edith pursed her lips. "Mr. Stuart, we are busy."

Mia and Elizabeth entered the parlor. Mia saw Mr. Stuart at the door and ran over. Colin squeezed past Edith, who had been blocking his entrance. Edith stood there looking cross.

Colin cautioned, "I can't stay long; I have a driver waiting."

"I'll get Mummy." Mia bolted from the room to Rose's bedroom.

Colin said, "Good morning, Elizabeth."

She replied in a warm tone, "Good morning, Mr. Stuart."

Rose and Mia came in. She stepped right up to Colin and held out her hands to him. He took them and smiled.

Rose beamed. "I was hoping to see you."

Mia echoed, "Me too!"

"I only have a minute. I wanted to tell everyone goodbye. Now first I'll start with Mia. You're my little angel and I have enjoyed getting to know you. When you come to Chicago, we must fly kites. I hear there are some great places to fly there."

"That sounds like fun."

She hugged him tight. He kissed her on her forehead.

"Now to Lady Rose, this trip has been astonishing because of you. I'll forever remember our dances together. I'll see you soon in Chicago."

She stepped toward him and like he did to her the night before, she cupped his face gently and kissed him.

Mia giggled, Elizabeth smiled, and Edith grimaced.

After the kiss, he declared, "I would miss every train and ship in the future for one of those kisses."

Elizabeth and Mia cooed, "Oh."

Edith murmured, "Oh no."

Rose blushed. "You're always so sweet to me."

"I'll see everyone soon." He kissed her again and walked out the door. Mia and Elizabeth rushed up to Rose and hugged her.

Elizabeth said, "That was so romantic. You were so bold kissing him that way."

Rose said, "I wanted him to know he would be missed."

"I bet he's counting his fortune now," Edith sneered.

Rose frowned and Elizabeth said, "Edith, that's a terrible thing to say!"

She replied, "The Scotsman might have you three fooled but not me."

Mia started to say something but Rose interrupted. "Now we must all get our things together. They'll be here any minute for our luggage."

Rose turned and went to her bedroom with Mia on her heels. Mia closed the door and locked it so Edith couldn't enter.

"Mummy, you would never intentionally kiss a frog!" Mia declared.

Rose tried to regain her prim and proper manner. She admitted, "I shouldn't have kissed him in front of you."

"Mummy, you like him. He likes you. Don't make it so complicated!"

Rose smiled. "Are you only nine? You seem so much older than that." She hugged her tightly. "Now get your things ready."

"Yes Mummy."

Mia unlocked the door and brushed past Edith, who stood outside. Mia smirked at her as she passed.

A few minutes later, several porters arrived and gathered the luggage. The ladies took a taxi to their hotel.

CHAPTER 22

———

THE DRIVER TOOK COLIN ACROSS town to the railroad station where he would be traveling in Mr. Jones' personal first-class Pullman car. The car had everything he needed for a comfortable ride to Chicago including a well-stocked bar. He immediately checked the liquor inventory. All the top-grade liquors were there including a bottle of GlenWilliams Heritage Whisky and several prominent Scottish brands, but not one bottle of Jones liquor was present.

He asked the porter, "I noticed Jones Whisky isn't in the bar. Do you know why?"

The porter observed, "Sir, I can tell from your accent that you're not from around here."

"I'm from Scotland."

"The Scots have some excellent spirits but the Jones brand is...." He paused for a second. "It's simply awful. Every time I put some in the bar, Mr. Jones' guests will throw it out the window. It's that bad."

Colin laughed. "I understand. Now tell me this, they seem to sell a lot of it. Who buys it?"

"In Scotland, you have...what's the word you use for a tavern?"

"A pub."

"That's it, pub. In the Scottish cities or towns, do you have pubs where nice people don't go? You know the type where the bums go?"

"Yes." Colin nodded.

"Those places buy Jones liquor. They buy it because it's cheap and it gets the job done. They call it Faster whiskey."

"Why do they call it Faster?"

"They call it that because it gets you drunk faster than anything else."

Colin laughed and shook his head. "I don't believe you."

The porter replied, "It's true. It's so cheap, even a poor man can buy a lot of it."

"Do Americans ever buy premium whisky?"

"The rich people do and some people who've had the better stuff. The Kentucky and Tennessee liquors are darn good, but most Americans buy beer or cheap whiskey. You can get Faster anywhere so it's popular. If you like, when we stop in Philadelphia, I'll get you a bottle."

"I would like that. How much does it cost?"

"A dollar."

Colin choked, "Only a dollar?"

"Yep, it can be even cheaper at some places."

Colin gave him two dollars. "You keep the other dollar."

"Thank you, sir."

Colin settled in and watched the scenery as it passed by. Once they were out of the city, there were miles of open farmland. Colin gazed in wonderment at all the openness.

After a stop in Philadelphia, the porter returned.

"I have your liquor for you." It was in a cheap, clear glass quart bottle. The label simply said, *'Jones Whiskey'*.

The porter poured Colin a glass. Colin sniffed it several times and held it to the light.

"This liquor wasn't aged properly," Colin began, "and was probably also put in a cheap barrel. What a shame! It's like taking a budding flower and cutting it before it blooms. This liquor never had the chance to come alive." Colin put the glass on the bar.

"Sir, are you going to drink it?"

"No, I know what it will taste like. You can have it and the rest of the bottle."

"Thank you!"

Colin returned to watching the landscape.

The next afternoon, Colin arrived in Chicago. Waiting for him on the platform was Mr. Babcock, the plant accountant.

"Mr. Stuart?"

Colin nodded at the pale, thin, short man. "Yes, I take it you are Mr. Babcock."

"I am. It's a pleasure to meet you."

They shook hands.

"We have two hours before our train leaves. Would you like to get something to eat?" asked Mr. Babcock.

"Let's go to a local tavern. I want to sample some of our competitor's liquors."

"We're going to a taverna?" asked Mr. Babcock with concern in his voice.

"I take it you don't go to taverns often."

"Never. I don't drink."

"You work for a distillery and you don't drink?"

"I don't drink."

Colin slapped him on the back. "Well, you are going to start."

Colin asked a porter where the nearest tavern was and he sent them to one nearby. A large Irish fellow was the bartender.

"Gents, what would you like?"

Colin replied, "One shot of your best whisky."

The bartender asked, "Do I hear a Scotsman?"

"That you do," said Colin with pride.

The bartender said looking down his nose at Colin, "I normally wouldn't serve a Scotsman, but I'm feeling generous today."

Colin fired backed, "I wouldn't generally buy from an Irishman, but I have a train to catch."

The Irishman paused for a second then laughed. He turned his back, poured from a bottle then handed the glass to Colin. He held it up to the light and sniffed the whisky.

The Irishman watched him closely. "Hey Scottie, here in America we drink it, not smell it."

Colin replied, "I always start by smelling it first. I'm a master distiller."

"Am I supposed to be impressed?"

"Do you see that bottle of GlenWilliams Whisky behind you?"

"Aye," the Irishman answered.

"Look at the name on the back, you will see the name Colin Stuart. I am Colin Stuart."

The bartender picked up the bottle and read the name.

"Well, I'll be. I would have cleaned your glass if I knew you were a celebrity."

Colin sniffed the whisky, "I made this whisky, it is GlenWilliams."

The bartender nodded. "You're right."

"Mr. Babcock, please drink this for me." Colin handed him the glass.

Mr. Babcock stammered, "Remember, I don't drink."

"You don't drink because of your religion?"

"No."

"Is it because of your health?"

"No."

"Do you work for me?"

Hesitantly he answered, "Ahhh, yes."

"Then you will learn how to drink."

"But sir—"

"If you don't drink it, this Irishman will be offended. He'll throw us out on our ear after he breaks our noses. Isn't that right, sir?" Colin winked at the Irishman.

The Irishman reached under the bar and grabbed an axe handle. He slammed it on the bar and bellowed, "I'll be greatly offended."

Mr. Babcock jumped at the sound then grabbed the glass and drank it. He coughed and wheezed but managed to finish it.

"Now give me a shot of your worst whisky. What's the name of it?"

"The whiskey is called Faster."

The Irishman poured him a shot.

Colin sniffed it and held it up to the light. "You sell a lot of this?"

"I do. It's awful but cheap."

"How much of the GlenWilliams whisky do you sell?" Colin inquired.

"Not a lot. It's expensive, coming all the way from Scotland."

Colin leaned forward. "What if I made a product better than GlenWilliams but at half the price. Could you sell it?"

"The Kentucky bourbons and the Tennessee whiskeys are that price and they sell well."

"Mine would be better."

"Why would yours be better?" the bartender asked skeptically.

"I know how to make the best whisky."

"Where would you make it?"

"Let's say Wisconsin," Colin replied.

"There is only one distillery in Wisconsin and they make this crap." He gestured at the Faster bottle.

"I know; I'm the new master distiller for the Jones Distillery."

"Well, I'll be. Are you going to stop making Faster because my customers will still want it?"

"I always give the customer what he wants, however, I also want him to be able to try something better."

The Irishman said, "I can agree with you there. If you can make what you say you can, I'll buy it from you."

"Done." Colin reached out and shook his hand. He turned to Mr. Babcock and handed him the Faster. "Mr. Babcock, drink this."

"Do I have to?"

"Yes," said Colin.

"You had better!" commanded the Irishman as he put his hand on the axe handle.

Mr. Babcock gulped it down. He coughed and made funny noises. He croaked, "That's awful."

"Mr. Babcock will now try the Tennessee whiskey."

"No please, please, I've had enough!"

Colin said, "Bring two glasses."

The Irishman poured two glasses.

Mr. Babcock moaned, "Sir, my head is spinning."

"This one will smooth out that feeling for you. This time sip it."

Colin sniffed the whiskey, examined it in the light then sipped it. "This is smooth and was aged properly. I can tell it's grainier than I'm used to."

The Irishman commented, "Someone told me they filter it though charcoal or something like that."

Colin replied, "Yes filtering is something a few distillers do. It adds cost but some say it makes the whisky smoother. Mr. Babcock, what do you think?"

The thin accountant was red in the face. "This is only the third drink in my life, so I'm not an expert, but I like it."

Colin smiled. "There you go. I will make you a whisky connoisseur yet."

They sat at the bar and finished their drinks. It was getting close to departure time.

"Sir, we need to settle our bill. What do I owe you?" asked Colin.

"Three dollars should do it."

Colin handed him five. "Thank you for your hospitality and for your future business."

"Thank you, Mr. Stuart."

"Mr. Babcock, drink up. We need to go."

Mr. Babcock finished the drink. "What is this feeling?" he wondered aloud. "I can't describe it. I feel warm and in charge, like I have a lot of confidence."

"Mr. Babcock, I have let you in on one of life's best secrets. Whisky gives a man the courage to say what's on his mind."

"I was thinking that. There's a thing or two I want to tell my wife."

Colin smiled and cautioned him, "You haven't had enough yet. Let's get you used to drinking before you decide to have a discussion with your wife."

"Mr. Stuart, I like you," said Mr. Babcock slurring his words.

They returned to the station and boarded the train to Lake Geneva. Mr. Babcock slept all the way. When they arrived, they took a carriage to Colin's new home, which was a two-story white house adorned with red shutters. It was a fine building on several acres. Down a gentle sloping hill from the house was Lake Geneva. It was a scenic and peaceful setting.

Mr. Babcock rang the doorbell and a woman answered. She was a portly woman in her fifties with black hair tied up in a tight bun.

Mr. Babcock said, "Good evening, Mrs. Bell."

"Good evening to you."

"Colin Stuart, this is Mrs. Bell, the housekeeper. She's responsible for all the servants and for managing your home."

"Mrs. Bell, it's an absolute pleasure you meet you." Colin held out his hand and took hers. He bowed and kissed her hand.

Mrs. Bell blushed. "Oh my, you're such a gentleman, certainly a rarity these days."

"Mrs. Bell, you have quite a responsible position. How many servants are there?"

"We have two cooks, two maids, and a groundskeeper."

"Well then, I promise I'll make your job easy by doing what you tell me to do."

She laughed. "I have always wanted a man to do that. Now let's get you inside and settled in. I'll have the driver bring in your luggage."

She introduced him to the staff and showed him the house. Colin told her how clean and tidy the house was. Mrs. Bell face lit up from the praise.

They returned to the parlor and she said, "Dinner will be ready in thirty minutes."

Mr. Babcock turned to Colin. "I'll pick you up on Monday at seven-thirty and take you to the distillery. Now…Mr. Jones *did* tell you about Mr. O'Brien, didn't he?"

"Yes."

"Mr. O'Brien wants to meet with you before you meet with anyone else. He wants to meet with you tomorrow afternoon at three if that is acceptable."

"It is," Colin said. "Where does he want to meet?"

"Mr. O'Brien's family owns a tavern in town called the Boar's Inn. He will meet you there."

"Will you be there?"

"I won't be there, Mr. O'Brien doesn't like me." Mr. Babcock pressed his lips together. "He calls me the bean counter."

"How will I know him?"

"Find an Irishman who likes to fight and that will be him."

"I look forward to it," Colin said.

"Mr. Stuart, I have some advice for you. Keep him at more than an arm's length away. He has been known to surprise a few men with his left hook."

"Mr. O'Brien sounds like an interesting man," Colin quipped.

"Not unless you think a man who curses and fights is interesting."

"Thank you for your advice."

Mr. Babcock said, "I hope you decide to stay after meeting him."

Colin grinned. "I will. Don't worry."

The next morning, Colin slept late and had lunch at home. It was Saturday and he walked to the tavern to see Mr. O'Brien.

Boar's Inn, a busy establishment, was in the town square. The inn had two sections: a restaurant with fifteen or so tables and a bar area. The bar ran the length of the building.

Colin stepped to the bar and spoke to the bartender. "I'm here to meet Mr. O'Brien; do you know him?"

The man replied with an Irish accent, "I'm Mr. O'Brien." He was an older distinguished man with a stocky build, grey hair, and mustache.

"Mr. O'Brien, I'm Colin Stuart from the Jones Distillery."

From over his shoulder, another man, also with an Irish accent, barked, "You're looking for me!"

The bar got quiet. Colin turned and a man about his age approached. Colin recalled the advice from Mr. Babcock and he took a step back. People started to crowd around them, sensing trouble.

Colin held out his hand. "It's a pleasure to meet you, Mr. O'Brien."

O'Brien flashed a wicked smile and he looked at the bystanders who seemed to be his friends. He held out his hand then grabbed Colin's hand and wouldn't let it go. The younger O'Brien pulled Colin forward and took a swing at him with his left hand—the left hook Mr. Babcock warned him about. Colin had seen this trick before. He ducked and O'Brien missed. Colin popped up, hit him with a left cross square on the nose. O'Brien fell back and hit the floor hard.

The older O'Brien peered over the bar at his son sprawled on the floor and crowed, "Looks like Mr. Stuart has been around the block once or twice. He's seen your trick!"

The younger O'Brien scrambled to his feet. Colin took a fighter's stance. The Irishman looked surprised Colin was going to defend himself. O'Brien took another swing, but Colin blocked it then hit him in the stomach hard. O'Brien groaned loud, bent down and Colin hit him in the jaw with a right uppercut. This punch stood him up and then Colin hit him directly in the nose. O'Brien collapsed, out cold, on the floor.

The older O'Brien leaned over the bar and looked at his son. "He deserved that. I told him to talk to you, but he always wants to use his fists."

Colin was panting and still riled up. He surveyed the bystanders. "Should I expect any more of this today from him or his friends?"

The elder O'Brien answered, "No, you've shown you're a man not to be messed with. Once he wakes up, he'll be more receptive to talking. None of his friends will get involved. Will you, boys?"

"No sir," said a couple of men. The men disappeared into the crowd.

Colin looked at younger O'Brien on the floor. "Should we get some smelling salts to wake him up?"

"Naw, he'll wake up eventually."

The tavern, which was quiet during the fight, returned to a normal noise level. The waitresses and customers simply stepped over the younger O'Brien lying on the floor.

The older O'Brien said, "Mr. Stuart, I understand you're from Scotland."

"I am."

"Why are you coming here and taking my son's job?"

Colin sat on a barstool. "I'm not taking your son's job. He'll still be the distillery foreman."

The older O'Brien sounded surprised. "Is that so? Then what will you do?"

"I'll be the master distiller."

"What does a master distiller do?"

"I'm responsible for making the whisky."

"Isn't that what he does?" He pointed with his thumb to his son, who was still unconscious on the floor.

"Let me show you what I do." Colin gestured to the bottles on the wall behind O'Brien. "I see you have many fine liquors. Please select ten of them. I would like you to put a small amount of each liquor in a glass. Write on a piece of paper what it is and put it upside down under the glass so I cannot see it. For each liquor I cannot identify, I'll give you two American dollars. You put the bottles on the bar and I'll put the bottle behind each glass after I determine which liquor it is."

"Do I have to place a bet or something?"

"No, you will win two dollars per glass if I cannot choose the right liquor. I'll pay you for the liquor if I get it right or not."

Mr. O'Brien smiled. "I can't lose on this one."

"I'll turn my back so I can't see what you're doing."

Colin turned his back and looked at the son still on the floor. Colin said loudly, "I'm worried about your son."

"He was a little drunk. Don't worry about him, he has a hard head."

The older O'Brien poured liquor into ten glasses and wrote the names down on small slips of paper. He said, "I'm ready."

People crowded around to watch. Colin started the sampling. He held the first glass up to the light and sniffed it several times. He didn't taste it. He put the glass down on the paper, took a bottle from the cluster of bottles O'Brien had left on the counter, and placed it behind the glass. He did the same thing with the next five glasses. On the seventh glass, he held it to the light and swirled it. He tipped the glass and almost let some drip out. He sniffed it several times then selected a bottle. The next three glasses, he quickly decided upon.

Colin said, "Let's see how I did."

The older O'Brien took the paper from under each glass and turned it over. Colin had them all correct. The crowd applauded.

"That's amazing!" the older O'Brien exclaimed. "How did you do it? It must be a parlor trick."

"There's no trick," Colin said with pride. "I'm a master distiller and I have sampled liquor all my life. Let me explain how I do it. This one is GlenWilliams Heritage Whisky. I made it so I know it well."

"You are *the* Colin Stuart on the back of the bottle?"

"That's me," said Colin.

"I think GlenWilliams Heritage Whisky is one of the best."

"It is. Now, these three are from island distilleries. I can smell the smoky peat in them. I can tell them apart because this one aged in a wine barrel, this one aged in a charred barrel and this one aged in a cherry brandy barrel. These two are from near my home in Scotland. One is a young whisky, bold and sharp. The other one is a twelve-year-old whisky, which is smooth and refined. This one is a blend from Scotland. This one is an Irish whisky. That left me three. This one is Faster, which is awful. That left only the Kentucky bourbon and the Tennessee whisky. The Tennessee whisky I had yesterday so I remembered it."

"Impressive," the older O'Brien said.

"I can take this and fix it." He pointed to the Faster and declared, "I'm an expert at taking alcohol and turning it into the best whisky in the world. I'll make sure it's made pure and clean. I'll put it into a proper barrel to age. I'll sample it over the years, nurture it, blend it with a better cousin if I need to, and make you the best whisky you have ever tasted. That's what I do."

"Now I understand, you're a chef and my son is a cook."

Colin considered his comment. "That's an excellent way to describe it. I went to school to learn to become a master distiller and I learned from the best."

"Mr. Stuart, if you still want him, on Monday at seven he will be on the job. You will never have any trouble from him again. I promise you that. By the way, were you a boxer?"

"I was. I was our school champion and almost won a championship in England."

"Almost?"

Colin confessed, "Yes, I hate to tell you this, an Irish boy whipped me in the championship."

The older O'Brien bellowed, "Now that is a difference between a Scot and an Irishman. An Irishman would have said he won!"

Everyone around laughed.

"Would you like a drink? You have a few to choose from on the bar," asked the older O'Brien.

Colin saw the son was starting to stir. He thought it would be the right time to leave.

"Thank you but no. How much do I owe you?"

"Nothing, I'll make him pay for it." He pointed to his son.

Colin nodded. "I'll stop in later in the week for a drink and dinner if that's acceptable."

"You're always welcome here."

Colin left the tavern and walked home.

On Sunday, Colin slept late, had lunch, and went for a long walk in the afternoon to get to know the area. Lake Geneva was a nice town and he felt comfortable there. Mrs. Bell served traditional Wisconsin food for dinner including beer soup, bratwurst, cheese curds and cream puffs which he enjoyed. He turned in early to be fresh for his first day at the distillery.

———➤———

CHAPTER 23

ON MONDAY MORNING, MR. BABCOCK brought Colin to the distillery. The first person Colin saw was Mr. O'Brien, who was sporting two black eyes. Mr. O'Brien held out his hand.

Colin held back. "I've seen this before."

Mr. O'Brien was apologetic. "I'm sorry for Saturday. I promise that will never happen again."

Colin put out his hand and they shook.

"I'm Shawn O'Brien."

"I'm Colin Stuart."

"How do you want to start your first day?" asked Shawn.

"We'll start in the distillery—at the beginning of the process. I want to see the grain."

"The folks in the office have coffee and cake for you."

"That can wait," said Colin.

Shawn took Colin on a tour through the distillery to the grain area and he introduced Colin to people along the way. Colin was friendly to everyone and greeting each person with a smile and a firm handshake.

Colin's reputation had preceded him. One worker, who was a giant of a man, teased him, "Do you plan to give a black eye to everyone?"

Colin laughed and replied, "Only to the Irish, the English, Democrats, and men who drink beer instead of whisky."

The man laughed heartily. "Everyone here will get a black eye then."

Shawn took him to the grain storage area. The area was dirty. Dust was in the air and thick on the floor. Colin reached to the floor and wiped up some dust with his hand. "So this, goes into the mash."

"I never thought of that, but yes."

"How often is this area cleaned?"

"Never."

"Starting today, this area will be swept and washed every day."

"Yes, sir," said Shawn.

They watched the milling of the grains—corn, wheat, barley, and rye—into cereal. Colin noticed the workers were not measuring the amount of grain used. "Who has the recipe for the cereal?"

"We don't follow an exact recipe to make the cereal. We know the number of shovels required of each."

"I see there are several types and sizes of shovels that tells me every batch is different."

Shawn replied, "In the end the cereal will ferment and make alcohol. Does it matter if the cereal varies some?"

Colin declared, "Absolutely, it matters! We must follow an exact recipe every time. I want samples of each batch of white dog we make today."

Shawn scratched his head. "What is white dog?"

"White dog is the pure alcohol before it goes into the barrel to age. I think folks in America also call it moonshine. You and I will sample them tomorrow morning and I'll show you there will be differences."

"Yes, sir."

Colin walked to a still, opened a cover and looked at the mash consisting of cereal and water. "Where does the water come from?"

"It comes from the lake."

"Is it filtered?"

"Why would we need to need to filter it?"

Colin instructed, "I saw ducks on the lake this morning, so you know what they're doing in the water. Yesterday I saw runoff from a farmer's cow pen spill into the lake. I wouldn't want to drink that. Would you?"

"Doesn't making the alcohol kill everything that comes in from the water?"

"Yes, but everything in the water will leave its imprint on the alcohol. The water must be clean and pure. I don't see any temperature gauges," commented Colin.

"We don't need them. We know from experience what to do."

Colin directed him, "You will install the gauges immediately. The mash temperature must be a minimum of 146 degrees and no hotter than 160. We will do it the same way every time. Now take me to the barreling area."

When they arrived there, Colin inspected some barrels. "How often are the barrels used?"

"Until they fall apart."

"As soon as possible, start using new barrels. Make sure the barrels are white oak and charred. You will see the whiskey looks richer and has a better flavor if we use a better barrel."

Shawn nodded. "Yes, sir."

"Take me to the warehouses."

They walked to a warehouse, which was a five-story wooden structure.

"How many warehouses do we have?" Colin asked.

"A dozen."

"How long does the whisky age?"

"The government specifies it must be two years," Shawn said.

"What if the whisky isn't ready?"

"It's always ready because if we have to, we'll doctor it up to make it look right."

Colin shook his head. "We will stop doctoring our whisky starting now. Let me make sure I understand. All the whisky in these warehouses is two years old?"

"No, some of the whiskey is as old as ten years," Shawn said. "We generally take the product from the nearest warehouse or the lower floors of the warehouses because it's easier on the men to move them. If we have a busy year, we will take more from the older inventory, however, our customers don't want it. They like the taste of our younger whiskey. They complain when it doesn't taste the same."

"Yes, that's what they're used to. We could sell the older whisky for a higher price," Colin said, thinking aloud.

"We have sold some but not much. We don't have enough customers for it."

"We must sell it to a different set of customers," Colin said. "I want you to get me a barrel of our two-year-old stock, three-year-old stock, and for every year after that. I also want an accurate whisky inventory by year immediately."

"Yes, sir."

Colin spent the afternoon meeting various people and then he met with Mr. Babcock for two hours to review the books.

That evening before O'Brien left, Colin reminded him he wanted to meet with him the next morning to sample the white dog from that day. That night Colin stayed up late to list the changes they would immediately make at the distillery.

The next morning, O'Brien and Colin tasted the white dog samples from the previous day.

"Shawn, please excuse me if I sound like a teacher, but that is a large part of my job. Everyone here must learn that making whisky is not an art, it is a science. The water must always be pure, our grains must be the best, the storage area, and the vessels we use must be clean like your mother's kitchen. The recipe will be followed the same way each time." He paused to make sure Shawn still followed him. "Lastly, not every barrel of whisky ages the same. A barrel of whisky on the top of the warehouse where it's hotter will age differently than a barrel further below. Trees shade several of our warehouses while others are on the ridge fully exposed to the sun. Everything affects the whisky and we must monitor it all. My job is to teach you and others how to do it. Do you understand?"

Shawn said, "I do."

"Now let's sample the white dog from yesterday."

Colin sampled each and talked to Shawn about it. He showed him how to sniff it and taste it.

Shawn asked, "I'm surprised, they are different. Why?"

"It's because we don't do it the same way every time. For example, this one smells fruitier to me. We probably added too much rye. This one smells sweet because we probably added too much corn. To make sure we are consistent in the future. This is the recipe I want used. It must be followed exactly." He handed a paper to Shawn.

"Was the grain area cleaned?" Colin asked.

"Yes sir."

"When will the barrels of whisky be here?"

"Any minute now."

"Pull the buggers out of the barrels and we will sample each one," Colin instructed. "Let me know when you're ready."

Colin went to the office and discovered that Mr. Jones had arrived. Colin told him what he had found so far.

Shawn stepped in the office, and with his head down to hide his black eyes, he said, "The whiskey is ready for sampling."

Mr. Jones saw Shawn's face. "What the hell happened to you? Did a horse kick you?"

He smiled and answered, "No, a Scotsman did."

"I see." Mr. Jones turned to Colin and winked.

Colin said, "Mr. Jones and Mr. Babcock, I would like you to please come with us. We are sampling our whisky."

Shawn asked, "Why is the bean counter coming?"

Colin answered in a firm voice, "Mr. Babcock will help us to decide what changes we can afford to make. He will be involved on every major decision. His name is Mr. Babcock not bean counter."

Mr. Jones noticed Colin's firm tone. They walked out to the warehouse. Nine barrels were there with the buggers out.

Colin declared, "Now, I learned from Shawn we have barrels in our warehouses that are older than two years. We're going to sample each year we have."

Colin collected samples from each of the barrels that were two to ten years old. He put them in glasses in a row by year.

"Gentlemen," Colin began, "look at the differences in color. Notice the richness after four years. Now sniff each one. You must sniff it deeply, allowing it to roll over your tongue, but don't taste it yet."

They sniffed it.

Mr. Jones said, "We all know the longer a whiskey ages, the better it is."

Colin said, "I respectfully disagree. Low-quality alcohol will be poor whisky no matter how long you age it. I think we might have enough stock that can become a decent whisky if we do the right thing. Please look at the four- to six-year whiskies. There's hardly any difference in visual appearance between them. Now look at the seven- to ten-year whiskies. There's a significant difference between those and the younger whiskies."

Mr. Jones said, "I can see where you're headed. You're going to ask my permission to age our product longer, aren't you?"

"Not exactly," Colin said. "If we age our whisky longer, it will taste different and our customers won't like it. We must continue to give the customer what they want. However, we can do some other things."

"Like what?" asked Mr. Jones.

"I'll get to that. Now let's taste the samples."

They tasted the two-year-old and three-year-old samples.

Colin said, "The two-year is young and aggressive. The three-year is about the same."

They tasted the four-, five-, and six-year-old whiskey.

"These are starting to be mellower and more aromatic. Smoother to the tongue."

They tasted the remaining samples.

"These are truly mellow and smooth. Do you agree?" asked Colin.

Mr. Jones was impatient. "I agree. However, we don't have the money to age it the way you want."

"I understand. Let me ask Mr. Babcock some questions. If we raise our current whisky price by five percent, could I take some of that money and invest in a larger inventory of aged whisky?"

"Yes," replied Mr. Babcock.

Colin asked, "Mr. Babcock, we are selling everything we make now, aren't we?"

"Yes," replied Mr. Babcock.

"Let me tell you a story. My brother has a dairy farm. He was selling every pint he could produce but wasn't making any money. He spoke to a wise businessman about it, who told him to raise his price. My brother did and he still sold every pint. He raised it again and still sold-out. He did it again and again. Finally, sales started to slow. He lowered the price a bit and his sales went up. He left it at that price. My point is every market has a price. I propose we raise our price and see if sales fall. When was the last price increase?"

Mr. Babcock answered, "Prior to the last business turndown and that was three years ago."

Colin stated, "We should try raising the price immediately. We will make more money so I can start to build an inventory of aged whisky."

Mr. Jones nodded. "I like that."

"Also, I'll take some of the aged stock and blend it to make a decent premium whisky. We'll have a better product that sells at a higher price."

Mr. Jones crossed his arms. "I also like that, but our customers won't buy the better product at a higher price."

"We must take the premium product to a new set of customers. Now let me make a blend so you can taste what it will be like."

Colin blended the older whiskeys together and swirled the combination in a glass. After a few minutes, he said, "Try this."

The men tried it and they smiled.

Mr. Jones nodded, "This is superb!"

"I agree!" Shawn exclaimed.

Colin said, "We will call it 'Diamond Whisky' and we will spell whisky with no 'e'. It will be in a clear bottle with a large diamond on the label. Mr. Babcock has a customer in Chicago already lined up to buy it."

Mr. Babcock stammered, "I do?"

"Yes, remember the Irishman you impressed with your drinking skills?"

"Oh yes, yes, of course, the Irishman, he said he would buy a premium liquor from us."

Colin boasted, "See, we have our first customer for our new product!"

"Why aren't we calling it Jones Diamond Whiskey?" asked Shawn.

Colin said, "Let me tell you another story. An English chef in London put goose liver on his menu because he heard it was selling well in Europe. He didn't sell any for the first month. He went on a trip to Paris to visit a friend who was also a chef. On his menu was foie gras, duck liver, and it was selling well. He came home and changed the name on the menu to foie gras. He sold out every night after that. My point is sometimes you have a new name to get people interested."

Mr. Jones nodded. "I agree with you. How will you let people know about it?"

"We would start at the art exposition; we could introduce it there."

"That's coming soon. Can you blend enough?" asked Mr. Jones.

"I won't have the bottle yet, but folks will be able to taste it. Also, I want to put bottles of our product in different high-class saloons across the country. We should also put it on your railroad cars."

Mr. Jones exclaimed proudly, "These are excellent ideas!"

"Ideas have to be put into action. Let's see how people react to them," said Colin.

CHAPTER 24

JULY 12, 1906 – NEW YORK CITY

———◆———

ROSE HAD BEEN IN NEW York for two weeks and was anxious to go to Chicago. New York had been exciting with its museums, theaters, and other attractions, but she missed Colin. He had planted a seed in her heart and it was growing. She thought of him constantly.

Mia was also looking forward to Chicago. She felt New York was simply another big, boring city. She had enjoyed her time with Colin on the ship and wanted to see him.

Rose and her party boarded a train to Chicago on Thursday and arrived the next day. They were staying in the penthouse, which was magnificent with three large bedrooms, a kitchen, and a parlor. Waiting for Rose on the parlor table was a letter from Colin.

Mia saw the letter first and read who sent it. She said excitedly, "Mummy, you have a letter from Mr. Stuart!" She handed it to her.

Letter in hand, Rose rushed into her room and closed the door. She fumbled, opening the letter.

My dearest Rose,
I have counted the days until your arrival. I'm so anxious to see you
again. Every day I have cursed myself for not staying with you in New
York. I would have enjoyed seeing all the city's glory with you and Mia.
I would have been proud to escort the two prettiest women in America. I
hope you enjoyed your stay.

The art exposition starts on Saturday and I have three tickets for us to attend the premiere that commences at one-thirty. I would be honored if you and Mia could attend with me. I will meet you at your penthouse at one o'clock if that is acceptable.

I would also be honored if you would attend a dinner with me on Saturday evening. There is a formal dinner party at your hotel and I will be introducing our new whisky.

If you do not have plans for Sunday, I would love for you, Mia, Edith, and Elizabeth to come to my home for tea. That evening, if I could be so bold, I would like to invite you for dinner at my home.

I have reserved a suite for you and Mia plus two additional rooms at the Lake Geneva Plaza. I will be your personal escort while you are here. I hope I haven't been too forward suggesting these plans. Please telegraph me with your reply.

I have missed you terribly and think of you nearly every minute. I often think about the dinners, the dances, and the romantic moments we had on the ship. I want so badly to recreate those feelings we had and I am anticipating we will.

I look forward to hearing from you!

With my deepest love, Colin

P.S. Please tell Mia I miss her and I have several kites ready for her. There is a hill not far from my home that looks out on Lake Geneva which is a perfect spot for flying.

Rose was relieved to know he shared the same feelings she did. She read the letter three times to drink in his words. Each time she read it, tears flowed down her cheek.

There was a soft knock on her door. "Mummy, may I come in?"

"Yes, dear."

Mia stepped inside and saw the tears. She closed the door behind her.

"Mummy, is something wrong?"

"No, dear. I was reading Colin's lovely letter." Rose took her handkerchief and wiped the tears away.

"May I read it?"

Rose chuckled. "No! You may not! You don't need to know everything about me."

Mia laughed. "That's my job. I always want to know the details."

"Not this time. However, you should know this. On Saturday, you and I are going with Colin to the art exposition."

"Wonderful!" exclaimed Mia.

"On Sunday, we are going to Lake Geneva with Colin. He said there is a great place to fly kites and he has invited us to tea."

"Only you and me?"

"Edith and Elizabeth are invited as well, but I have arranged for Elizabeth to see the city with some ladies from the consulate."

Mia grinned. "She will love that. I knew coming to Chicago would be better than New York."

"Also, Colin invited me to attend a dinner here at the hotel. He is introducing a new whisky and he wants me there."

"I can't wait for Saturday!" Mia exclaimed.

"Neither can I." Rose felt the excitement rise in her. "Now I must send a telegram to him accepting his invitations."

Rose composed a telegram to Colin. Mia watched as her mother wrote the message. Mia tried to read it but could not. Rose put the note in an envelope and called for a porter.

"Mummy, I was wondering if we can bring your swan and put it on the lake."

Rose laughed, "I'd forgotten about that. We can test to see if Colin's story is true."

"I bet it will come true," said Mia.

"We will see."

"Mummy, how far is Lake Geneva from here?"

"I'm not sure. Let's look it up."

Rose got out a map and they looked for Lake Geneva. In a few minutes, there was a knock at the door.

"My lady, there's a porter here," said Edith. "May I come in?"

"Yes please," replied Rose.

Edith came in and Rose handed her the note.

"Please have the porter make sure the telegram is sent immediately."

"Yes, madam."

Edith left.

"How long will we be there?"

Rose replied, "We can stay until Tuesday."

"That doesn't sound like nearly enough time to me."

"I wish now our stay in New York had been shorter," Rose said sadly.

"So do I."

CHAPTER 25

———◆———

COLIN RECEIVED THE TELEGRAM FROM Rose and was extremely pleased. He wanted everything to be perfect when they arrived. He had ordered new china, crystal, and some new furniture. He was busy both at home and at the distillery.

He worked night and day at the distillery to make sure the new whisky was ready. It took longer than he expected to make the blend. The distillery workers thought what Colin was doing was a waste of time. They didn't consider it a high priority and complained about how much labor it required, but once Colin let them taste the new product, they changed their minds and worked hard to get the blending done. They were ready with three barrels two days before the Chicago event.

On Saturday, Colin traveled to the Chicago Grand Hotel. After he checked in, he changed into a new suit he purchased for the day.

Promptly at one o'clock, he knocked on Rose's penthouse suite door. Edith opened it.

"Good afternoon, Miss Kelsey."

Edith didn't smile. She said stiffly, "Lady Rose and Miss Cavendish are almost ready. Please have a seat."

Colin entered and sat on the couch. Edith stood in the parlor like a guard. She frowned and had a furrowed brow. Colin could tell she didn't want to talk to him so he decided to tease her a bit.

"It was a long and hot trip here. I am thirsty."

Edith ignored him.

"I wonder if there is any whisky around here?"

Edith replied, "No, we don't have any whisky!"

"Is there any water?"

"I didn't know I was supposed to provide refreshments for you," she said, irritated.

"In Scotland, we always offer our guests something to drink. We're known as hospitable people."

Edith sighed and looked irritated. "Alright, I'll get you some water."

Colin laughed to himself because he didn't want it. Edith brought him a glass of water.

Colin looked at the glass. "Do you have any ice?"

Edith glared at him and frowned. She went to the bar and added ice. She returned and shoved it at him.

He didn't hold out his hand. "Are you sure there is no whisky?"

"Yes, I'm sure."

"Can you order some?"

She said, "No!"

He took the glass and said, "Thank you." He took a small sip and put the glass on a coaster on a nearby coffee table.

Seeing how little he drank, she snapped, "I thought you were thirsty."

"I was," Colin said, "but I'm fine now."

Edith fumed silently.

Colin continued to tease her. "So how is your dragon?"

Edith said, "My what?"

"I made you a dragon. How is it?'

"I gave it to Mia."

"I see. I take it you don't like dragons?"

"No, I don't," she growled, her patience wearing thin.

"I see. Should I make you something else? I have some paper here in my jacket," he lied.

"No."

"A rose or perhaps a small bird?"

Aggravated, she said, "No! I don't need anything. I'm going to check to see if they are ready." Edith knocked on a bedroom door then went in. About the same time, the other bedroom door opened and Mia and Elizabeth came out. Mia saw Colin and smiled.

"It's so good to see you!" She ran to him and hugged him.

"My little angel, I have missed you so." He kissed Mia on the forehead. "Miss Carpenter, it's good to see you as well."

"You too, Mr. Stuart," Elizabeth beamed. "Mia has been counting the minutes until you arrived. She has so much to tell you."

Colin replied, "I'm anxious to hear. Mia, you must tell me everything you have seen and done."

Mia and Colin sat on the couch and Elizabeth sat in an armchair. Mia told him about New York and the train trip to Chicago. Colin didn't get to ask a question because she was talking so fast and was so excited. Colin enjoyed it; she reminded him of his nieces and the way they got excited over everything.

Ten minutes passed before Rose came out with Edith following behind her. Rose was wearing a white afternoon dress with long sleeves and a U-shaped neckline. Her slightly curly, golden-blonde hair flowed over her shoulders.

Colin stood and beheld Rose. "Now who is the radiant beauty? An English angel must have come because no normal woman could be so striking."

Mia and Elizabeth said, "Oh!"

Edith said under her breath, "Malarkey."

Rose said, "That's so nice." She stepped close to him and he gave her a long hug. Colin wanted to kiss her but was reluctant.

Edith cleared her throat several times to show her displeasure. Rose ignored her and hugged him back.

Rose pulled back after a few seconds. "I have missed you!"

"And I have missed you!" he replied. "You look amazing. Is this a new dress?"

Rose beamed. "Yes, I bought it in New York."

Mia stood and spun around. "Did you notice anything else?"

Colin turned to Mia. "Of course, your dresses match. I love your dress too. I'll be with the two prettiest ladies in Chicago." He clapped his hands together. "Now we must get going because the grand opening will be starting soon and we can't be late."

Colin paraded arm in arm with Mia and Rose on the short walk from the hotel to the exposition. It was a warm day with a slight breeze. They arrived as the grand opening was beginning. It was a champagne, chocolate, and cheese affair. Colin's knowledge of the exhibit's paintings impressed Mia and Rose. They spent three hours at the exhibit and had quite an enjoyable afternoon. Colin returned them to the hotel so Rose could dress for dinner.

When they entered the suite, Edith was standing guard with a surly look on her face. Colin decided not to display any affection for Rose and left after a quick goodbye.

After Colin left, Rose went to her room with Mia close on her heels. Mia closed the door before Edith could enter.

"I had a marvelous afternoon, didn't you, Mummy?"

"Oh yes, the exhibit was superb."

"I noticed that Colin kissed you when he thought I wasn't looking."

Rose grinned and playfully, she said, "Mia, shame on you! You aren't supposed to spy on your mother."

Mia smiled. "Of course I am."

Rose laughed as she removed her jewelry. Mia helped to unbutton her dress in the back.

"Were we too conspicuous?"

"No, it was discreet and he kissed you only when a few people were around. You two looked happy together."

Rose sighed wistfully. "I'm so thrilled to see him again."

"So was he. He smiled the entire time."

There was a knock on the door. Edith's muffled voice asked, "My lady, may I come in?"

Rose answered, "Yes."

Edith entered. "My lady, may I help you change?"

"Yes please." To Mia she said, "You should go change."

Mia replied, "I will. Please tell Colin how much I enjoyed today."

"I will."

Mia stepped past Edith as she came in. Edith closed the door.

Edith asked, "How was the exhibit?"

"It was outstanding. We had an enjoyable time. Colin knows impressionist art well."

Edith retorted, "I'm sure he has been doing his homework."

Rose shot her a look. "What do you mean by that?"

"The Scot is going to do everything he can to impress you."

Rose objected, "He wasn't trying to impress. He was simply being himself."

"My lady, can't you see what he is doing?"

Annoyed, Rose replied, "Apparently not, but I expect you will enlighten me."

"Madam, my job is to always look out for you. This Scot uses smooth and clever language, plus I'm sure he studied up on everything he thinks you like. He is a clever one. You must stay on guard."

"I should be on guard for what? Do you expect him to whisk me away?"

"You must guard your heart."

"Nonsense, he is a charming, kind, and loving man."

"I see him as he is," Edith said harshly. "You see him only with your heart."

"My heart has never been wrong before."

"You must be careful because he is a charmer."

Rose replied, "I like that in him. Now let's focus on getting me prepared for dinner."

Edith was silent as she helped Lady Rose get ready.

CHAPTER 26

———◆———

COLIN RUSHED TO HIS ROOM to change. He was so anxious about the dinner he got ready nearly an hour before he was to meet Rose. He opened the drapes in hopes of finding something interesting to watch. He was in luck—there was a building across the street under construction and so he watched the men working until he left to get Rose.

Promptly at seven, he knocked on the door and Mia answered.

"Miss Lady Cavendish, it's a pleasure to see you. It has been much too long since our last encounter." Colin bowed to her.

Mia giggled and curtsied. "Yes, it has. Please come in."

Colin entered and Mia closed the door. She asked, "What have you been doing with yourself since our last encounter of so long ago?"

"I have been busy. I didn't think I was going to make it here in time."

Elizabeth entered and smiled at Colin. "Good evening, Mr. Stuart."

"Good evening to you. I was about to tell Mia what I have been do-ing since our last encounter. It was quite an adventure. Would you like to hear?"

"I would."

Colin sat in an armchair as Mia and Elizabeth sat on a couch.

Colin began to spin his story. "After I left here, I went to my room. Soon there was a loud and urgent knock on my door. I answered it and a nervous porter was there. The porter asked me, 'Mr. Stuart, you're from Scotland, aren't you?' I replied, 'Aye, I am.' He said, 'My boss told me Scots know everything about dragons, is that true?' I replied with pride: 'We do. We are experts on the subject and most other subjects as well.'"

Elizabeth laughed and interjected, "I have learned that about Scots."

Colin winked and continued, "Yes, Scots are an intelligent people. The porter said there is a dragon on the roof and no one in the hotel knows what to do about it. I asked, 'Is he a fire-breathing dragon or a man eater?' The porter said he didn't know, because he was afraid to go on the roof. He asked, 'What difference does it make?' I asked him if he would rather be eaten or burned to death."

Mia was intently listening as Elizabeth smiled.

"The porter's eyes got wide and he said, 'Neither.' He said his boss wanted me to go to the roof immediately. I walked with him to the top floor and he slowly opened the rooftop door. I crept outside and the porter slammed the door behind me. Guess what was there?"

Mia replied, "A dragon."

"You're right. Guess what kind?"

"A fire-breathing one?" asked Mia.

"Luckily no, but he was the meanest looking dragon I have ever seen. He was definitely a man eater."

Mia was hanging on to every word.

"His eyes glowed and blood ran from his mouth. I could tell instantly he was a stone dragon."

Mia asked, "What is a stone dragon?"

"A stone dragon is a dragon banished for his bad behavior to live forever in stone, but something allowed him to escape and he was mighty hungry. He growled and said he would eat me alive. He moved toward me, his eyes glowing."

Mia's eyes were wide open.

"I put my hands up and shouted for him to stop! I told him according to the legends of my people and his ancestors we can do either one of two things: one, we could fight to the death. Either he would win, or I would. I told him the fight would be difficult and bloody. I said to him I didn't want to fight but I would if I had to. I told him the other choice was he could ask me a riddle, and if I answered it correctly he must return to stone. I told him if I didn't answer it correctly, after dinner with Lady Rose I would return and he could eat me alive."

Mia's eyes grew even wider.

"The dragon roared. 'Only the Scots know this tradition and I must follow it. Here is my riddle: Come a riddle, come a riddle, come a rote-tote-tote; a wee, wee man, in a red, red coat, a staff in his hand, and a bone in his throat. Come a riddle, come a riddle, come a rote-tote-tote.' I said to the dragon, 'I must hear it one more time.' The dragon repeated, 'Come a riddle, come a riddle, come a rote-tote-tote; a wee, wee man, in a red, red coat, a staff in his hand, and a bone in his throat. Come a riddle, come a riddle, come a rote-tote-tote.'"

Colin continued, "The dragon leaned forward toward me and said, 'I have three questions and you must answer all three. First, what is the wee, wee man, in a red, red coat? Second, what is the staff in his hand? Third, what is the bone in his throat?' The dragon laughed because he knew his riddle was difficult. I struggled to think of an answer. Soon the dragon got impatient and said I'd had enough time. He said he would not wait until after the dinner and would eat me now. He lunged toward me."

Mia gasped.

"I jumped back and it struck me what the answers were. I said, 'Wait a minute, Mr. Dragon. I know the answers to the riddle. The wee, wee man, in a red, red coat is a cherry, the staff is the stem, and the bone in the throat is the pit.' This surprised the dragon who got even angrier and he roared loud."

Colin roared for effect. Mia jumped, then giggled.

"He got up on his hind legs and opened his mouth wide to eat me. I shouted to him, 'Mr. Dragon, I answered your riddle and I get to determine your future. You will return to stone forevermore.' The dragon screamed a bloody yell, flew up into the air and disappeared."

Mia, with her eyes wide opened, asked, "Oh goodness, do you know where he went?"

"I do."

Elizabeth said, "Mr. Stuart, you have outdone yourself on this Scottish yarn."

Colin replied, "It's not a yarn."

Elizabeth gave him a look. "How can you prove it's not a yarn?"

"I can prove it."

Colin took them to the window and opened the drapes. He said, "There he is across the street."

Across the street on the corner of the building was a stone dragon.

Surprised, Mia stared at the dragon. "Elizabeth, have you see that dragon before?"

Elizabeth shook her head, baffled. "I looked out this window many times since we've been here and I've never seen that."

They looked at Colin. He smiled and folded his arms across his chest. "See, my stories are always true."

Rose and Edith entered the room. Mia rushed up to her mother. "Mummy, there is a dragon across the street and Colin caused him to be there."

Rose had a confused look on her face for a second then she smiled and turned to Colin. She teased him, "You're talking about dragons again! Do Scots ever talk about anything else?"

Colin chuckled. "We do. We often talk about how beautiful angels are, and you look like one."

Rose blushed. "You always say the nicest things. I have never known a man to know more about dragons, angels, and butterflies."

Edith, who was standing behind her, quipped, "I have noticed that he seems to be full of—"

Rose shot her a glance. Edith bowed her head and finished her statement. "Knowledge."

Mia said, "Let me tell you the story." She was excited and gestured with her arms as she told the tale. She got to the riddle and asked Colin to say it with her.

Together they said, "Come a riddle, come a riddle, come a rote-tote-tote; a wee, wee man, in a red, red coat, a staff in his hand, and a bone in his throat. Come a riddle, come a riddle, come a rote-tote-tote."

Mia finished the story. Rose was smiling and Edith acted peeved.

Rose commented, "Colin, you have been busy since we saw you last."

Edith asked, "Now where is this dragon? I want to see it."

Colin took them to the window and he pointed to the stone dragon.

Astonished, Rose said, "I looked out this window this morning and he wasn't there."

"I know how to handle dragons. You will always be safe with me," said Colin with a smile.

Edith opened her mouth to say something, but instead, she left the room. Everyone watched her leave.

Mia giggled and whispered, "Edith doesn't like dragons."

Everyone laughed quietly.

Colin turned to Rose. "You will be the belle of the ball tonight. You're absolutely gorgeous!"

Around her neck was a stunning diamond necklace with matching earrings. "I bought this dress in New York. We had to leave New York before I spent Mia's inheritance on clothes."

Colin laughed. "I once saw a sea shell on a beach in France and the inside of the shell was the color of your dress. It's such a delicate pink."

"You're correct on the color—it's called soft shell pink."

"I would be honored to escort you to the dinner." Colin bowed.

"I must ask you an important question first. Are you certain there are no more dragons lurking about?" She winked at Mia.

"I'm sure."

Rose said, "Then we are off. Mia, you aren't to wait up for me. We leave for Wisconsin tomorrow morning and I want you rested."

Mia smiled and replied, "Yes, Mummy."

"Elizabeth, if she doesn't go to bed by nine you have my permission to ask the dragon from across the street to come and get her."

"I will."

Colin held out his arm and led Rose to the door. They took the lift down and walked across the grand lobby to the ballroom. It was the largest ballroom in the city and three hundred guests were there in attendance.

The grand introduction of Colin's new whisky occurred during cocktails. The bartenders were Jones Distillery workers. People lined up and kept going back for more. Colin had instructed his men to mix the whisky with different juices for the ladies. The women were fond of the mixed drinks and many went back for seconds and thirds. The evening was successful; they ran out of whisky and the guests ordered over one hundred cases of the new Diamond Whisky.

People complimented him often on the whisky. Rose was beside him, hearing it all. She stayed at his arm throughout cocktails and sat next to him during dinner.

After dinner, the orchestra started and Colin and Rose danced. After several dances, they strolled outside to the terrace.

Rose said, "I'm so proud of you. Your whisky was so well received."

Colin smiled and nodded. "How did you like it?"

"I liked it, especially when it was mixed with the juices. How did you come up with that idea?"

"I wanted something that would appeal to women."

She nodded. "I think you have a great idea. You're so creative."

"Thank you! Coming from you, that means a lot to me."

"I can see clearly now, your talent with whisky." She smiled at him. "I'm looking forward to coming to Lake Geneva and seeing the distillery and your home."

"So am I. I hope you like my humble abode."

"I'm sure we will. Colin," she said, changing the subject, "I loved your dragon story."

"I'm glad."

"I liked the riddle."

"It's actually an old Scottish riddle, not mine."

"I liked it; I hadn't heard it before. I want to know how the dragon got on the building. I know there wasn't a dragon there earlier in the day."

"Mia told you in the story how it got there."

Rose mocked an angry face. "Colin Stuart, I'll leave this minute if you don't tell me the truth!"

Colin wrung his hands. "This goes against centuries of Scottish storytelling tradition by you forcing me to tell the truth. Please write this date down in your diary because a Scot telling the absolute truth is a momentous thing."

Rose laughed. "I promise I'll write this date down. I'm waiting for your answer."

Colin smiled at her. "Did you know the building across the street is new?"

"No I didn't."

"When I got to my room from the art exposition. I was so anxious to see you that I got ready too early. To pass the time, I opened the drapes and to my surprise across the street I saw a dragon in the air."

She hit him playfully. "Colin Stuart, I asked you to tell me the truth."

"I'm sorry, my Scottish flair for the dramatic is coming out again. I did see a dragon in the air because workmen were installing it on the building. It was fascinating to watch them hoist it into place."

"You Scottish rascal! How did your story come from watching that?"

"I love telling Mia stories and somehow the story came to me."

"She does love your stories." She leaned against the terrace railing. "You know she loves you."

Colin smiled. "Does she now?"

"She does. I can tell by the way she talks about you."

"How about her mother? Does she love me?"

Rose acted insulted and pointed a finger at him. "Colin Stuart! That's such a forward thing to say. I'm surprised at your question."

Colin smiled and quoted from Shakespeare, "The lady doth protest too much, methinks."

"There you go surprising me again. You know *Hamlet?*"

Colin smiled. "Scotland isn't in the middle of a jungle. We *do* go to school and read some."

Rose laughed. "I'm sorry. I forget sometimes that you're a special Scotsman."

He smiled wide and nodded. "That I am."

Rose teased him. "Now I'm supposed to be angry at you for asking me that question, aren't I?"

"Yes, I asked a forward question and you were greatly offended."

Rose tried to appear concerned. "Yes, I was. My daughter loves you, but I'm still trying to decide about you."

"How about those romantic moments we had on the ship? Have you forgotten those?"

Rose teased him, "Sir, you must have me confused with someone else, or perhaps you dreamt that like your dragon story."

"I see. Let me tell you about the woman on the ship. Maybe you know her?"

"I'll try to help you. What color eyes does she have?" Rose turned away.

"Her eyes are the color of emeralds, a dazzling green which would cause any man to get lost in."

"And her hair?"

"A woman at the exposition today had hair like hers. It's a silky golden color. The finest Egyptian gold pales against her hair."

"Is this woman fat?" she asked playfully.

"On the contrary, her figure is lovely."

"Her smile? She probably has only a few teeth."

"Her smile melts the heart of every man she meets."

Rose nodded slowly. "She sounds like a unique woman."

"She is, but there's one other thing. Her lips are so sweet a man cannot be without tasting them for long."

Colin cupped her face with his hands and kissed her gently.

He said afterward, "I think I have found her again."

Her eyes filled with tears of joy and she said, "I think you have too." She put her arms around him and kissed him softly.

She pulled back from the kiss. "I have had a splendid day. I hate to tell you this, but I need to return to my room. It's late. Tomorrow morning, a dashing Scotsman is picking my daughter and me up for an adventure in the wilds of Wisconsin."

"I understand. May I have one more kiss?"

Rose looked around and there were too many people around the terrace. "At my door would be a better place for that."

Colin said, "Off we go to your door!"

They walked through the ballroom to the lift and took it to her floor. Outside her room, they kissed passionately several times.

Rose said out of breath, "Colin, I must go in. Tomorrow will be here before we know it."

"I know. I have had a glorious day with you."

"So have I."

"I'll pick you and Mia up at nine," he promised.

"Remember Edith is coming too."

Colin wrinkled his nose and frowned. "I forgot. You know she doesn't like me."

"She doesn't know you yet. Once she knows you, she will like you."

"I hope so."

Rose had a concerned look on her face. "Please don't worry about her opinion of you. It's my opinion that counts."

"I hope that's true."

"It is." She squeezed his hand.

"Now, I'll see you tomorrow."

Rose kissed him and went in. Colin wanted to follow her but didn't. He returned to his room.

Once in his room, Colin opened his drapes and looked across the street at the dragon. He said, "You have done me a great favor today. You're released to become a dragon again if you would like."

Colin was sure the dragon winked at him.

CHAPTER 27

———◆———

THE NEXT MORNING AT NINE, Colin arrived with a porter. Elizabeth opened the door. Mia, Rose, and Edith were ready to go.

"Good morning, ladies. I hope everyone slept well."

Mia said, "I could hardly sleep at all. I'm so anxious to see Wisconsin."

Rose said, "I slept well although I didn't want to get up because someone kept me out late."

Colin teased her, "I told you not to drink so much of my new whisky."

Everyone stared at her as she tried to defend herself. "I didn't drink too much, but I saw several ladies who did. They loved Colin's whisky. They had several drinks apiece!"

Colin said, "I brought some for the trip. Edith, would you like some before we leave?"

"I'm not dignifying that with a reply," she said.

"I'm joking," said Colin, half-serious. He thought a drink might improve her disposition.

"Drinking is not a thing to joke about," Edith snapped.

He ignored her. "I have a taxi waiting downstairs. He will take us to the train. I had the hotel pack us a lunch for the trip. When we arrive, I have a man waiting to take us to my home. We will have afternoon tea then Rose will be attending dinner at my home later tonight. I have a boat at our disposal later today if you like. On Monday, I'll take you to the distillery."

Rose said, "It sounds delightful."

"When do we put Mummy's swan on the lake?"

Colin had forgotten about Rose's swan and he didn't know what to say.

Mia saw his blank look and said, "Remember, you said we could put Mummy's origami swan on a lake and it would turn into a swan."

Edith thought this could be her chance to show up this Scot. She smiled and said mockingly, "Oh yes, I'm looking forward to seeing the live swan."

Colin stared at Edith and he understood what she was trying to do. "Of course, we can do that." He had no clue of how he would create a real swan from the paper swan, but he would find a way. "Now let's have this fine man help us with your bags."

Rose said, "Elizabeth, I left some money for you and if you need anything, ask the hotel for it."

"Madam," Elizabeth exclaimed, "thank you! That was so kind. Mia, you have a fun time."

"I will," said Mia.

Elizabeth hugged Mia and kissed her on the forehead.

The porter gathered the bags on a dolly and they were soon in the taxi. Colin thought about the problem he had with the swan as they drove to the train station and he devised a plan. Once they arrived at the station, he told Rose he needed to send a telegram to make sure someone was meeting them. It was a rouse to let him execute the first step in his swan plan.

He sent a telegram:

Shawn O'Brien: I need a live white swan for the lake. Make it a priority to find one today. Tell no one. Colin Stuart.

Rose, Mia, and Colin enjoyed the train ride to Wisconsin. Edith stayed by herself.

Mr. O'Brien greeted them at the train station. As a porter loaded the luggage into the carriage, Colin took Mr. O'Brien to the side. "Shawn, did you get my telegram?"

"I did. Finding a swan on a Sunday will not be easy. I have three men looking for one. Why do you need it?"

"I have put myself into a tight situation with a promise I made to Rose."

"I see."

Colin pleaded, "You have to come up with one."

"I have them looking, but it's Sunday and two of the workers are still hung over from last night."

"Did you tell them anything? We have to keep this secret."

"I simply told them I needed a swan."

Colin said, "Good! Once you have it, when I tell you to, you're to release the swan on the lake behind my house."

"Do you want to see the swan before I release it?"

"Yes, come and get me when you get it."

They returned to the ladies and drove to the hotel. After Rose and her party had checked in and changed, they went to Colin's home for tea.

Mrs. Bell met them at the front door and showed them in. Compared to Rose's estate in London, Colin's home was quaint, but Rose and Mia loved it and the view overlooking the lake. Rose, Mia, and Colin walked to the lake while Edith stayed inside with Mrs. Bell.

Rose said, "I love your home. Mrs. Bell said you bought new furniture."

"I did." Colin nodded. "Also, I bought new crystal and china for our tea. Americans don't know what we use for tea. I wanted you to feel comfortable."

Rose said, "That was thoughtful of you to make us feel at home. I do love it here. There is so much room. Unlike London, it is not cramped and the air is clean." She took a deep breath in to prove her point.

"Look over there." He pointed to a vacant field. "That's 500 acres of the best farmland in Wisconsin and it's for sale. Anyone can buy it and it's incredibly cheap. My brother would die to have a piece of property like that for his dairy farm."

Rose peered at the land. "Are you thinking about buying it?"

Colin winked at her. "A man could raise a family there."

Rose smiled and agreed, "Yes, he could."

Mia pulled on Colin's sleeve. "Can we take the boat out?"

"If your mother doesn't mind."

Rose said, "I would love that."

It was Sunday and many people were boating on the lake. They had spent an hour on the water when Colin noticed Shawn waving to him from the dock.

"Ladies, I have some business with Mr. O'Brien," Colin said apologetically. "There's a park with a lovely garden not far from here. I'll meet you there in a few minutes." Colin pointed the way for them.

Colin pulled into the dock and Shawn helped the ladies get out. Rose and Mia walked around the lake to the park.

Shawn said, "I have something for you." He took Colin to a shed out of sight from the house. Inside there were three cages.

Colin looked in the first cage and exclaimed, "That's not a swan! It's a duck!"

"I know, I sent out a drunk guy and he saw a white feathered animal with webbed feet and he thought it was a swan. I told him it wasn't a swan. He thought I was calling him a liar and he took a swing at me." Shawn sighed. "I brought it along to appease him."

Colin looked at the second cage, there was a grey swan inside. "At least this one is a swan even though it's not white."

"I know."

Colin looked at the third cage and gasped, "That is the ugliest swan I have ever seen. What's wrong with it? It only has half of its feathers."

Shawn shook his head. "I don't know. It must be molting or something."

"You have to find a white swan. Get men who aren't drunk and send them out again. Give them a reward for finding the best swan. Remember, we have to keep this a secret."

Shawn scoffed. "This is a small town and a Scotsman wanting a swan will be hard to keep secret for long."

"We have to keep it secret until after the ladies leave," Colin insisted. "I'll try."

Colin left the shed. On his way to the park, he saw Mrs. Bell on the pack porch of the house, waving frantically at him. He waved back and started toward the house. She turned and went inside.

When Colin entered the kitchen, he saw Mrs. Bell with her hands on her hips and the cook was sitting at the kitchen table crying. "What's going on here?"

Mrs. Bell demanded in a loud voice, "Either that English witch stays out of our way or we will quit!"

Shocked, Colin asked, "What are you talking about?"

Mrs. Bell revealed, "Edith told me I'm doing everything wrong. She said the tea settings are wrong. She hates my brewed tea. She tasted my chocolate cake and spit it out. She said my award-winning strudel is gooey. I have never heard a woman who is more hateful."

Colin frowned. "Let me see what's going on."

Colin walked into the dining room where Edith was rearranging the tea settings.

Edith shot him a disgusted look. "Your servants should all be released. I have never seen such incompetence in my life. The settings are wrong. The crystal and china are filthy. The food is awful. I have to straighten this mess out."

"Edith, you're a guest in my house. I'll handle it."

"No, I will. I don't need any help from you."

Colin bit his tongue, trying to control his temper. He said in a calm yet firm voice, "Edith, this is my home. Mrs. Bell is my housekeeper and we will do this our way, not your way."

Edith scoffed. "My lady cannot have tea in these conditions. I will not allow it."

"You will allow it because nothing is wrong here."

Edith hissed at him, "Lady Rose and Lady Mia are accustomed to elegant and proper teas."

"They will enjoy what we have planned."

Edith's eyebrows rose. "I know them and they will not. I can fix this and make this right."

"There is nothing you need to fix."

"Let me repeat what I said earlier: I will not allow it. I should have known a Scot would be living like a pig." She scoffed, "You have fooled everyone else but not me!"

That was the final insult for Colin. "Edith, you're my guest and you may stay if you like, however, you will not have anything to do with preparing or serving the tea. If you don't want to do that you will return to the hotel. Do you understand?"

Edith turned up her nose at him. "I refuse to take any orders from you."

Colin's face reddened. He yelled over his shoulder, "Mrs. Bell, please come here."

Mrs. Bell came into the dining room.

"Mrs. Bell, is Earl still here?"

"Yes, sir."

"Please have Earl take Miss Kelsey to the hotel. She is no longer welcome here."

Edith protested, "I will not go!"

Colin glared at Edith. "If she refuses to go, have Earl put her over his shoulder and carry her there." He turned to Mrs. Bell. "Do you understand?"

"Yes sir. I'll do it with pleasure." She couldn't hide her smile. "I'll get him now." She left in a hurry.

Edith was shocked and she insisted, "You cannot treat me this way!"

"You will leave now or Earl will carry you out."

Edith looked furious. "I'll leave on my own, but I'll tell Lady Rose all about this," she threatened.

"I hope you do."

Edith grabbed her coat and bag then stormed from the house. Mrs. Bell returned with Earl.

"Earl, please take the carriage and offer Miss Kelsey a ride. If she doesn't take it, follow her until she gets to the hotel. You don't let her return here. Do you understand?"

"Yes sir," said Earl.

After Earl departed, Mrs. Bell said, "Thank you for defending me." She paused. "Aren't you going to be in trouble with Lady Rose?"

"Not if the tea goes well. Are we ready?"

"I thought we were, but now I'm worried about it. It may not be fancy enough."

"You don't worry about that. You get ready and I'll get them."

Colin left the house and walked to the park. Rose was on a bench watching Mia on a swing. Colin sat next to her. "Are you having a good day?"

"Absolutely." Rose turned to him and beamed. "It's so pretty here."

"I'm glad. It looks like Mia is enjoying herself."

"She loves it and wants to move here. She said Wisconsin is her favorite place in the whole world."

Colin laughed. "Please don't tell Edith that. I don't think she likes America."

"Yes," Rose said, raising an eyebrow, "Edith is only comfortable in London and she doesn't like change of any kind. I seldom take her to my mother's house in the country because she says it's too dirty there."

Colin said, "Oh by the way, Edith went to the hotel."

Rose looked at him surprised. "She did? Do you know why?"

"Mrs. Bell had the tea under control so I mentioned to her she could return to the hotel. I thought she might be more comfortable there. Earl escorted her back."

"Did she say anything before she left?"

"Oh yes, a lot about one thing or another and I'm sure she will fill you in later. She can be a peculiar person at times. Are you ready for tea?"

"I am."

Colin said, "Let's see if we can pry Mia from the swing."

They coaxed Mia away from the swing. As they walked back, Colin said, "Now, the tea we are having is an American tea."

Mia asked, "What is American tea?"

"Tea in America is more informal and the food is different. There will be cakes, strudel, and small animal shaped chocolates. It's different and I think you'll like it. Mrs. Bell hasn't served tea for English folks before and she's rather nervous about it. Most Americans who are away from the big cities don't have formal tea in the afternoon like we do at home, but the American ladies do like to get together."

Rose said, "I don't want it to be like home. I want it the American way."

Colin smiled. "I thought you would."

They returned to the house and sat at the dining room table. Mrs. Bell started serving the tea. Rose and Mia commented on how pretty the new china was. Mia loved the tiny chocolates and especially loved having chocolate milk instead of tea. Rose and Mia sampled the chocolate cake, which they thought was delicious, but the apple strudel was what they enjoyed the most. Rose and Mia complimented Mrs. Bell several times on how excellent everything was, to which Mrs. Bell smiled happily.

After tea, Colin took them to the hotel. In the lobby, Colin asked to speak to Rose privately. He reached out, took her hand, and walked away from Mia.

"Rose, I must be honest with you about something. Edith didn't return to the hotel on her own. I told her to leave."

"What happened?"

"Edith upset Mrs. Bell by taking charge and bossing her around. I told her Mrs. Bell was my housekeeper and we would do it her way. Edith wouldn't take any direction from me so I sent her home. I know she is your servant and I should have asked your opinion, however, she insulted me and I was angry. I felt she should leave."

Rose thought for a few seconds. "It was your home and Mrs. Bell was in charge. She did an excellent job and we had such an enjoyable time." She looked contrite. "I apologize that my lady's maid misbehaved in your home."

"Edith doesn't like me and my actions today made it worse," Colin went on. "I did something you should know about. She didn't seem as if she was going to leave when I told her to. I said if she didn't leave, Earl would carry her out."

Rose was shocked. "Colin!"

"I was only bluffing, but she believed it and she left immediately."

"Threatening to carry her out like an old dirty rug was too much." Despite the seriousness of her tone, a smile toyed at the corners of Rose's lips. "You must apologize for that."

"I was angry at the time because she wasn't obeying me," Colin said.

"I understand," Rose said, "but in the future, should I expect that you will pick me up and have someone carry me out if we disagree?"

Colin thought for a second. "You're right. I'll apologize to her, but she should also apologize to me for her actions."

Rose nodded. "I think she should. She has always had the best manners in the past. I'm sure she will."

"Well, we will see if she does. I hope this issue hasn't ruined your day."

"No, not at all! It's funny because when you said she left for the hotel I suspected there was something more to it."

Colin said, "I didn't want to tell you about our argument because I wanted you to form your own opinion of the tea. It's clear now everything she said about the tea and the food was wrong. She said Mrs. Bell's food wasn't fit for a dog."

Rose shook her head. "I thought it was delicious."

"So did I."

Rose asked, "Did she say anything else?"

Colin paused and thought of some of the hateful things she said, but he decided not to discuss them. He replied, "Nothing of any real significance. So, are you upset with me?"

"No," Rose said. "Thank you for telling me. I'm pleased you defended Mrs. Bell. It would have been easier to do what Edith wanted because you know she is close to me."

"She doesn't think much of me."

"She will learn to love you like…." Rose caught herself. "Like Mia does."

Colin grinned. "You almost said 'like I do.'"

She ignored her near stumble and smiled. "I don't know what you're talking about. Now what time are we going to dinner?"

Colin replied, "I'll pick you up at seven. Mrs. Bell has a scrumptious meal planned. She proposed several things and I hope you like what I picked."

"I'm looking forward to it."

CHAPTER 28

EDITH HAD BEEN IN THE hotel suite stewing about what happened. She heard the door open and she stood, ready to tell her story to Lady Rose.

Rose interrupted Edith before she could get a word out. "We had a delightful day, didn't we Mia?"

Mia was exuberant. "Oh yes, the tea wasn't like the boring ones we have at home. It was casual and fun. The food was delicious and instead of tea, which I absolutely hate, I had two glasses of chocolate milk. The milk was fresh from a chocolate cow and it was divine. I didn't know about chocolate cows until today."

Edith sneered, "I bet that Scot told you that. You do know chocolate cows don't exist!"

Mia giggled. "I know. I'm teasing you. Colin told me there were chocolate cows and I believed him. He later told me the truth."

Surprised, Edith asked, "You call him Colin and not Mr. Stuart?"

"Yes, he asked me to call him Colin."

Edith went to speak but Rose interrupted, "Mrs. Bell also made this delightful apple strudel. I can't remember when I had such an enjoyable time at tea."

Mia rubbed her tummy. "We also had chocolate cake, which was so yummy!"

"You seemed like you filled up on desserts today." Edith couldn't hide the disgust in her voice—and didn't try to.

Mia giggled. "We did. We ate things we wouldn't normally have for tea but it was so good. Also, Colin told the funniest stories. Have you ever heard of how they catch monkeys?"

Edith didn't hear her question because she was trying to absorb everything. She had misjudged what their reactions to the tea would be. They had enjoyed it. It was clear to her she couldn't attack Mr. Stuart on what they argued about. She was trying to decide when or if she could tell Lady Rose about how a gardener escorted her home.

Mia asked again, "Edith, have you ever heard of how they catch monkeys?"

Edith snapped back to the present. "I'm sorry, dear. I have not, but maybe later we can talk about it. I need to help madam get ready for dinner."

Rose said, "You're right. Mia, please change and rest while I'm getting ready."

"I will. I think I'll read a bit in my room."

Edith followed Rose to her bedroom and helped her change from her day dress. Rose put on a robe and sat on a chair in front of a dressing table. Edith started brushing her hair.

Rose looked at Edith through the dressing table mirror. "I was surprised to learn you returned to the hotel."

Edith was cautious with her response. "Mr. Stuart assured me his servants could manage the tea properly. He thought I would be more comfortable here."

"I see. How did you like Mr. Stuart's home?"

Edith smirked and thought this was an easy way to undermine Mr. Stuart. "It was an ordinary house with poorly supervised servants," she continued, "I noticed Mr. Stuart doesn't seem to manage his house well."

"Everything and everyone seemed fine to me."

"Madam, you must admit our home in London is grand and your staff there is the best there is," Edith countered. "Your taste in furniture and furnishings are superb. His furniture, china, and crystal are simply pedestrian. His home fits a man who ekes out a living making whisky."

Rose shrugged. "I felt comfortable there."

"A common home like his would never suffice for a lady with discerning tastes." Edith paused brushing Rose's hair. "I have yet to see a home in this dreadful place that holds a candle to a fine London home."

"I'm sure there are," Rose sighed.

"On his salary, he will never have much more than he has now," Edith stated.

"There is more to life than fine homes and china."

Edith replied, "Yes there is…but there is security in a fine home and land. There is no long-term security in whisky." Edith had measured her comments carefully and made her points clear. It was time to move on. She asked, "My lady, would you like to rest for a while before I help you get dressed?"

"I would, thank you."

Edith left her room and went to Mia's room. She wanted to try to find out if Colin spoke to Rose about the incident at Mr. Stuart's home. Edith knocked on the door.

Mia's voice came muffled through the door. "Come in."

Edith turned the doorknob and entered. Mia was lying on the bed reading a book. Edith sat on the bed. "You had a fun time today, didn't you?"

"I did." Mia sat up. "We went for a boat ride and to a park. I love Wisconsin. It's so nice here."

"Don't you miss your cat and London?"

"Of course I miss King Richard, but I'm sure he's fine. I miss my room but I don't miss London. I have seen more of the world now. I like America."

"I wanted to ask you something." Edith put on her best friendly face, trying to get Mia to talk. "Did Mr. Stuart seem upset about anything this afternoon?"

Mia thought for a moment. "No, not that I noticed. He and Mother seemed to have a fun time today."

"That's good, my dear. Did Mr. Stuart ever have a private talk with your mother?"

"Yes. They spoke for a few minutes in the lobby."

"Was either one of them upset?"

"No, Colin held her hand and they talked. He kissed her afterward." Mia sighed. "He's so romantic and handsome, don't you think?"

"He does seem to be an overly friendly man."

Puzzled, Mia stared at Edith. "Why are you asking these questions?"

"I want to make sure everything went well. I had to correct a few things for Mrs. Bell before you and your mother arrived. I wanted to make sure no one was upset about it."

Mia shrugged. "Everyone seemed fine to me."

"That's good to know." Edith paused. "I wanted to ask you about you calling Mr. Stuart by his first name. In England, a young lady would never address an older man by his first name. Even though we are in America, we must keep up our standards."

"Colin said in America people are more informal. He asked Mother's permission and she agreed, so I thought it was fine."

"I understand, but we will return to England soon and we must remember our proper manners."

A dreamy look came over Mia's face. "I pray we don't return to England. I like it here and I want to stay."

Edith's brow furrowed. "Have you told your mother your feelings about this?"

"Oh yes, at the park today we talked about it. We had a long chat when Colin was in the house."

"How does your mother feel about America?"

"She likes it."

Edith didn't like her reply because she hated Wisconsin, she patted Mia's hand. "You have had an exciting day. I think I should let you rest. Please let me know if you need anything."

"I will."

Edith went to the parlor and sat on the couch. It was clear to her Colin didn't say anything, or much, to Lady Rose about their disagreement. She decided it would be best to forget about it.

CHAPTER 29

———

COLIN KNOCKED ON ROSE'S DOOR punctually at seven o'clock, hoping Mia or Rose would answer, but it was Edith who did.

He tried to be upbeat. "Good evening, Edith; I hope you are well."

"I'm fine." She didn't say come in but Colin did anyway. She closed the door behind him and they were alone in the parlor.

"Edith, I wanted to apologize for the way I sent you back to the hotel. I shouldn't have threatened to have you carried out."

Her eyebrow rose. "Yes, you were certainly wrong to do that and your behavior was some of the worst I have ever experienced."

Colin winced because he felt attacked and he made a conscious effort not to strike back. He took a couple of deep breaths to let the anger pass then said. "Again, I apologize."

Edith put her hands on her hips. "Is that all you're apologizing for?"

"Yes." He paused. "Is there something else you think I should apologize for?"

"Of course there is!" she exclaimed. "I should have never been dismissed. I was doing what I felt was right for my lady."

Colin nodded. "I understand and respect that, but neither you nor anyone else can tell me what I'm to do in my home."

She stamped her foot. "Mr. Stuart, you're wrong! What I did was what a lady's maid should do. I must protect Lady Rose. If you don't apologize for all the behavior you showed today, I'll not accept a partial apology."

Colin was shocked. She was ignoring her behavior completely. "Miss Kelsey, did Mia tell you the story about how to catch monkeys?"

"Why are you talking about monkeys? I'm talking about your behavior today."

"Let me tell you the story of how you catch a monkey. First, you put small holes in a barrel a little bigger than the monkey's hand. You put a peanut in the barrel. The monkey will reach in the barrel and grab it. When he withdraws his hand, his hand is too big. He won't let go of the peanut because of his stubborn pride. He will drag the barrel though the forest until he tires and gets caught."

"What does that have to do with me?" asked Edith. Her face was sour, worse than normal.

"Your stubborn pride and your view of me as a lower-class Scot keeps you from seeing I love Rose. I want her to always be happy. You have to let go of your poor view of me like the monkey needed to let go of the peanut."

"I resent the fact you're referring to me as a monkey."

Colin sighed. "I'm not calling you a monkey. I'm using an illustration."

"I don't understand it. Let me make my point clear. To me this situation with you is simple." She stood straighter and took a deep breath. "In my opinion, you only want her money!"

Colin fired back, "I would love her if she didn't have a shilling to her name. I don't care about money. I have enough."

"I have never known a man who has enough money," Edith sneered.

"You don't know me and what I want," Colin said brusquely. "I see you won't accept my apology and I'm sorry you can't. I won't ever bring it up again. I think it would be better if you asked Lady Rose to meet me in the lobby."

Colin slammed the door as he left, leaving Edith fuming.

Rose closed her bedroom door softly, recounting the heated parts of the argument she heard between Edith and Colin. Colin had tried to apologize but Edith's pride and her poor view of Colin would never let her see what a good man he was. Rose thought of her mother and some of her other friends in England. They would see Colin and probably treat him the same way.

Rose heard a soft knock on the door. "Come in."

Mia entered, closed the door, and walked up to her. Rose had tears in her eyes.

"Mummy, why are you crying?"

"I'm sad about something."

"Are you going to dinner?"

"I don't know about dinner now. Some things have happened and maybe I shouldn't go."

Mia took her hand and put it on her mother's arm. "I think I know what happened. Mummy, did you hear the discussion between Colin and Edith?"

"Yes, I did. I shouldn't have eavesdropped on them, however, I wanted to see how he would talk to Edith about something that happened."

"Edith asked me some odd questions earlier and I was curious so I listened too," Mia confessed. "Colin tried to apologize for something. Do you know anything about it?"

"Yes, something happened at his house with Edith. He said he would apologize to her for it."

"He tried then he left because he was upset. I don't blame him for being cross. She makes me angry, too."

Rose shook her head. "Edith is only trying to protect me."

"Elizabeth told me something and I think you should know." Mia hesitated. "But I don't want Elizabeth to get into trouble."

"You can tell me."

Mia paused, choosing her words carefully. "Elizabeth told me Edith doesn't like Colin because she's trying to hold on to her old life in England. She doesn't want anything to change. Elizabeth thought Edith was thinking about herself, not you."

"Do you think so?"

"Yes. I think Colin is amazing and so does Elizabeth."

"I do too, but Edith thinks about Colin like others in England will. Colin won't be liked by many of our friends at home."

"I don't care what others think. I like him."

"I don't think your grandmother will like him."

"She will, once she knows him. I know she will. She'll see how much we like him."

"I'm doubtful."

"Mummy, there's something else. Did you hear him say he loved you?"

"Yes, and I should be delighted but this whole situation is so complicated." Rose put her head on her forehead.

Mia put her hands on her hips. "There's that word again! There is nothing complicated about this. Mummy, he loves you. He said so."

Rose thought about what she said for a few seconds. "At times, I think you know more about life at almost ten than I know at thirty."

"I don't know about that but I like things simple." Mia smiled.

"I agree. I tend to overthink things at times and worry too much about what others think. At this moment, I think we should go to dinner with Colin!"

"We?" Mia's face lit up. "I'm going too?"

"Yes, I want you to go and I'm sure Colin won't mind. I want your company tonight. We need to get going. Let me fix my makeup."

Rose kissed Mia then touched up her makeup from the tears. They went into the parlor.

"Edith, Mia will be going to dinner with me tonight. Could you help her get ready?"

"Yes, madam."

"I heard Colin's voice, where is he?"

"He is waiting for you in the lobby."

"Mia, you get ready and meet Colin and me in the lobby. Edith, don't wait up for us." Rose left.

Colin was standing by the fireplace in the crowded lobby. He worried about what had happened, and was afraid of Rose's reaction when Edith talked to her. He was certain Edith would.

Rose came down, beautiful in her yellow dress. She glided across the lobby to him, put her arms around his shoulders, and kissed him.

Colin pulled back from the kiss and the words poured from his mouth before he could stop them. "I was standing here worried you might be upset with me. I tried to apologize to Edith but it didn't go well."

Rose put up her hand. "I know you did, and thank you, but let's forget about Edith for tonight."

Colin smiled and was relieved. "That's fine with me."

"I have made a couple of decisions about you tonight."

Colin could feel his foul mood dissipating. "You did? What are they?"

"A lady has to keep some of her secrets, but the kiss in front of all these people should tell you something."

"I think it does. May I have another?"

She kissed him again. After the kiss, she pulled back a bit. "Would you mind if Mia attends dinner with us?"

Colin's face lit up. "That would be ideal!"

"Do you think Mrs. Bell would mind?"

"Not at all, she likes you both."

"Mia can share my plate if there's not enough to eat."

"We are only having cabbage and potato soup anyway."

Rose wrinkled her nose. "Cabbage and potato soup?"

"I'm teasing; there will be plenty of food."

Mia arrived a few moments later.

Colin kissed her on the forehead. "I'm with the two prettiest ladies in Wisconsin. I hope you're hungry."

Mia said, "I ate like a pig at tea but now I'm starved again."

"Me too," Rose echoed.

"That's good because we are having a feast. Now Mia, have you ever heard of a cow that gives strawberry milk?"

"Colin, is this like the chocolate cow you tried to convince me of?" asked Mia.

"Well, this story is true. You're having strawberry milk tonight and it came from a strawberry cow."

Mia smiled at him. "Do Scots ever tell the truth?"

Colin laughed. "My dear, the truth is a matter of perspective. We Scots have a unique perspective on things."

Mia and Rose laughed. As they left the hotel, Colin began his astonishing tale about the first strawberry cow.

CHAPTER 30

———————

THE NEXT MORNING, COLIN WENT to work with the plan to pick Rose and Mia up at the hotel midmorning to tour the distillery. The first thing Colin wanted to do was to check on the status of the swans. Shawn waited for him in his office.

"Did you find a swan?"

Shawn smiled. "Oh yes, we have swans."

"How many do we have?"

"We have four pairs of swans plus a grey swan, an ugly swan, and the duck. Each man returned with a pair. Swans mate for life and the farmer wouldn't sell only one. Unknowingly the men all eventually ended up at the same farmer. The first man paid regular price for two swans but when the second man came in and the farmer learned he was also from the distillery, the farmer thought he could raise the price. Each man after that paid twice as much as the first man." Shawn laughed.

"I'm desperate at this point so the money is not a concern. Where are they?"

"Follow me."

They went behind the distillery to a tool shed.

Colin gasped when the shed door opened. "These are exactly what I wanted; you did an excellent job! Tonight, turn them loose behind my house after dark. Make sure there is plenty of feed on the shore for them. Rose and Mia will be there tomorrow and see the swans. I'll be off the hook."

Shawn chuckled. "So, it's like magic, you make swans appear."

"Something like that."

"These swans are expensive. You're going to turn them loose and hope they stay. That is your plan?"

Colin smiled with confidence. "If there is food around, they'll stay."

Shawn scratched his head. "How do you explain there are so many swans if they all stay around?"

"I'll think of something."

"I hope this works out for you. She must be a special woman."

"She is."

Colin went to the hotel and picked up Rose and Mia. They returned to the distillery and Colin took them on a guided tour. The complexity of the process and the distillery's size impressed Mia and Rose. At the end of the tour, they stopped for Rose to sample the liquor. Shawn waited for them in the warehouse.

Colin and Shawn selected a barrel to draw samples from as Mia and Rose sat on wooden cases. Through an open door, a duck started to walk across the floor. The duck walked calmly across like it had done so many times before. Colin saw the duck and he grabbed Shawn's arm. Both men froze. They knew immediately the duck and probably the swans had somehow gotten out of the tool shed. They stared at the duck, which was standing there quacking.

Mia laughed and pointed to the duck. "What's a duck doing here?"

Colin and Shawn sprang into action, shooed the duck outside and looked out back. There had been a poultry breakout. Swans were everywhere. The ugly swan had followed the duck to the door and looked up at them as if Colin or Shawn should acknowledge its presence. They slammed the door so Rose and Mia couldn't see what was happening.

"Is the duck the distillery's pet?" Rose called.

Colin was red faced and didn't know what to say so he replied, "Yes."

"What is the duck's name?" asked Mia.

Colin looked at Shawn who shrugged his shoulders. Colin uttered the first thing that came to his mind: "Supper."

Rose and Mia laughed then Mia asked, "Why is it called Supper?"

Colin answered, "Because if it comes in here again, I'm having it for supper."

Mia and Rose laughed again.

Colin whispered to Shawn, "Please round them up."

"I will."

"Please do it quietly."

"I'll try."

Colin tried to draw Rose and Mia's attention away from the duck. He showed Mia and Rose the proper way to sniff the whisky and taught Rose how to taste it.

Rose remarked, "This is good. I think this is better than what you had at the Chicago party."

"Yes, this is a ten-year-old whisky."

Mia asked, "How do you know when a whisky is ready?"

"It takes years of experience to be able to tell when it's ready." Colin held the glass up to the light and asked, "See this color? This is a fine whisky—not as good as what I made in Scotland or will make here in the future but still commendable. I'm using this to mix with the younger product to mellow them out."

Mia asked, "Do you sample the whisky often?"

"Yes, you have to stay in touch with it, like your mother does with you. In a glance, your mother can tell if you're feeling well or not because she knows you. I can tell in an instant what I need to do for a whisky. Do I let it stay in the barrel longer, do I blend it, or is it ready to sell?"

Mia thought for a moment. "Has a woman ever been a master distiller?"

"That's an excellent question. I don't know of one."

Mia stated, "Maybe I could become the first."

"Why not? You're smart. I'll take you on as my assistant."

Rose said, "I thought I was going to be your assistant."

"You're right. I did promise you that. I'll have two assistants."

Rose giggled and teased Colin, "Mia, part of your job would be to keep the ducks out of the distillery."

"That would be fun," said Mia.

Rose observed, "You told me a lot about making whisky when we were on the ship but seeing it in person makes such a difference. It's impressive. I wish now Edith was here."

Colin and Mia wrinkled their noses.

Rose laughed. "I can see you both think that's a bad idea."

"Mummy, Edith would hate it here and would take the fun out of it."

"You're probably right," Rose agreed.

Shawn returned from rounding up the fowl, Colin took him to the side. "Have you solved our problem?"

"Almost, but there are two still missing. Supper and the ugly swan have escaped. I have two men working on it."

Colin and Shawn walked back to the Rose and Mia. Colin looked at his watch. "It's close to lunchtime and we will be going to Mr. O'Brien's father's restaurant." Shawn took them to lunch, which was delicious. Afterward, Colin took the ladies to the hotel.

"Now ladies, this afternoon starting around three, we will be flying kites. Tonight, we will have dinner at my house. Tomorrow morning before you leave for Chicago you will be coming to my house for brunch. Also, tonight before dinner we will put the origami swan on the lake. I promise tomorrow morning there should be a magnificent swan on the water."

Rose was skeptical. "Colin, are you sure about that?"

"Yes, I heard a swan in the paper when we were on the ship. I'm sure it will come out."

Mia said, "I can't wait to see the swan. All this sounds like fun."

Colin kissed Rose and Mia then he returned home to prepare for their visit.

Rose and Mia arrived at Colin's home that afternoon. There was a good breeze and the nearby hill was perfect for flying kites. All three of them flew kites until an hour before dusk.

"Ladies, we have to get to the lake before dark to release the swan."

Rose got the origami swan from the house and they walked to the lake.

At the shore, Mia asked, "What do we do? Do we say something?"

"No, you only need to put it gently on the water," said Colin.

Mia set the origami swan on the water. The wind was blowing gently, the swan moved across the lake and disappeared. Mia waved to it as it went.

CHAPTER 31

———

ROSE WOKE UP EARLY FEELING a heavy sadness because they were returning to England. Mia had brought up the idea of them staying along with Elizabeth and sending Edith home. However, there was business Rose needed to attend to in England. She knew she needed to go home.

As Rose got ready, Edith came to help her. Edith was the most cheerful she had been since leaving England.

Colin had also risen early and was in a panic because there were no swans on the lake. Shawn had turned nine swans plus the ugly swan and the duck out last night and not one was there except Supper, who was on the shore eating the remaining food. Not even the ugly swan was there. Colin had considered having Shawn get a search party but decided against it. He gave up on the swans.

Colin was sullen as he arrived to pick up the ladies. He was gloomy not only because his swan plan had failed miserably but also because Mia and Rose were leaving.

He knocked on their door and Edith answered. She was smiling. "Good morning, Mr. Stuart!"

"Good morning, Miss Kelsey."

"It's a fine morning, isn't it?"

"It is. You seem to be in a cheerful mood."

"I am because we are headed home."

"Yes. I know," said Colin with despair.

She smiled, clearly displaying her pleasure due to his sadness. "The ladies are almost ready. So, I understand we are going to see a magical swan today. Is that right?"

Colin winced. "That's the plan."

Edith laughed and said cynically, "If this works, I want you to make me an origami pot of gold. Can you do that?"

Colin had opened his mouth to reply but Mia and Rose came into the room. Mia went to Colin and hugged him tightly. She looked up at him. "Colin, you must allow me to stay here or you have to come to England with us."

His shoulders sank. "I'm sorry, I can't go to England. My life is here now. I would love for you to stay."

Mia looked down and looked sad. "Then I'll have to stay in Wisconsin. I'm sure there is an orphanage that will take me. You can visit me on weekends."

Rose chuckled. "Now Mia, please stop being so dramatic. We agreed we would not talk about this, didn't we?"

"We did, but as soon as I saw Colin my heart started breaking."

"Yes dear, I know." Rose sighed. "Now we shouldn't dwell on this. We need to get to Colin's home and check on our swan."

Colin grimaced.

Edith saw his reaction and said slyly, "Mr. Stuart, I suspect the swan isn't there."

Colin looked around. "I'm sure it's somewhere nearby. I didn't see it this morning. We may have to look for it."

Edith smiled. "I knew you would have some kind of excuse."

Rose looked at her sternly.

Colin escorted the women to his home. Edith immediately asked to go to the lake because she wanted his swan story to end badly.

Colin reluctantly took them to the lake and as they got closer he saw there was something on the shore. Colin thought it was Supper, but when he got closer he realized it was a magnificent white swan. Its mate swam in the water nearby. As they got close, the swan moved into the water.

Colin beamed as they got close.

Mia exclaimed, "Look! There are two swans!"

Colin explained, "I must have been wrong. There were two swans in the paper, not one."

Edith argued, "I'm sure there have always been swans on this lake."

Colin straightened up and said with confidence, "I can promise you there haven't been any swans on this lake until after Rose put the origami swan into the water."

"We know Scots never lie!" replied Edith cynically.

"You can ask Mrs. Bell if she has seen swans on the lake before today."

Edith rebutted, "She works for you."

"She will tell the truth. You can ask anyone around here. Before last night there have never been swans on this lake," Colin replied.

"This has been a fairy tale that has come true." Rose smiled and winked at him.

Mia looked at the lake and a duck was swimming up. "Colin, is that Supper?"

"Yes, one of my men caught him and dropped him off here to get him away from the distillery. I think he likes it here."

Mia cocked her head. "How do you know it's a male?"

"I'm guessing it is."

The duck swam up and waddled right up to them. It acted like it expected to be in the conversation. Mia fed it some grain.

Edith was quiet because Colin somehow had pulled this off. She intended to ask Mrs. Bell privately about the swans.

Colin said, "We should go up for brunch because you will need to leave for the train soon."

They went to the house and Supper followed.

Mrs. Bell greeted them and saw the duck. "Who do we have here?"

Mia replied, "His name is Supper."

Mrs. Bell laughed. "This is the first time I have ever had a duck visit us here. Also, this morning for the first time ever, a pair of white swans was swimming on the lake. I hope they are a mating pair. It would be delightful to have other swans here."

Colin smiled wide and looked at Edith. He hadn't told Mrs. Bell to say anything and she brought it up at a perfect time.

Rose and Mia looked at Colin. He winked at them. "See, I told you."

Mia smiled and looked at her mother, who was smiling and had a twinkle in her eye.

Mrs. Bell held out her arms. "Please come in. The food will be ready soon."

Colin, Rose, and Mia went to the dining room with Mrs. Bell. Edith stayed behind in the parlor, eyeing a letter on the table.

She stepped closer and looked down at the letter. It was from Abigail McCarthy of Aberlour, Scotland. She picked up the letter and turned it over—it had a distinctive wax heart seal. "No woman seals an ordinary letter with a heart seal," Edith muttered. "Some woman in Scotland sent him a love letter." For an instant, she thought about opening it but reconsidered and put it back.

Rose called out, "Edith, are you coming?"

"Yes, I was admiring the pictures here in the front room." She hurried to the dining room.

"Rose," Colin said, after they had enjoyed a delicious brunch and were ready to leave, "if you don't mind, there are two carriages here. I would like Mia and Edith to ride in one and we will ride in the second one. I must talk to you privately."

Edith started to speak, but Rose interrupted her. "I would like that."

Once inside the carriage, Colin immediately took her hands and held them close to his chest. "Rose, I have been trying to gather my courage to say this all morning. I don't want you to go. Can't you please stay?"

Rose shook her head. "I have to return to England before the weather turns. Why don't you go with us?"

"Rose, you know my life is here now."

She pleaded with him. "But you could make a new life in England with us."

"I have to make a life here. You know my feelings about that."

"Yes, I do."

"Rose, I have something I have wanted to tell you since we were on the ship." He looked at her seriously. "I love you. I know in my heart that I do."

Her eyes softened. "Colin, that's so sweet. You're so gentle, kind, and loving…you're an amazing man."

Colin looked disappointed. "I expected you might say you loved me too."

Rose paused. "I need more time."

"You're hesitant because we live in two different worlds."

"We do," she admitted, "and I want you to be welcomed in my world."

"I'll never be welcomed in your world. In America, as you have seen, no one cares about titles. Here they say there is a man who loves a woman and nothing more." He looked down. He didn't know what else to say.

"I know, I know," she stifled back a sob. "What do we do?"

Colin pleaded, "You can stay."

Rose shook her head. "I can't."

There was a long pause.

Colin suggested, "I think there is only one thing to do. You need to take some time to think about it. Go home to England and think about what we could be together. Think about what our lives would be here. You, Mia, and I would have a fantastic life here. However, you must write often to me so I know how you are."

"Is every day too much?" Rose smiled.

He laughed. "No, but twice a day would be better."

"Thank you for being patient with me. Also, thank you for everything you have done."

"I want to do much more. I want to be part of your life. I love you, Rose."

He kissed her, long and passionately.

She pulled back after the kiss and was about to say something. He held his breath, but she changed her mind. She buried her head in his shoulder for the rest of the ride to the station.

They exited the carriage and Colin guided everyone to the train. Edith immediately boarded without saying a word to him.

Colin kneeled on the train platform. He looked at Mia as tears ran down her face.

"I don't want to go," she cried.

"I know," said Colin and he wiped her tears. "Let me tell you this, I love you and whenever you want to come here, you can."

"I love you too." Mia hugged him and kissed him. "I'm worried about Supper. Can you please look after him?"

Colin laughed. "I'll try, but that duck has a mind of its own."

She said, "I consider Supper to be our duck now."

"I'll treat him that way. I promise I'll take care of him."

He kissed her again. He stood and turned to Rose.

"Rose my dear, this is your last chance to stay. I love you and I will care for you both always."

Rose said, "I have no doubt of that. Thank you again for everything."

Mia nudged her mother. "Mummy, you heard what he said. He said he loved you. Tell him how you feel!"

Rose exclaimed, "Mia!"

"Mummy, tell him how you really feel. You must tell him now! You may never have the chance again."

Rose stared at Mia then she looked at Colin. His expression begged her to say something more to him. A sob escaped her. "Colin, she's right! I love you! I should have told you earlier in the carriage. I have to go, but I promise I'll be back. I promise *we* will be back!"

Colin took her in his arms, kissed her and twirled her around. He put her down. "Thank you, Rose! Thank you! I can make it until you return."

"I can too."

Mia laughed and added, "So can I."

The three of them hugged.

Edith watched from the train. She could see a momentous event had occurred. She couldn't hear them, but she saw their reactions. She knew she had to return to England and try to stop this. She remembered the name Abigail McCarthy and wondered who she was.

Mia and Rose stayed with Colin until the last minute. Colin kissed them one more time. He stayed on the train platform waving to them until they pulled away from sight.

As the train was on its way from the station, Rose whispered to Mia, "Not one word to Edith, do you understand?"

"Why?"

"She only wants what is best for me and I'll slowly get her to warm up to this."

"Mummy, I don't think you can."

"I'm sure I can," Rose continued, "but until then, no discussion of what we said to each other. Also, don't say we are coming back."

Mia looked like she was going to cry. "We are returning, aren't we?"

"Absolutely, we are coming back. I love Colin!" She paused. "I love saying that. I love Colin! I love Colin!"

Mia's face brightened and she giggled.

"Mia, you gave me the courage to tell him. Thank you for pushing me."

"I knew you loved him. Everyone needs a gentle push at times, even mothers."

"Yes, you're right about that." Rose hugged Mia and watched as Lake Geneva faded into the distance.

CHAPTER 32

THE TRIP TO NEW YORK and on to England was uneventful. Rose and Mia missed having Colin on the journey home. Each day that passed, Rose regretted more her decision to leave. Distracted and irritable, Mia could not concentrate on her studies no matter what Elizabeth tried and so she gave up until the voyage was over. The only person who seemed happy was Edith, who spent her free time thinking of how she could put a wedge between Rose and Colin. By the end of the voyage, she had devised a plan.

Immediately upon arriving home, Edith contacted her uncle, Theodore, who was Lord Richard's valet. He was her mother's older brother, her favorite uncle. She asked if she could visit him in London. He replied saying he would love to see her. They agreed to meet at a popular restaurant downtown.

When Edith arrived, Theodore was already there. He was a thin, balding man, in his sixties.

He stood when she approached. "My dear, it's splendid to see you."

"You as well."

They exchanged a hug and kiss then sat next to each other. Their table was close to the window. The restaurant was in a bustling shopping area and people jammed the sidewalk.

Ted asked, "Have you had lunch yet?"

"No, I'm famished. This is a busy place."

"It always is. They have an outstanding location here in the shopping district. They have excellent fish and chips. How was your trip?"

"Long and exhausting. I'm not sure why everyone raves about America. I found the people crude and unsophisticated."

"I have never been there, but I would like to. Maybe I will when I retire."

Edith was anxious to get to her plan. "One reason the trip was so hard was my lady met a Scotsman on the voyage who was terribly rude and obnoxious to me. Then to my surprise she agreed to visit him in Chicago and also after the art exposition in a terrible hamlet of a town, Lake Geneva, Wisconsin. He is a former well-known Scottish whisky maker."

Edith waited to see his reaction.

"A Scottish whisky maker? Is his name Colin Stuart?"

"Yes...how would you know that?" Edith acted surprised.

"He was the master distiller at the GlenWilliams distillery. I know him well."

"You do?"

"Yes, after Lord Williams and Mr. Stuart had a dramatic falling out, Mr. Stuart left for America. Lord Williams always talks badly about him. You said he was rude and obnoxious to you."

"Yes he was, on several occasions. The Scot fell in love with Lady Cavendish and he knows I'm suspicious of him. I have tried to protect her from him, but he is a handsome and skilled courtier."

"Yes, he's a handsome man," her uncle conceded. "I knew his wife. She was lovely and many men tried to court her but Colin won her heart. Did Lady Cavendish and Colin spend much time together?"

"Yes indeed, they were together alone often. Lady Rose and her daughter went to his home several times."

"That is shocking!"

"I agree. Lady Cavendish's mother doesn't know anything about this escapade."

"So, she is hiding this from her mother?"

"Yes, I'm afraid the Scot has turned Lady Cavendish's head and I'm not sure what to do about it."

Ted replied, "I know what you mean. I often must guide Lord Williams away from these poor, common wenches he brings home. Our job is to protect the houses we serve and try to keep our masters from making unwise decisions. Should my master or your lady marry lower, it affects us."

"I agree it definitely does." Edith smiled innocently and slyly added, "If only someone like Lord Williams could become interested in her."

"I have urged Lord Williams to pursue Lady Cavendish."

"You have?"

"Oh yes, I encouraged him many times to see her. He tried but the relationship with her never blossomed."

"I know why it didn't," Edith said.

"You do?"

"Yes, but I'm not sure I should tell you. It's confidential to my lady."

"I understand." Ted sat back. "I won't pry."

Edith wanted him to ask so she baited him, "Well, if it's for the benefit of our houses maybe I should. Do you think it would be proper?"

"If it's for the benefit for our two houses, you should share it with me." He leaned toward her.

"Well," Edith began, "Lady Cavendish was definitely interested in Lord Williams until he said something about her daughter going to a boarding school."

"I'm not surprised. Lord Williams doesn't like children. He considers them a nuisance and he would especially not be interested in another man's child."

"Most gentlemen wait until after they have married to encourage the wife to send the stepchildren to boarding school."

"Yes, but Lord Williams is impetuous and often blunt."

Edith suggested, "Maybe we can help him with her."

"What do you have in mind?"

"Lord Williams must understand Lady Cavendish and Mia are close. Mia isn't going to a boarding school. It wouldn't be sound for him to ask about that."

"I see your point."

Edith added, "If Lord Williams calls on Lady Cavendish again, you should encourage him to express interest in her daughter."

"I agree. That would be easy for me to coach him."

"If Lord Williams knew Colin was pursuing Lady Rose, it might motivate him to renew the relationship."

"If he knew, I'm sure he would."

"Think you could tell him about this?"

"Absolutely," her uncle replied. "I can and I will immediately. Do you know of any event approaching where we could get them together?"

"Yes, Lady Rose's mother, Countess Winston, is having her annual Harvest Ball soon. Lord Williams should ask her about it."

"Excellent! Lord Williams is an expert at getting invitations to parties."

Edith grinned. "Theodore, this has come together nicely. I think we have a good plan."

"I do too."

"There is another topic I want to discuss with you. I need to ask you about a Scottish woman who wrote love letters to Colin."

"Love letters?"

"Yes, I saw a letter from Abigail McCarthy to Colin."

"I know Abigail well. She is Colin's sister-in-law and she is definitely in love with Colin. Everyone in her village knows that. She also has a lovely voice, she reads poetry and short stories aloud at the coffeehouse in town once a month. Many people go there to hear her."

"Does he or did he love her?" asked Edith.

"I don't know, but I have seen him at her parents' home and at the coffeehouse with her many times."

"Sounds like there's something there. If Lord Williams is successful in his pursuit of Lady Rose, Abigail can have the Scot. At this point, please don't tell Lord Williams about her. I'll save that for later if I need to."

"I won't."

"Teddy, you have helped me with a big problem. I feel so relieved. Thank you!"

"You're welcome, my dear. Our job as servants is to protect our houses. The combination of the Williams house and the Cavendish house would benefit everyone."

"I agree."

CHAPTER 33

LONDON – LORD WILLIAMS LONDON ESTATE

———

THE NEXT MORNING, THEODORE WOKE Lord Richard Williams at his customary eleven o'clock time. He had to be discreet because a young woman was in bed with him. Richard had an appointment at his London club at one in the afternoon and after a late Friday night, it would be difficult for him to get going.

The young woman also woke up. Theodore recognized her; she had been there before. He knew he had to help her go out the back door and pay her, which he did.

When he returned, Richard was drinking coffee in bed and reading the paper.

"Good morning, sir."

Richard grunted some unintelligible reply. Theodore opened the drapes, flooding the room with sunlight causing Richard to whine his displeasure.

Theodore turned to Richard. "Sir, do you have an invitation to Countess Winston's Harvest Ball?"

"No."

"Did you know Lady Cavendish has returned from America?"

He didn't reply.

"Did you know Lady Cavendish visited Colin Stuart in America?"

Richard dropped the paper. "What did you say?"

"I asked if you knew Lady Cavendish visited Colin Stuart at his home in America?"

"I didn't. How in the devil did he meet her?"

"On the voyage to America."

Richard barked. "How did you learn this terrible news?"

"Through her servants."

"Are you positive about this?"

Theodore nodded. "Absolutely."

"I can't let a commoner take the most eligible woman in England. Lady Rose and I were close for a while until she backed off. I don't know why," Richard grumbled.

"I know why."

"You do? Then tell me, man! Tell me now!"

"It was because of her daughter."

Richard thought for a few seconds. "I don't remember meeting her daughter."

"Lady Cavendish is close to her daughter and you asked her when her daughter would be going to boarding school."

"I did?"

"Apparently, she felt your question indicated you don't like children."

Richard laughed. "Well, she's right about that."

"Sir, a woman with a child can't know that. You have to show some interest in the child, at least until you're married."

He nodded. "I understand. How serious is her relationship with Colin?"

"Serious enough that she visited him in Chicago and in Wisconsin." Theodore continued, "Lady Cavendish and her daughter visited Mr. Stuart at his home several times."

Alarmed, Richard said, "She never visited my home!" He got out of bed and began to pace the floor. He stopped after a few seconds and had an idea. "I'm sure Countess Winston will be at Duke Clarke's party tonight. I have an invitation and I could see her tonight. I'll get an invitation to the Harvest Ball from her."

Theodore added, "Lady Cavendish has hidden all this from her mother. The countess would be upset to learn her daughter is interested in a Scottish commoner."

"Yes, she will be," Richard said. "She might put a stop to this for me. I know the woman who can tell her. Duchess Clarke loves gossip and I'm sure she will run right to Countess Winston with this news as well as tell everyone else."

"Excellent idea, sir, allowing someone else to bring the shocking news. I would suggest soon after their discussion, you meet with Countess Winston. You can provide a shoulder for her to cry on."

"That is exactly my plan! A London gentleman can outmaneuver any Scottish commoner."

"I'm sure you can, sir."

CHAPTER 34

LONDON – DUKE AND DUCHESS CLARKE'S LONDON HOME

———————

RICHARD ARRIVED EARLY FOR THE duke's reception. Normally he would be fashionably late, but he wanted to talk to the duchess as soon as he could. When he arrived, the duke and duchess were greeting the guests at the door. He took the duchess to the side.

She was a short, plump, and rather plain woman. Her tight corset unsuccessfully tried to stuff her pear-shaped figure into her expensive, lavender evening dress. She could barely breathe because the corset was so tight.

"My lady, you look so lovely in that dress."

"Thank you, that is kind of you!"

"Are you expecting a large turnout today?"

"Yes, we are, nearly everyone accepted."

"Did Countess Winston accept?"

"She did; do you know her?"

"Yes, I know her and her daughter well. I'm surprised to hear she is coming."

"Has something happened?"

"Apparently, her daughter Lady Cavendish went to America to see a Scottish commoner without the countess knowing and she saw him without a chaperone many times."

"What? Do you know this for a fact?"

"I do. The man's name is Colin Stuart. He used to work for me. I had to let him go because of some irregularities. As many people know, I was seeing Lady Cavendish before she left for America and I'm shocked to hear she did this."

The duchess put a hand to her chest. "I'm shocked as well. Did Lady Cavendish's daughter go with her to America?"

"Yes, they visited the Scottish man at his home in Wisconsin several times."

"No!"

"Yes," he replied.

"I'm sure the countess is devastated. I'll seek her out to console her."

"Please don't tell her I know about this. I'm still interested in Lady Cavendish."

"Of course, I understand completely. Lord Williams, thank you for sharing this with me."

"You're welcome."

"More guests are arriving so I must get back." The duchess hurried off with the juiciest gossip of the night.

Lord Richard watched her from a distance. She looked like she was going to burst until she told someone. Several times, she pulled ladies away as they were arriving and talked to them about what she learned. Richard sought out these women and told them more awful lies about Colin. He insinuated Colin had to leave the country because the authorities were investigating him. The entire party buzzed with the gossip.

Countess Winston arrived and the duchess immediately took her to the side. Richard spied on the conversation from the shadows. It was an animated conversation and when it ended, the countess escaped to the garden. Richard caught up with her and stopped her next to a water fountain.

"Your Ladyship, you look distressed. Is there anything I can do to help?"

The countess tried to wave him off. "I need to be alone."

"I'm sure you will feel better if you talk to someone."

The countess thought for a second then disclosed what she heard. "I heard some distressing news about my daughter. Apparently, she met a Scottish man on the voyage to America and visited him at his home there."

Richard said in a soothing tone, "Oh, I'm sure it was nothing significant. She would never do anything to bring shame on you."

"Apparently, this man is an unsavory commoner who makes whisky."

Richard knew this was his chance. "As you know, I'm in the whisky business. Maybe I know him or I could find out about him for you. What is the man's name?" inquired Richard.

"Colin Stuart."

"No!" Richard said in an overly dramatic fashion. He turned and took a step away from her. He waited to see if she would react.

She stepped toward him and put a hand on his shoulder. "Do you know him?"

Richard turned around and answered, "Unfortunately, I know him only too well. I let him go a while back for some irregularities. He is an unsavory character to say the least. I wonder…." He trailed off.

"Wonder what?" she asked.

"I have something delicate and revealing that I must tell you first."

"Of course, please do."

"You know I'm interested in your daughter."

"Yes, I do."

"The truth is I love Lady Rose dearly but unfortunately she hasn't returned my affection." He put his head down.

"I'm so sorry." She put her hand on his arm.

He lied again, "Colin Stuart knew I loved your daughter. Do you think it's possible he deliberately targeted her because of his hatred for me?"

She blinked several times. "Could anyone be that devious?"

"Colin Stuart is a cold and calculating man."

"He is?"

"Yes, he tried to steal my business away by playing up to my father when he was ill. Mr. Stuart knows how to get people to like him quickly."

She thought for several moments. "Is he smart enough to ensnare my daughter?"

"Yes, he is devilishly cunning."

The countess started to tear and shook her head. "I'm too upset to stay here. I must go home."

"I have my carriage and driver; I will take you home. I'll get my hat and our coats."

"I'll tell the duchess I'm not feeling well."

Countess Winston sought out the duchess and told her she was leaving. Richard gathered their belongings and summoned his carriage.

Once inside the carriage, he moved to put his arm around her, consoling her. As they traveled, he made up the story of how well his business was doing since he fired Colin. He told her how Colin hid barrels of whisky and how he discovered the whisky barely in time to save the business.

The countess invited him into her London home and since they missed dinner, she offered him some wine and cheese. As they sat in the parlor and enjoyed the wine, he casually asked about the Harvest Ball. She immediately invited him to it. Richard stayed until they finished the wine and she walked him to the door. Pleased with what he had accomplished, he went home feeling he had struck back at Colin.

CHAPTER 35

—

THE NEXT MORNING AFTER THE Clarkes' party, Rose received a hand-delivered note from one her mother's servants.

Rose, I need to speak with you. I'm staying at my London house. I would like to meet you today if possible. Please come alone. Love, Mother

Rose concluded her mother must have a health problem and took a carriage to her home immediately. When she arrived, the butler said her mother was resting in her room and he took her to the parlor. A few minutes passed and her mother entered looking pale and tired.

"Mother, you don't look well. Are you ill?"

"No, I had a terrible shock last night when I went to the Clarke party. Duchess Clarke told me some disturbing news that caused me a sleepless night."

The countess sat on a chair and Rose stood next to her. She put her hand on her mother's shoulder.

"What is the news?"

"I heard you visited a Scottish commoner at his home in America." She turned to look up at her daughter. "Please tell me it isn't true."

Rose removed her hand from her mother's shoulder. She wondered how she could have learned so fast.

She carefully worded her response. "Yes, it's true. I met a brave, kind and handsome gentleman on the ship. While I was in Chicago for the art exposition, I saw him. I also went to his home in Wisconsin for dinner." She decided not to tell every detail.

The countess began her inquisition. "Were you chaperoned during this time?"

Rose stepped away from the chair and turned her back so her mother could not read her face. She didn't tell the complete truth. "Edith, my lady's maid, was with me along with Mia."

In a shocked tone, the countess asked, "You didn't invite anyone else to be with you? I know several women from the consulate who were also in Chicago. They could have gone with you."

Rose turned, glared at her mother and defiantly protested, "I'm a grown woman and I don't need a chaperone!"

The countess scoffed. "Apparently, you do! You were the talk of the party last night." She pointed to several letters on the table. "See those? I received them this morning. Everyone wanted to make sure I know about what you did and they are trying to console me."

Still defiant, Rose sat in a chair near her mother. She leaned toward her and responded, "Console you for what? I'm not ill or dying. I simply met a man I like. Let me correct that. I met a man I love."

In a mocking tone, Louise said, "Love? You fell in love with a Scottish commoner? You must be joking! Please tell me you're joking!"

Rose leaned back in the chair. "I'm not joking. He is brave, kind, handsome, intelligent and he loves Mia."

The countess dismissed what she said. "This is simply a voyage romance and infatuation. He is someone you shouldn't be with. He is the forbidden fruit you shouldn't have. It's natural you might be taken in especially if he is handsome and used the right words."

"No, it's more than that."

"How long have you really been with him? A few days at most. I'm so glad you are home and away from him. Once you have spent time with your people, your yearning will fade."

Rose's face reddened and her voice raised. "What do you mean *yearning*?"

"I heard you were alone with him several times. I'm sure he caused you to rekindle the feelings of being with a man."

"Mother," she said, exasperated, "I don't know what you heard or dreamed up. There was nothing but gentle romantic moments, nothing else."

"That's good to know. Now, what are we going to do about this?"

"I don't intend to do anything."

The countess rebutted, "We must let people know that nothing happened while you were in America."

"Something did happen," Rose countered. "I met a man and fell in love with him. I'm not ashamed of it."

"Rose, you cannot fall in love with a commoner. That simply won't do!" Louise's eyes flared.

Rose stood and stepped away from her mother. She turned and asked, "Why not?"

"Because you are a titled woman and was raised better than that."

"If you were to meet him, you would see he is everything I have told you."

"I heard things about him that are unsavory."

Rose fired back, "What have you heard?"

"I understand he was relieved of his last position and left the country because the authorities are pursuing him."

Rose's voice heightened in anger. "That's absolute nonsense! He left his position to become a partner at a distillery in America. I went to the distillery so I know it's true. I also have met his partner who is a well-known businessman in America."

"I can tell you have an answer for everything."

"I do because I know the truth. You have only heard gossip."

"I have learned in my life that where there is smoke, there is fire."

Rose replied, "Sometimes what we think is smoke is only dust. Dust that people sweep into the air to hurt others!"

The countess paused and in a softer tone said, "I can see we are not going to resolve this today. Are you still coming to the Harvest Ball?"

Rose sighed. "Yes, of course, Mia and I will be there. I won't give anyone the pleasure of thinking I'm shying away from Colin."

"I was hoping you wouldn't cancel. The best way to deal with a tempest is to stare it in the face with a stiff upper lip."

"I have done nothing wrong so I don't feel like there is a tempest."

The surprised countess asked, "You don't see what you have done is wrong, do you?"

"Wrong? I found a man who loves me. You should be happy for me." Anger returned to Rose's voice.

"I would be if he was from our class and loved you for you and not your money."

"He doesn't care about money!" replied Rose.

Countess Winston shook her head. "I suppose he told you that."

"Yes, he said it to me and to others."

"He is a liar because all men care about money. In fact, they love it more than their women."

"Mother, this is a side of you I haven't seen before. I didn't know you were so distrustful of men."

"I have learned men want what they want and not what we want."

"How about Father?"

"He was different. He let me worry about the money. He cared about me, you, and William."

"Colin is like that. Money is secondary to him. He wants a family."

"Yes—he will want his own children, not Mia."

"No," Rose countered. "I have rejected others because of that. He truly loves her."

The countess said frankly, "Men tell women with children that so the women will let their guard down."

"Not Colin! He loves Mia. I know he does."

"So, what are your plans?"

Rose replied, "Mia and I will return to America next year. I'll decide then."

"Has he asked you to marry him?"

She shook her head.

"When you go to America, I'll go with you," her mother stated.

"I would like you to go. You will find as I did that Colin is an amazing man."

"I hope so." The doubt was clear in her voice.

Silence filled the room. The countess studied Rose. "I can tell you're upset with me. If Mia was older and she did this, you would have done the same thing."

"I would have handled it differently."

"How so?"

"I would have trusted she was making the right decision and would talk to her about her trip without an inquisition. She would tell me everything. I would have told you everything when we had the time."

"I'm not sure of that."

"I always have in the past."

The countess wanted to move past talking about Colin. "When may I see Mia?"

"You can always visit her. She adores you. However, I won't be coming here or to the country estate for a while."

Rose started for the front door.

"I see. You are punishing me."

Rose stopped and turned. "No, I'm disappointed and hurt. I need some time to recover."

"Be angry if you want, but I don't think I did anything wrong."

"I know you don't think you did anything wrong." Rose paused. "That makes me sad."

Rose got her coat and left. In the carriage, she cried all the way home.

CHAPTER 36

Late September, 1906 – Countess Winston's Estate

———◆———

A LARGE PART OF THE Countess Winston's and Rose's income came from the crop harvest. Every year Countess Winston celebrated the end of the harvest. Foremen and workers from both her and Rose's properties attended a party on the estate during the day. In the evening, there was the exclusive Harvest Ball which was a must-attend event for the nobility and aristocrats of England.

Mia looked forward to this day every year. She played games with the children from her grandmother and mother's farms during the day and then there was a children's party at night.

On the carriage ride to her mother's home, Rose was unusually quiet and had been for the past several days. Mia could tell something was wrong.

"Mummy, are you not feeling well?"

Rose looked up. "I'm fine; why do you ask?"

"You haven't been yourself recently."

She shook her head. "I'm not looking forward to today."

Surprised, Mia inquired, "Why? This is one of the best days of my year. I love the Harvest Ball."

"I normally do too. However, your grandmother and I had a disagreement recently and it has been bothering me."

"Over what?" inquired Mia.

"I shouldn't talk about it."

"You always tell me that I'll feel better if I tell you what I'm struggling with. You should do the same."

Rose said sharply, "Mia, this isn't about dolls and little girl things!"

Hurt by the comment, Mia replied, "Mummy, you know I don't play with dolls anymore. I'm almost ten."

Rose saw her upset look. "I'm sorry, you're right. I shouldn't have said that."

"I often talk to you about other things. I told you recently how I was missing Colin and what I write to him about. I tell you everything."

"Yes, you do." Rose sighed. "So, I'll tell you about my problem. Your grandmother and I had a disagreement about Colin."

"I thought so."

Rose cocked her head. "How would you know that?"

"You used to talk about Colin and returning to America all the time but you have stopped."

"Yes, I know. The discussion with Mother has made me sad."

"She's upset that Colin is a commoner, am I right?"

"Yes."

"Why does everyone worry about that? I overheard Edith talking to you and Elizabeth about it recently. Does it matter? You know Colin is a wonderful man and not having some silly title doesn't matter."

Rose shook her head and reached for Mia's hand. "It does matter to many. When I was growing up, I loved that my father was an earl and my mother was a countess. I loved having the title - Lady Rose. I insisted everyone call me Lady Rose even when I was little. I went to all the balls and all my friends were from titled families. Because my father was an earl, I met the royal family many times. I never considered my husband wouldn't be titled—and he was, Baron Cavendish." Rose's eyes softened. "But your father was a different kind of gentleman. He worked for a living and he enjoyed it. His father insisted he work on the docks and on the farms when he was young and because of that, he saw the world differently. I loved him not only because he was handsome and smart but also because he was humble and didn't care about being a baron."

"I remember going with him to the big ships," Mia said, smiling. "The docks were always so busy and everyone knew him. People would stop us and everyone would talk to me."

"Yes, everyone liked him. Colin is the same way. When we walked around the distillery and the town, everyone talked to him."

"Yes, I noticed that."

Rose's expression changed and her eyebrows furrowed. "Mother has heard some gossip about Colin that is absolute rubbish and it upsets me."

"What did she hear?"

"I won't go into that, but people can say awful things about people at times."

"Did you correct her?"

"I did," Rose said, "but your grandmother has her own way of doing things."

"Do you still love Colin?"

Rose didn't hesitate. "Oh yes, I love him more than ever. With each new letter from him, I fall more in love. His letters to me are so sweet."

Mia grinned. "His letters to me are funny and always cheerful. Did he tell you the ugly swan has gotten all its feathers back?"

"He did tell me. What does he call it?"

"Snowy. I think the name fits since, according to Colin, he is as white as snow."

"I like that name too." Rose smiled at her daughter. "Talking to you has made me feel better. Today, if anyone says something wrong about Colin, I'll correct them and walk away with my head high."

"I will as well."

"Now Mia, young ladies don't get into arguments with grown-ups. You smile and walk away."

"I'll try."

When Rose and Mia arrived, they saw a large white tent in the meadow. Under the tent were tables filled with food and there were many barrels of beer. Many people were already there.

The carriage stopped in the courtyard and they got out. The countess was greeting guests at the tent and, to Rose's surprise, next to her was Lord Williams. He looked like a country gentleman with a brown shooting jacket, white open collar shirt, brown pants, and brown boots. Rose and Mia went to the tent.

Countess Winston said, "My dear Rose and Mia, thank you for coming."

Rose looked directly at her mother. "We would never miss a Harvest Ball."

Mia added, "I couldn't wait to get here."

"Rose, you know Lord Williams."

Lord Williams bowed. "It's a pleasure to see you again."

Rose smiled. "You as well."

"Lord Williams, this lovely lass is my granddaughter, Lady Mia Cavendish."

Lord Williams bowed. "My lady."

"My lord," replied Mia and she did a proper curtsey.

"I have heard from others that you're as lovely as your mother…and you are."

"That is kind of you! My mother is by far the beauty in my family," said Mia with a smile.

"I see your mother has raised you well."

"Thank you, sir."

Richard turned to Rose. "Lady Rose, I hoped you enjoyed your stay in America."

"I did." She looked right at her mother. "The people there were so kind to us."

Lord Williams said, "I have been to America and I found it to be somewhat backward when compared to England."

"It's a young country and you could feel its vibrancy everywhere," offered Rose.

"That you can." Richard nodded. "May I get you and Mia something to drink?"

"Yes, please," answered Rose.

Mia shook her head. "Nothing for me, thank you."

Richard left.

"Mummy, may I go see the other children?"

"Yes, please try to stay somewhat clean."

Mia took off running. Rose asked her mother pointedly, "Is this your doing?"

Her mother faked ignorance, looking away from her. "What are you referring to, dear?"

"Lord Williams has never attended a Harvest Ball before. Why is he here?"

The countess replied without looking at her. "Several eligible gentlemen will be here including Robert Mawbray."

Rose reached out and held her mother's arm to get her attention. The countess looked at her. Rose whispered, "Mother, I have told you before about doing this sort of thing."

The countess replied, "You aren't engaged and my role as your mother is to make sure you meet eligible men."

Rose continued in a quiet voice, "If I had known I was going to be put on parade, I would have stayed home."

The countess replied smugly, "That's why I didn't tell you."

Richard returned with a glass of lemonade and handed it to Rose.

Rose said, "Thank you."

He nodded.

Rose drank some lemonade and looked away from them. There was a long, awkward silence. Richard sensed something was wrong between mother and daughter based on their expressions and their unwillingness to look at each other. He stood there smiling and shifting his weight from foot to foot hoping someone would say something.

The countess finally offered, "You two should go to the lake. They're sailing small boats there."

Richard agreed. "That sounds interesting. Rose, would you like to walk with me?"

Rose shot an icy glare at her mother. "I would." She shoved the half empty glass at her mother, who had no choice but to take it.

As they walked, Richard held out his arm for her but she ignored the gesture. He dropped his arm.

Rose asked, "How is your business?"

Richard was taken back. "I'm surprised you would be interested in my business."

Her eyebrows rose and in a tone that came out sharper then she intended, she said, "Richard, I own the largest import and shipping company in England, plus I have thousands of acres of farmland. I know something about business."

He had dug a hole with his comment then he dug it deeper. "I thought you had men who ran it for you."

She stopped and turned to him. "I have men who work for me. I make the important decisions and decide where my money goes. No one else does!"

He blinked and realized the mistake he had made. "I understand, I'm sorry if I offended you."

Rose saw his reaction and paused. She realized she shouldn't be rude to him because of her mother. "Let's start this again. I'm sorry I was short with you. Please tell me how your business is doing."

He smiled. "No apologies are necessary, my lady. My business is doing well. Since I won the award for the best single malt whisky, my business has been booming."

His comment surprised her because she knew who had actually won the award. As they walked, Richard continued to brag about his whisky business.

She interrupted him. "How long do you age your whisky?"

"For as short a period as I can. The faster I sell it, the more money I make."

"But if you sell it too soon, it doesn't taste as good."

"There is a balance you have to have," he acquiesced, "but I would rather sell it sooner than later."

"How long do you use your barrels?"

"Until they won't hold whisky," he answered and thought for a second. "You ask insightful questions. How do you know so much about whisky?"

"I met a man on the voyage to America who taught me a few things."

"Yes, I understand you met Colin Stuart," Richard said. "I know him well."

Rose expected him to say something bad about Colin, but he went on to boast about his land holdings and his harvest.

Mia, who was already at the lake, saw Richard and her mother approaching. She noticed her mother was talking to him, but she wasn't glowing and smiling like she did with Colin. However, she could tell this man was interested in her mother. He seemed to hang on to every word her mother said.

Mia approached them, "Mummy, aren't the boats pretty? They are all handmade."

"Yes, they are," said Rose.

"There is a strong wind today, I should have brought my kites." Mia asked, "Lord Williams, do you fly kites?"

"No, I don't."

"Did you fly them when you were a child?"

"No," he answered. "Do you fly kites much?"

"I do. I have also learned to make them. I also do origami."

Lord Williams looked puzzled. "I'm sorry...what is that?"

"It is an art of folding paper to make things like flowers, dragons, and butterflies."

"I see."

"Maybe I could teach you how to do it."

"I'll give it some thought," he said, brushing her off. "Ladies, let's walk to the house. I have welcome home gifts for you."

Surprised, Rose said, "That's kind of you, but you shouldn't have."

"I wanted you and Mia to know you were missed when you were in America."

Mia thought it was odd he brought gifts to a girl he had never met. She decided she was right—this man was definitely interested in her mother. As they walked to the house, she decided to quiz him a little further.

"Lord Williams, do you like animals?"

"I like horses."

"I do too. Do you have a cat?"

"No, cats make me sneeze."

"Oh, that's a shame. I love cats. I have one; his name is King Richard. Do you have a dog?"

He shook his head.

"Do you like dogs?"

"I do but I'm a busy man and taking care of a dog takes time which I don't have. You ask a lot of questions, don't you?"

Rose interjected, "Lord Williams is right; you're asking a lot of questions."

"I'm sorry. I'm only trying to get to know Lord Williams. Sir, I hope I'm not a bother."

"You're not; I find you quite charming," answered Lord Williams in a stuffy tone.

"I have another question if you don't mind?"

"Of course."

"Do you know anything about dragons?"

Richard laughed, "I don't. Where does that question come from?"

"Mummy and I saw a dragon when we were in America. I was wondering if you knew anything about them."

"You saw a dragon?"

Rose interrupted, "It's a long story. I'll have to tell you about it sometime."

Mia looked at Lord Williams, "I have another question, do you know anything about butterflies?"

"I see them in my garden from time to time, but I don't know anything about them."

Rose smiled because now she knew what Mia was doing. Mia was pointing out to her that Richard had nothing in common with her. Everything she asked was something she and Colin shared an interest in.

"I have one last question. Do you know how they catch monkeys in the jungle?"

Richard was unsure if he had the right answer. "With a net?"

Mia replied, "That's a good answer and maybe some monkeys are caught with a net. Let me tell you a story that a close friend of mine told me." As they walked to the house, Mia told him the monkey and barrel story.

He laughed when she finished. "The next time I go to the jungle, I'll bring a barrel and some peanuts. Now, your gifts are in the house. Let's go inside and let me get them for you."

They entered the parlor and the ladies sat down. Richard left to get the gifts.

Rose whispered, "I saw what you were doing."

Mia acted innocent and whispered, "I'm not sure what you're talking about."

"Yes, you do! Should I expect this line of questioning with every gentleman who says hello to me?"

Mia smiled. "Until we are safely back in America with Colin, you can."

"I love you."

Mia replied, "I love you too."

Richard returned with his gifts. "I hope you like them. Mia, let's start with yours." He handed it to her and she gently unwrapped the box. Inside was an adorable porcelain doll with long brown hair.

Mia noted in a monotone and underwhelmed voice, "Mummy look, it's a doll."

"It's pretty; don't you think?" asked Rose in an uplifting voice, hoping Mia would act happier about it.

However, Mia didn't. "Yes, it is," she said lifelessly. "Thank you, Lord Williams, for your thoughtful gift. I love to play with dolls."

Rose tried not to laugh.

"You may call me Richard."

"I respectfully cannot call you Richard. That's much too informal for a young lady of my age. Out of respect for you and your title, I will continue to call you Lord Williams. I hope you're not offended."

Rose nearly giggled when Mia finished. She knew why Mia responded the way she did because Mia told her how Edith talked to her about Colin and using his first name.

He didn't understand the subtle point she was making and her response didn't surprise him because it was proper etiquette. "That's fine dear, I understand completely. Rose, this is for you." He handed her a small wrapped box.

Rose opened it to find an ornately jeweled perfume bottle.

"Richard, this is so thoughtful. Thank you."

"I took the liberty of having it filled with French perfume. I hope you like it."

"I'm sure I will."

"Would you like to try it?"

She dismissed him with a wave of her hand. "I will later. Richard, you have been so kind. Now you must excuse us. Mia and I need to retire to our room to rest for a while."

He nodded. "Of course, of course."

Mia looked alarmed because it was early afternoon and she hadn't visited with all her friends yet.

"Mummy, I…."

Rose said hurriedly, "Tell Lord Williams thank you again."

Confused, Mia looked at her mother then at Richard. "Yes, Lord Williams, thank you."

"You're welcome."

"Now Mia, please come with me." Rose took Mia's hand and led her up the stairs.

Once they were inside their room, Rose said, "Thank you for playing along with me. I couldn't think of another way to get away from him. In a few minutes, you can go outside."

"Oh good, I thought I had done something wrong."

"No dear, you were gracious as always."

Rose sat on the bed. Mia carefully placed the box with the doll on the dresser.

"Mummy, I don't know what to do with the doll. It's lovely but..."

"I know, dear. We will take it home and I'll think of something. It might make an ideal gift for a needy girl at Christmas."

"Are you going to keep the perfume bottle and perfume?"

"Absolutely not! It's a gaudy bottle and the heavy perfume is too much for me. I could smell it when I opened the box. I much prefer the delicate French perfumes."

"You should give it to Edith." Mia suggested.

Rose laughed. "You don't want us to keep anything from him, do you?"

Mia smiled and didn't reply.

"I understand perfectly. I'll stay here and read for the afternoon. My mother has other gentlemen lined up for me. I refuse to be on display like a prized cow."

Mia giggled.

"You can go outside now."

"Mummy, are you going to the ball tonight?"

"I'll go to the dinner; however, I think I'll have a headache before the dancing starts."

Mia smiled. "I'll check on you later."

"Try not to return looking like a little pig."

"I can't promise but I'll try."

"Now Elizabeth will be here later today and will go with you to the children's party. You know the rules!"

"Yes Mummy, I'm to stay with Elizabeth. May I please go now?"

Rose nodded.

Mia ran out the door.

As soon as Rose and Mia left, Richard looked for Countess Winston. He found her in the stables showing off one of her prized stallions.

"Countess," he said after taking her off to the side, "my idea to get gifts for Rose and Mia was excellent. They are pleased with them."

"That is good news! Now tonight you will be sitting next to her at dinner. How did it go with Mia?"

He grinned. "We seemed to get along famously. She asked me all kinds of questions. She is a bright and well-mannered young lady."

The countess looked smug. "Remember the way to Rose's heart is through Mia."

"Yes, I think I did well in that regard."

"Now you must also ask Rose for the first dance tonight."

"I will. Thank you for helping me."

"You're welcome."

Richard walked away, confident he had hit his mark.

CHAPTER 37

THE HARVEST BALL WAS HELD at a resort not far from the countess' estate. They decorated the large ballroom in fall colors along with baskets of barley, corn, wheat, and pumpkins. The tickets were expensive with all the proceeds going to charity. The ball was well known for the number of couples who met at this event and later married. Richard hoped it would bring him luck too.

Normally, the countess and Rose would ride together to the ball but not that night. When Rose arrived, Richard was in the lobby waiting for her.

"Good evening, Lady Cavendish."

"Good evening, Lord Williams."

"I trust you and Lady Mia had a good day."

"We did. It was relaxing for me and Mia enjoyed herself with all her friends."

"I noticed this afternoon she stayed with the commoner children. It seemed unusual to me."

Rose raised an eyebrow and replied, "There is nothing unusual about it. She knows most of them. Many of the families work at my properties and my mother's so she sees them often."

He lectured her in a snobbish tone, "I never associated with any lower-class children when I was growing up. My mother warned me to stay away from them. All those nasty diseases they seem to have. It was excellent advice then and still is."

Rose bristled at his comment. She stared at him and started to reply but stopped, realizing the futility in trying to change him. "I could use something to drink. Would you mind getting me a glass of white wine?"

"Of course."

Richard walked away and she immediately tried to hide from him in the crowd. As she weaved through the people, she saw Lady Florence Mitchell, the woman from the ship with the dog, talking to her mother. Rose approached them.

"Lady Mitchell, it's good to see you."

"You too, my dear. I was telling your mother about my trip and how Mr. Stuart saved my dog and possibly Mia."

"Rose, you didn't tell me what a brave man this Mr. Stuart is."

Rose said coldly, "There are many interesting things about him I wanted to tell you."

"Lady Mitchell said not only is he brave, but he is also charming, intelligent, successful, and handsome."

Rose added, "That and much more."

"I also learned he introduced a whisky at the art exposition and it's all the rage now in America."

Rose nodded and smiled. "Yes, it was well received."

Countess Winston put her hand on Rose's arm. "Lady Mitchell heard some ladies gossiping about you visiting Mr. Stuart. She told them if she were single, she would visit him and probably never come home. Lady Mitchell, did I quote you correctly?"

Lady Mitchell blushed. "Yes, you did. I don't mean to say anything improper about Mr. Stuart, but in my opinion, he is a remarkable man. Rose, I told you this before. I wouldn't care if he is a commoner—he's a catch for any woman. I heard the terrible gossip from other ladies and I stopped it immediately. You were always a lady on the ship with Mr. Stuart, at the art exposition, and I'm sure you were when you visited his distillery. This is 1906, not 1806. We have progressed in what women can do and should be allowed to do without criticism."

"Thank you for defending me. I'm glad someone did." Rose glared at her mother.

"Lady Mitchell, as you can tell her remark was for me. Rose, I'm sorry I reacted the way I did when I heard the gossip regarding you and Mr. Stuart. I should have trusted you more."

Rose, fighting back tears, said, "Thank you, Mother."

"Your mother said she will be going with you to America to meet Mr. Stuart. I told her she will love him like you and I do although maybe I shouldn't have said that."

Rose smiled. "Lady Mitchell, you're right, I do love him."

Lady Mitchell nodded. "I'm glad to hear it. I can see you two need to talk. I'll leave you now. Before I go, I have one piece of advice, no woman should wait long to decide about that man. In America, the women will see he is handsome, kind, smart, and ambitious. Women there don't care about titles and they will act fast."

Rose reached out and took Lady Mitchell's hand. "Thank you, you have been a life saver."

Lady Mitchell said, "You are welcome, dear." She offered a smile and nod to the countess then left.

"Rose, I have made a mess of you coming home, haven't I."

Rose smiled and reassured her. "You're only being a protective mother."

"Overly protective."

Rose looked at her mother knowingly. "Maybe a little. I'm so glad Lady Mitchell spoke to you."

"She wasn't the first. Several ladies who were on the voyage spoke to me today. It was clear I was getting a one-sided view. However, I still haven't accepted the fact he is a commoner."

"Once you meet him, you will."

The countess joked, "Maybe I should talk to King Edward and convince him to give Mr. Stuart a title. If his whisky is as superb as I hear, the king, who loves whisky, might do it."

Rose laughed. "Good idea!"

"I have all these single eligible gentlemen here for you tonight. What do I do now?"

"I feel a headache coming on right after dinner," Rose said with a smile.

The countess laughed. "I have done that before."

Rose hugged her. "I'm so glad we are past this."

"So am I."

"Mia and I look forward to you coming with us to America."

"Can you and Mia stay with me here for a few days?"

"We will stay until you send us home."

"I would like that. Now let's mingle and let all the men see what they aren't going to get from us tonight."

"Mother!"

She smiled. "Dear, I mean our companionship."

Mother and daughter mingled with the crowd until the dinner started and Rose managed to avoid Richard until she sat at the table. Richard sat to her left and Robert Mawbray to her right. She was friendly and talked to them during dinner, although she thought of Colin often, wishing he were by her side instead.

At the end of the dinner, she said had a headache and left. Robert and Richard were disappointed that she didn't stay.

CHAPTER 38

———————

EDITH RECEIVED A LETTER FROM her uncle Ted two days after the Harvest Ball. She hadn't gotten any news on the happenings at the ball because Rose and Mia had stayed longer with the countess. Edith opened the letter.

My Dearest Edith,

I wanted to send you this brief note to tell you of our success at Countess Winston's Harvest Ball. All the information you provided has enabled Lord Williams to renew his relationship with Lady Cavendish. Lord Williams believes a formal courtship will start soon. He sent an invitation to Lady Cavendish today for dinner. This is so exciting! Imagine the possibilities of our two houses uniting and us working together before I retire.

The manner in how you described Lord Williams should engage with her daughter worked well. It is clear to Lord Williams that the young Lady Cavendish likes him. In an aside on the boarding school, he said the young Lady Cavendish talked entirely too much and asked too many questions. It convinced him she would be going to boarding school once they marry.

I suggested to Lord Williams he give welcome home gifts to Lady Rose and her daughter. I purchased the gifts for them. For Lady Cavendish, it was French perfume in a wonderfully adorned perfume bottle. I picked out the perfume myself so I am sure she will like it. I purchased a por-celain doll for her daughter. It is simply lovely and rather expensive. Apparently, they loved the gifts.

Thanks to you, our houses will be united soon!
I hope you are well. All my love, Theodore.
P.S. I forgot there is something regarding Abigail McCarthy that I want-
ed to share with you. I saw Abigail's father recently. I asked him about
Abigail and Colin. He talked on and on about how close Abigail and
Colin are. He and Abigail are going to America to see him next summer.
He was sure a wedding was in their future. You should consider letting
Lady Cavendish and Countess Winston know about their relationship.

Edith's smile stretched across her face. Her plan had worked. She had gotten back at the Scotsman and he didn't know it. She had to go somewhere and celebrate. She left the letter on her nightstand and went out.

Back from a short holiday at her parents' home, Elizabeth knocked on Edith's door to see if she knew when the ladies would return. There was no answer, she opened Edith's door and realized she wasn't there.

An open letter was on the bed stand. She knew Edith had snooped through her room before so she picked it up and read it without a tinge of guilt. The letter shocked her. Edith had done conniving acts in the past such as pitting one servant against another to gain favor, but this was going too far. Edith had betrayed the trust of her lady. She also couldn't believe Colin loved some woman in Scotland or that Lady Rose would be interested in Lord Williams. No one would believe her if she did not have the letter. However, she couldn't steal it.

An idea came to her: she would copy its contents. She took the envelope and letter to her room, copied the letter, and returned it. She left the envelope and letter on the bed stand. She hid her copy in a secret place. She wasn't sure what she would do with it, but she had it in case she needed it.

An hour later, Edith returned. Elizabeth went to her room and knocked on the door. She wanted to make sure Edith had not noticed anything unusual about the letter.

"Good afternoon," she said when Edith opened the door. Elizabeth stepped in, looked at the night stand and didn't see the letter.

"Good afternoon to you," Edith said cheerfully. "When did you get back?"

"A short while ago."

"How was your trip?"

"It was fabulous!"

"I bet you saw that young barrister, didn't you?" asked Edith with envy.

"I'll never tell."

"I can tell. Your cheeks are flushed."

Elizabeth decided Edith was in a good mood so there wasn't any issue with the letter. She changed the subject. "Enough about me, when do the ladies return?"

"By four."

"I'll get changed and be ready for them. Did you hear how the Harvest Ball went?" Elizabeth knew Edith had learned some news in the letter.

"I know it went well."

"How do you know that?" Elizabeth inquired.

Edith turned away. "I have heard from others."

"Can you share anything?"

Edith thought for a second then turned back. Her face showed she had some juicy news. "Do you remember Lord Williams?"

"Oh yes, I saw him once. He's a handsome gentleman."

"He is. I heard from a trustworthy source he and Lady Cavendish are seeing each other again. It is wonderful news because I can finally forget about that Scot in America."

Elizabeth shook her head. "I like Mr. Stuart and I find it hard to believe that suddenly Lady Rose and Lord Williams are now seeing each other."

"I know you like him but what I told you is true. I'm sure Lady Rose will tell us all about it. I don't want to talk about the Scot anymore because I'm having a good day and my lady is coming home."

Elizabeth nodded slowly. "I'll see you with the ladies soon."

———

CHAPTER 39

Rose and Mia returned from their extended stay with Countess Winston. They were cheerful and talked about what an enjoyable time they had as Edith and Elizabeth helped them unpack.

Mia unwrapped the porcelain doll and turned to Elizabeth. "We need to package this carefully and save it until Christmastime. I'll be giving it away when we make our donations to the needy."

Because of Theodore's letter, Edith knew it was the doll from Lord Williams. "Mia, this is an expensive doll. Are you sure you should give it away?"

Rose spoke up. "Yes, the gentleman who gave it to her doesn't know Mia and he doesn't know she no longer plays with dolls. It would be a shame to let it lie around unused. Some young girl will love it."

Edith was shocked. "Mia, doesn't it have any sentimental value for you?"

Mia shrugged. "None to me."

Elizabeth smiled because she also knew the doll was from Lord Williams. She eyed the doll. "My niece would love it. May I give it to her?"

Rose replied, "Of course you can!"

Edith glared at Elizabeth, but she ignored her.

Rose had the perfume bottle in her hand. "I also received this bottle of French perfume. The scent is too strong for me, one of you might like it."

Edith tried to hide her shock. Nothing so far that her uncle told her in his letter was accurate. If Rose and Mia gave away Lord Williams' gifts, that meant they had no affection for him at all.

Elizabeth sampled it. "I love it."

Rose said, "You may have it if you like."

"Thank you!"

Edith asked, "Did you see or meet anyone interesting?" She couldn't give up on Lord Williams yet.

Elizabeth interjected, "She means interesting *gentlemen*."

Rose smiled. "I know she does. Lord Williams and Lord Mawbray were there. Mia met Lord Williams and spent quite a bit of time with him. I'll let Mia describe what she learned about him."

Mia took a deep breath. "Well, since you asked, Lord Williams does not have a dog, cats make him sneeze, he doesn't fly kites, and he knows nothing about dragons or butterflies. He had no idea what origami is. I suspect he doesn't like children because he was always formal and stiff. He is, in my opinion, a typical London gentleman who picked his words carefully but isn't loving or caring—at least not with me. However, I could tell he liked Mummy a lot."

Elizabeth chuckled. "Oh my, what a thorough review. You certainly gave it a lot of thought."

"Lady Rose, I'm guessing the relationship with Lord Williams hasn't improved?" asked Edith.

Rose shrugged. "He is no different than before except I know something about his business now. The things he told me about how he is running his distillery tells me there will be tough times ahead. He is doing all the things Colin said will hurt his business. I think the future for Lord Williams is bleak."

Edith looked pale. Elizabeth glanced at Edith and offered a smile. "Edith, you don't look well."

Edith fired back, "I'm fine. Lady Rose, how about Lord Mawbray? Did you see him?"

"I did. He never asked me one thing about my trip or anything about me. He talked the entire time about a bird-hunting trip he took to Ireland and his new custom shotgun. He's such a boring man. I sat at dinner between Lord Mawbray and Lord Williams, however, I could only think about Colin. I miss him so." Rose let out a sigh.

Edith felt defeated. Lord Williams was no longer in the picture even if he thought he was and the opportunity with Lord Mawbray had evaporated.

Edith said, "My lady, I don't feel well. May I be excused?"

"Yes."

Edith returned to her room. She took the letter from her uncle, tore it into small pieces, and threw it into the trash. She needed to develop a new plan to drive a wedge between Rose and Colin.

She lay in bed and thought about the situation. She was disappointed with Lord Williams because even with her coaching, he made no progress with Lady Rose. Lord Mawbray also had no chance of improving his position. With no gentlemen on the horizon for Lady Rose, playing her Abigail McCarthy card was her only real hope.

She thought of her uncle again. He was her link to the woman. Edith wrote a letter to him and asked if he could introduce her to Abigail.

A week later Edith got a reply and an invitation to visit Theodore in Aberlour. Theodore said he would arrange a meeting with Abigail at the coffeehouse, where Abigail always recited holiday poems and short stories the week before Christmas. Edith made plans to travel to Aberlour to see Theodore and Abigail.

CHAPTER 40

DECEMBER 1906 – LAKE GENEVA, WISCONSIN

———◆———

THE PAST FEW MONTHS HAD been busy and successful for Colin. The plans he made to improve the distillery were working. They had increased prices twice and sales had not fallen, and they planned another increase in the spring. The higher profits allowed them to age more whisky. They had also introduced the new line of premium whisky and it was selling well.

Colin thought about Rose constantly and he wrote to her often. The more they wrote letters back and forth, the closer they became. Colin also received sweet letters from Mia. She told him how much she missed him and what she was doing. She wrote pages on her kite flying and about her cat King Richard and his adventures. Colin wrote to her and sent her a book on kite building. He told her he fed the swans plus Supper every day. He also mentioned he was thinking about getting a cat and a dog. He asked Mia her opinion on what to get. She sent him a ten-page letter on the pros and cons of each cat and dog breed.

Colin also received letters from Abigail. It was clear she believed their relationship was much further along. Her frequent letters dripped with her love for him. He had replied only once and he only told her what he was doing. Mr. McCarthy had written to Colin and established a date of early June for a visit. They planned to stay for two weeks in Wisconsin after first traveling out west for several weeks. Mr. McCarthy requested first-class tickets for the voyage and for the trains, however, Colin sent them second-class tickets instead. Colin prayed their visit wouldn't overlap with the time Rose would be there. He decided not to tell Rose about Abigail because he thought he had the situation under control.

Colin sent Christmas gifts to Rose and Mia. He had a diamond swan necklace designed for Rose. In the same package, he put a note to Rose asking her permission to give a special gift to Mia. It was a sterling silver heart locket that belonged to his grandmother. He had given it to his wife and now he wanted Mia to have it. He said he would understand if she felt it wasn't appropriate. He also sent Mia a smaller diamond swan necklace just in case. He mailed the package, hoping it would arrive on time and prayed they would like the gifts.

CHAPTER 41

DECEMBER 18, 1906 – ABERLOUR, SCOTLAND

LATE SATURDAY MORNING, EDITH ARRIVED in Aberlour to visit her uncle and meet Abigail. As she stepped from the train, he was there on the platform and they embraced.

"I'm so pleased you came to see me. I have a room reserved for you at the inn. Later today, I have arranged for you to meet Abigail McCarthy."

"Splendid," Edith said, exhausted. "I'm tired from the trip so I hope I may rest for a while."

"I assumed you would be. I thought after we have lunch I would drop you off at the inn."

Theodore took her bag and they walked down the street to a crowded restaurant in the village square. They took a table near the front window.

"Your letter to me explaining how Lady Cavendish and her daughter viewed Lord Williams was so disappointing."

"Yes, it's a shame."

"Lord Williams has tried to have lunch or dinner with Lady Cavendish so far he hasn't been successful."

Edith talked louder because of the noise. "I know. You should encourage him to keep trying. However, their relationship won't improve unless we do something about Colin Stuart."

Theodore looked around to make sure no one heard her. "You should lower your voice. Colin has friends here."

Edith pulled closer to him. "We have to do something about him or Lord Williams won't have the chance to improve his relationship with Lady Rose."

"I agree and I'm willing to help."

"Now this Abigail McCarthy, are you sure she's still interested in Colin?"

"Oh yes, I asked her about him last week. They write to each other frequently. She said she is visiting him in America with her father next year in June."

She nodded slowly. "That's good. We will be there in June as well. I have an idea as to what we can do, but we will need her help."

"How do you expect to get Abigail to help?"

"I have to see how much she loves him. If she is devoted to him, she will do anything to keep him."

Theodore was curious. "What exactly are you going to have her do?"

"I want her to be in America when Lady Rose and her mother are there. I want the countess to see Abigail and Colin together. She will be outraged to learn of a sordid affair with another woman."

"How are you going to make it look sordid?"

"On the trip to America, I'll have the opportunity to talk to the countess. I'll make her aware Colin has another woman and make it sound immoral."

He nodded.

"However, I must gauge for myself if Abigail is truly in love with Colin," Edith went on. "She must be willing to be blatant in her affection for Colin in front of Lady Rose and Countess Winston."

"Edith, do you hate the Scot this much?"

"I don't want to go to America to live as a lady's maid."

"Can't you go to a new lady in London? I'm sure you could get a reference from Lady Cavendish."

"Why should I have to change my life for that low-class Scot? I have a respectable position with a decent salary. He is disrupting my life."

He paused. "Your plan is risky."

She waved him off. "I don't have any other choice. Now let's have lunch so I can rest before my meeting with Abigail."

After lunch, Theodore took her to the inn. It was a typical small village inn run by a husband and wife with six rooms and a communal bathroom. The rooms were small with a double bed and a simple oak dresser.

At four, Theodore returned to get Edith. As they walked to the coffeehouse, she described her plan.

"After her reading, you will introduce me to her. Then you will leave us alone to talk. I'll make sure she knows I met Mr. Stuart and there is some confidential information we need to discuss privately. I hope she will ask me to lunch or to tea. There I'll try to get her involved in my plan."

"What if she doesn't go along with you?"

Edith replied, "I'll improvise as I need to."

They arrived at the crowded coffeehouse. Apparently, Abigail had a large following. She was sitting on a stool on stage, reading a series of popular short stories. Abigail's reading, which lasted nearly an hour, was impressive. Abigail had a flair for drama and a lovely voice. The crowd applauded for an extended period when she finished.

Abigail stepped off the stage and the audience crowded around, congratulating her. After a few minutes, Abigail moved through the crowd to a table near the front door. She was resting at a table sipping tea when Edith and Theodore approached.

Theodore said, "Abigail, your reading was impressive; I always enjoy it."

"Thank you!"

"This is my niece, Edith Kelsey. I talked to you about her recently."

"Yes, I remember."

"Abigail, it's a pleasure to meet you." Edith sat close to her.

Theodore said, "I must talk to an acquaintance of mine. You two please get to know each other." Theodore walked away.

"How did you learn to read so well in public? I would be scared to do it."

Abigail replied, "I enjoy being in front of people."

"You have a talent for it. Have you ever considered the stage?"

Abigail smiled. "I have many times. My dream is to someday be on the London stage."

"I would pay to see you."

"Thank you. I love London. Were you born there?"

Edith talked for the next few minutes about her history and her job with Lady Cavendish. Abigail listened intently and sipped her tea. The two women hit it off, which was what Edith had hoped for.

"Edith, I understand you recently returned from America."

"I did. It was an exciting trip. I was in New York, Chicago, and in a town in Wisconsin, called Lake Geneva."

Abigail got excited. "I have a close friend who lives there!"

"You do?"

Abigail replied, "I do. His name is Colin Stuart."

Edith enthusiastically replied, "I know Colin. I met him on the voyage to America. He gave me an origami dragon."

"Did he now? He loves origami and he is skilled at it."

"Yes, he is. He is certainly handsome and all the eligible ladies on the voyage swooned over him."

"Oh my!" exclaimed Abigail.

Edith knew she had her interested. "Listening to your tone, I take it you must be close to Mr. Stuart?"

Abigail blushed. "We are close."

"How close?"

"I'm going to America to see him in June. I expect him to ask me to marry him."

"Oh no!" Edith exclaimed and acted upset.

"What's wrong?"

"I'm in possession of some confidential information about Mr. Stuart."

"What is it?"

Edith looked around the room. "I shouldn't talk here in public."

"You must tell me. Is he in poor health or something dreadful like that?"

"No, it is a matter of the heart. If I divulged it and Lady Cavendish found out, I could be dismissed."

Edith paused for dramatic effect. Abigail leaned forward hoping she would tell her. Abigail pleaded, "Please tell me."

"I have grown to like you and this is something two friends should discuss discreetly. Maybe tomorrow we could meet for lunch or tea?"

"Of course," Abigail said. "How about tea at my home at three?"

"I can be there, but I'm still somewhat conflicted about sharing this information. I would get in trouble with my lady if she found out."

Abigail put a hand to her heart. "I'll never tell a soul."

"For my ease of conscience on this matter, I must ask you a couple of questions. Are you truly in love with Mr. Stuart?"

Abigail's expression softened. "I love him terribly and my heart is only for him."

"You have no other men you're involved with?"

"None."

"My conscience is clear on this because you love him so. I promise to share it with you tomorrow. It was a pleasure to meet you."

"You as well."

Edith stood and sought out Theodore. He was outside, smoking a pipe.

"Did you succeed?" he asked.

Edith smiled and answered, "I did. I'm having tea with her tomorrow."

"Excellent! Maybe this is the rebuilding step in bringing our houses together."

"At least it's a step in keeping the Scot away from my lady."

CHAPTER 42

———

THE NEXT AFTERNOON, EDITH WALKED to Abigail's home. It was cold and rainy, but fortunately it was a short walk. Abigail met her at the front door and welcomed her in. The home was modest and simply decorated.

A proper ladies' tea was ready in the parlor. After a few minutes of small talk and sipping tea, Abigail said, "I have been waiting anxiously for your information."

"Several times, I have told myself I shouldn't discuss this with you, however, as I said yesterday, I have grown fond of you." Edith paused. "I feel as we have been friends for a long time even though it has only been for a day."

Abigail was impatient. "Edith, please share with me your information. I can't wait any longer."

"You know my lady and I went to America and we met Mr. Stuart on the voyage over."

"Yes."

Edith took a breath and revealed the secret, "Lady Cavendish told me she has fallen in love with Mr. Stuart."

Abigail paled, sat back and her breathing seemed to have stopped. She asked in a disbelieving whisper, "A baroness has fallen in love with my Colin?"

Edith nodded and secretly reveling in Abigail's anguish, she responded, "Yes."

Tears sprung to Abigail's eyes. She covered her face and let out a sob. "This can't be true. I have waited for him for so long!"

"You must hear me out first," Edith said. "Please don't cry."

Abigail dabbed her eyes with a handkerchief. "Go on."

Edith lied, "Lady Cavendish loves him, but he hasn't told her he loves her."

Abigail's face lightened. "That's good news."

"Yes, it is and Lady Cavendish's mother, Countess Winston, is adamant she can't get involved with a commoner."

"That's good news too." She hesitated. "I don't understand. Why are you telling me this? Shouldn't you be glad Lady Cavendish is in love with someone?"

"My job is to protect my lady," Edith said. "Lady Cavendish is a titled woman, and in my opinion, she should stay within her class. If she marries a commoner, it would lower my station."

"I see." Abigail paused for several moments and thought about the situation. "Do you think I still have a chance against a baroness?"

"Yes, but we must intervene so he doesn't get his heart set on her simply because of her wealth. You should know she is one of the wealthiest women in England. Any man could get his head turned simply because of her money."

"Oh dear." Abigail sat back and sighed. "This seems to be a monumental task."

"Please be heartened though; I will help you."

"Has she been writing to him much?"

"Yes."

"Has Colin written to her?"

Edith lied. "Only two letters."

"I'm not surprised; he doesn't write much." She sat up and looked serious. "How can we deal with this?"

"We must make your relationship known to her mother, this way she can end it before Lady Rose's infatuation for him goes too far. It cannot be gossip. She must see something with her own eyes. Something like seeing you two together in Lake Geneva holding hands or some other proof he loves you."

Abigail thought for a minute. "What if she saw one of Colin's love letters to me?"

"Love letters?"

Abigail lied. "I have his love letters."

"Having a love letter would be much better than trying to get you and Mr. Stuart to be seen by Countess Winston. You would lend me one?"

"Yes," Abigail nodded. "I still want him to be my husband. Lady Cavendish's money and power may have turned his head, but I still love him dearly and I believe he still loves me."

Edith thought about what had fallen into her lap. "Having a love letter to show her would be so powerful. I could say I heard about your relationship with Mr. Stuart and I came here to meet you. I'll say I didn't believe you when we met then you proved it with a love letter."

"Why wouldn't you show Lady Cavendish the love letter? Are you not close to her?"

"I'm only her lady's maid. I have some influence, but her mother has the greatest influence." Edith lied, "The countess has ended other relationships Lady Rose had before they went too far. Her mother has told her many times she will cut her out of the will if Lady Rose embarrasses her or violates her wishes"

Abigail blinked, thinking. "I thought Lady Cavendish was already wealthy. Why would she care about her mother's money?"

Edith dismissed her question with a wave of her hand and a smug reply. "My dear, the aristocrats and the nobility love wealth and power. Lady Cavendish's wealth would double with her mother's estate and so would her power. She would become one of the largest landowners in England. Land means power."

Abigail nodded. "I understand."

"When will I get the letter?" Edith asked.

Abigail paused. "Soon."

"Isn't it here somewhere? Can't I have it today?"

Abigail continued with her lie, "I need to select the right one. His love letters are personal and quite revealing regarding things we have done."

Edith blushed and bowed her head. "Of course, take your time. You can send it to me."

"I will."

"Abigail, it's important we keep this conversation confidential," Edith stressed. "You cannot write to Colin and mention one word of our talk. Also, you must make sure you're in Lake Geneva when we are so Countess Winston can possibly talk to you."

"I'll make sure I'm there when you are."

"Abigail," Edith said with a sly smile, "we will be lifelong friends now because we are helping each other."

"Yes, we will be."

After Edith left, Abigail went to her room and retrieved a box from her closet. In the box were letters from Colin. He had never written her any love letters; however, he had written many to her sister. Abigail's sister left all her personal items to her. Colin didn't know the letters were among her personal items when he gave everything to Abigail or he would have kept them. Abigail had read the letters; she knew the letters always started with "My Love," and most had no dates so no one other than Colin would know the letters were not to her.

She looked through them and picked one that didn't have a date on it. She mailed it to Edith with a personal note.

CHAPTER 43

CHRISTMAS EVE 1906

———

THE AFTERNOON MAIL ARRIVED AT Lady Rose's estate in London. The butler received it as he did every day. He divided the mail into three bundles: mail for Lady Rose and Mia, whom he delivered to personally; mail to the lady's maid, governess and the upstairs staff, he gave to Elizabeth; and finally mail for the downstairs staff, cooks, and coachmen.

The first three letters were to Edith and one of the letters was from Abigail McCarthy. Elizabeth recognized the name immediately. She kept the letter and delivered the other mail to Edith and the other staff. She went to her room and, having done it before, she steamed the envelope open. Inside were two letters, one from Abigail and the other from Colin.

Abigail's letter said:

Dear Edith,
I enjoyed meeting you. I appreciate you so much helping me win back Colin.
The enclosed letter from him shows clearly his love for me. I hope it will help Countess Winston see that Colin is truly in love with me. As I said to you, I forgive him for having his head turned by Baroness Cavendish. I love him so and I want us to marry soon.
Thank you for your help! I'll see you in America soon.
Yours truly, Abigail

Elizabeth read Colin's love letter. It was a long, sweet letter expressing his deepest love for her. The writing talked of things lovers share with each other. He also mentioned a heart-shaped locket he had recently given her; he hoped she liked it because it was his grandmother's.

Elizabeth was shocked and sickened by the letter. Perhaps Edith was right about Colin. He was leading a double life and this letter proved it. Elizabeth knew this revelation would devastate Rose and Mia. She re-sealed the letter and put in on Edith's nightstand with her other mail.

On Christmas Eve, the tradition was for Lady Rose and Mia to give gifts to her staff. Lady Rose and Mia asked Elizabeth to come to the great room where there was a large Christmas tree. All the other ser-vants had received their gifts. Edith would normally be there too but she left that morning for home because her mother was ill.

Elizabeth noticed Lady Rose was wearing a diamond swan necklace. "My lady, that is such a lovely necklace. Is it new?"

Rose smiled and looked at the necklace. "It's from Colin. He wants me to remember the swans on the lake."

Elizabeth tried to be upbeat. "Of course, that's so romantic."

"I got something from Colin too." Mia showed Elizabeth a sterling heart-shaped locket. "This locket belonged to his grandmother. He had given it to his wife, but now he wants me to have it."

"Mia, I don't understand. You said the locket belonged to Colin's wife?"

"Yes."

Rose tried to clarify. "The locket was his grandmother's and it's spe-cial to him. I thought it was endearing that he gave it to Mia."

Elizabeth's head was spinning now. How could Colin send a love let-ter to Abigail describing a locket Mia now had? She wondered if there were two lockets.

Lady Rose handed Elizabeth a gift. She opened it and it was an expensive scarf and well chosen for her as always. After the gifts, Mia and Rose went to their rooms to finish packing for a trip to Countess Winston's for Christmas. Elizabeth followed Mia and closed the door.

The locket intrigued Elizabeth. She asked to see it and examined it closely.

Mia said, "There is something unusual about it."

She took the locket from around her neck and opened it. It opened like a normal locket. Inside was a picture of Colin. She pushed on the inside and a hidden compartment opened, revealing a delicate jeweled butterfly.

Elizabeth gasped, "Oh, that's beautiful."

"This is special to Colin because his grandmother loved butterflies and she told him the butterfly story. Colin's grandfather was a watchmaker. He made this. See his initials on the inside: C.K.—Colin Kirkpatrick. Colin's maternal grandfather."

Elizabeth concluded, "There can only be one of these in the world."

"You're right. This is the only one."

"This is so lovely. I'm so happy for you."

"I love Colin so much. Weren't his gifts so thoughtful?"

"They are. Thank you for showing them to me. I'll miss you during the holidays."

"If you would like to, please come after Christmas and stay with me at grandmummy's country estate."

"I think I will. I'll go home tomorrow to be with my family for a few days then I'll come to see you. I need your help on a mystery I'm trying to solve. I'm trying to guess the ending of a book, but I'll tell you about it when I see you again and we can guess what the ending is together."

"That sounds like fun," Mia said. "I love mysteries."

"You have an enjoyable Christmas and I'll see you soon." Elizabeth kissed her on the forehead and left.

CHAPTER 44

———

AFTER CHRISTMAS, ELIZABETH WENT TO Lady Winston's estate. Everyone was happy to see her and after putting her luggage away, Elizabeth went to see Mia in her room. They sat on the bed and talked about Christmas. Mia asked about whether the young barrister had visited her. He had, so Elizabeth told Mia all the romantic details.

Mia said, "I have been waiting to learn about this mystery you described in the book you're reading."

"Oh yes, well I have spent a lot of time on this and I could use your help. Let me tell you the story. A young Scottish woman is in love with a man who must travel to America. On the voyage, a lovely and wealthy princess falls in love with the man. The young Scottish woman wants the man back but doesn't know how to do it. A servant of the princess doesn't want the man to marry her princess. The servant conspires with the young Scottish woman to try to break up the man and the princess. Do you understand so far?"

Mia listened intently and studied Elizabeth's face. "Who is Edith conspiring with?"

Shocked she figured it out so easily, Elizabeth replied, "Mia, this isn't about Edith."

Mia looked at her knowingly. "Elizabeth, I'm nearly ten. I know about these things. Also, if it was a book, you would have already read ahead."

"You're right. I'm struggling with a problem with Edith and I don't know what to do about it."

"Tell me and we can think it through together."

"I can't. I'm your governess. My job is to help and guide you, not share with you my problems."

"This involves me and my mother, doesn't it?" Mia's eyes narrowed.

"It does," Elizabeth admitted, "but I did something wrong to find out the information. I might be released if your mother finds out what I did." Elizabeth wrung her hands.

"I won't tell her."

"Are you sure you'll keep this a secret?"

"Yes."

Elizabeth told her the entire story starting first with the letter she copied about Lord Williams and about the love letter from Colin to Abigail.

Mia was shocked and shook her head in disgust. "What a mess this is! Edith dislikes Colin more than I thought. She has so many people involved in this conspiracy. I must tell you I have some doubts about this letter from Colin to Abigail."

"So do I. Also, I don't believe there are two lockets. One Colin gave to you plus one he gave to Abigail."

"Neither do I." Mia paused and thought about the situation. "I can't believe Colin is in love with two women. I can tell he loves Mummy completely."

"I do too. I believe the love letter is a lie. I think Abigail wrote it."

Mia stated with confidence, "I can tell Colin's handwriting. It's unique. Do you have the letter?"

"I can get it."

"When we get home, I'll examine it with you. What do we do if we discover the letter is a fraud?" asked Mia.

"We should wait. We will see if Edith acts on this in some way. Maybe she will reconsider and not do anything wrong."

"I hope so."

"I do too. Could you put away the locket when Edith is around? I don't want her to piece this together."

"I will. I also received a swan necklace from Colin. I can wear that. Let me show you."

Mia got it.

"This is stunning!" Elizabeth cooed. "It's like your mother's, only smaller. Colin really loves you."

"I know."

"Now the next step is for you to examine Edith's letter."

CHAPTER 45

———

AFTER THE HOLIDAYS, EDITH RETURNED to Lady Rose's estate. Edith read Abigail's letter and felt she had exactly what she needed to put a wedge between Colin and Rose. Her plan was to talk to Countess Winston during the voyage and use the letter to prove her point. She was quite confident of her strategy.

Elizabeth looked for the right time to get Abigail's letter from Edith's room. Twice she had planned to get it but Edith or others were around. The opportunity finally came when Lady Rose would be attending a dinner and Edith would be going with her. They would be away for the weekend.

Elizabeth snuck into Edith's room and retrieved the letter. She took it to Mia's room where they read it together. Mia got Colin's letters and they compared the handwriting.

Elizabeth concluded, "It's clear to me the handwriting is the same. Do you agree?"

"Yes, it is Colin's handwriting. I was praying someone else had written it," Mia said, dejected.

"So was I. Now what does this tell us?"

There was silence for a few seconds as they thought about the situation.

Elizabeth pointed to the beginning of the letter. "It says, 'To my dearest love'—that could be his wife or Abigail. There is no date so we are guessing who it is to. I feel the letter was to his wife, but we can't prove it."

"How would Abigail have gotten the letter?"

"She was her sister. I'm guessing she has access to her sister's old letters," offered Elizabeth.

"Sounds like a good guess to me. Now do we wait or should I go to Mother and talk to her?"

"No, I'll be in severe trouble if we go to your mother and Edith wiggles out of this in some way. I know it's hard, but we must wait until Edith shows herself. I think it will be on the voyage to America. Edith will not have any opportunity to be alone with Countess Winston before then."

Elizabeth let Mia read the copy of Lord Williams' letter.

"I knew I didn't like him. He was pretending to be nice to me, but he actually was planning to send me away."

Elizabeth nodded. "Yes, this shows you how conniving people can be. Edith doesn't care if your mother loves Colin or that he is a moral and upright man. She simply doesn't want her life changed in any way. Edith only cares about herself and no one else."

CHAPTER 46

JUNE 1907 – LIVERPOOL, ENGLAND

———◆———

THE TIME ARRIVED TO LEAVE for America. On departure day, Rose, Mia, the countess, and their large entourage arrived at the ship. Like the last voyage, Mia and Elizabeth watched the loading from the first-class deck. It was as exciting as last time, but this time there was no lost dog.

Mia had thought about what she could do to help prevent Edith from hurting her mother and Colin. She conceived a plan, however, she needed her grandmother to participate without the countess knowing she was helping. Mia knew her grandmother was smart and she decided to use the countess to help foil any plan Edith had to use the letter from Abigail.

The second day of the voyage, Mia sent an invitation to her grandmother for tea. The countess accepted, elated her granddaughter had invited her.

Teatime was in the grand dining room. Mia was there waiting for her grandmother, dressed in her best. She had the locket hidden until she got to tea so Edith couldn't see it. Mia put it on.

Her grandmother arrived on time and Mia stood and curtsied. "Good afternoon, Countess Winston."

The countess loved how grown up Mia was acting and responded, "Good afternoon, Lady Cavendish."

They sat and Mia immediately started to play with the locket to catch her grandmother's attention.

"Mia, what a lovely locket. Where did you get it?"

"Mr. Stuart gave it to me. There is a story behind it if you would like to hear it."

"I would."

"Colin received this locket from his grandmother. He later gave it to his wife but she died during childbirth. Colin asked Mummy if I could have it. She agreed and so I got it for Christmas."

Mia showed her the secret compartment and the butterfly inside.

"Colin's grandfather was a watchmaker. He made this. See his initials on the inside—C.K. for Colin Kirkpatrick, Colin's maternal grandfather. This locket is special because Colin's grandmother loved butterflies and had told him a heart tugging butterfly story. Would you like to hear the butterfly story?"

"I would."

Mia told her the story of Emily's butterfly and the countess teared.

At the end, the countess said, "Mia, that's a remarkable story. Did Mr. Stuart tell it to you?"

"Yes, he has told Mummy and me many interesting stories."

"You love him, don't you dear?"

"I do. Grandmummy, I think this locket is unique. Don't you think so?"

"I do."

"I believe Colin Kirkpatrick only made one."

"I'm sure Mr. Stuart's grandfather only made one because he made it for his wife. I'm sure it's unique and very special."

"Have you ever seen anything like this before?" Mia asked.

"Never."

"It makes me feel loved because Colin gave it to me and knowing no one else in the world has one."

The countess nodded. "You should feel that way."

"Grandmummy, do you fly kites?"

"No."

"Tomorrow if the weather is willing, I want you to fly a kite with me."

The countess balked. "Here on the ship?"

"Yes, Colin taught me and I think you will like it."

"I'm willing to try."

The discussion went exactly how Mia had hoped it would. If Edith showed Countess Winston the letter, Mia was sure her grandmother would notice the mention of the locket and would have questions about it.

While Mia was having tea with her grandmother, Edith asked the countess' lady's maid if she could have a few minutes alone with the countess on a confidential matter before they docked. The lady's maid arranged a meeting the next day after breakfast in the countess' room.

The next morning, Edith knocked on the countess' stateroom door and the lady's maid let her in.

"The countess is expecting you. Please have a seat."

Edith sat nervously. The countess came in and Edith stood to greet her.

"My lady, thank you for meeting me."

"You're welcome, my dear. Please sit."

They sat in the parlor alone.

"I have a confidential matter I need to discuss with you."

"Is it about Mr. Stuart?"

Surprised by her question, Edith replied, "Yes, my lady, it is."

"Let me guess, you're concerned he is a commoner."

"Yes, my lady."

"So am I, however, I'll reserve judgment until I meet him."

"My lady, I have come upon some information regarding Mr. Stuart you should know."

"Have you told this to Lady Rose?"

"No, my lady."

"Why not?"

"Lady Rose is infatuated with Mr. Stuart. She has been from the beginning and I'm afraid she will ignore what I have learned."

"What information do you have?"

"Mr. Stuart has a woman in Scotland whom he is in love with. He has been writing love letters to her."

The countess waved her hand to dismiss her statement and shook her head. "I have heard a lot of gossip about Mr. Stuart and none of it has ended up being true."

"I know this is true."

Sharply, the countess asked, "Who is this woman and how do you know about this?"

"The woman is Abigail McCarthy. She is Colin's sister-in-law. They fell in love after his wife died. My uncle lives in her village. I met the woman innocently at a poetry reading. One thing led to another and she told me she knew Colin Stuart. She said she loves Mr. Stuart and he loves her."

"She could be lying," the countess rebutted.

"I'm confident she isn't."

"What makes you so confident?"

"She gave me one of her love letters from Mr. Stuart. I have it here."

The countess took the letter and read it.

"Is this letter recent? There is no date on it," the countess asked shrewdly.

Edith nodded. "Yes, it is recent."

"How do you know?"

"She told me it was."

"I don't understand why the woman would give you a love letter. Love letters are precious and women always guard them."

"She still loves him and wants him back."

The countess probed further. "She wants me to intervene in the relationship between Rose and Colin. Am I correct?"

"Yes, my lady."

"You also want me to intervene?"

Edith sidestepped the question. "I want the best for Lady Rose."

There was a long pause. Edith sat there, uncomfortable.

"Is there anything else?"

"No, my lady."

The countess looked stern and handed the letter back. "You shouldn't share this with anyone else."

"Yes, my lady."

"You may go."

Edith left, unsure of what would happen next. Would the countess say something to Lady Rose? Edith was now having second thoughts.

Once Edith left, Countess Wilson thought about the conversation. Mia's locket kept rising in her mind. If the letter was from Colin and the woman was in love with him, she would have the locket because it would be a prized procession. The key to this mystery was the locket.

The countess wrote a note to her business manager, Mr. Compton, a hard-nosed man who always got every job done.

Mr. Compton. A woman in Aberlour, Scotland, Abigail McCarthy, has a locket made by Colin Kirkpatrick, a famous watchmaker. Tell her you are a jewelry collector and you heard from members of the Kirkpatrick family she might have the locket. Go there immediately and offer her five hundred pounds for it. Do not mention me. I must authenticate it before you buy it. Countess Winston.

She put the note in an envelope and wrote Mr. Compton's address on it. She called a porter and gave the note to him with instructions to send a telegram immediately.

CHAPTER 47

———◆———

THE MORNING THEY DOCKED IN New York, Countess Winston received a telegram from Mr. Compton.

Countess Winston. Abigail McCarthy is living in London. I have her address and will talk to her in person tomorrow. R. Compton.

The countess smiled because Mr. Compton was making progress. She had been thinking a lot about the love letter. Mr. Compton's next update would confirm for her the direction she would take.

The porters arrived and loaded their luggage into cabs for the short ride to the train station. Mr. Jones had made his first-class Pullman car available for them. The ride to Chicago and on to Lake Geneva was uneventful.

At the train station in Lake Geneva, Colin paced up and down the sidewalk. He was nervous not only because Rose and her family were coming but also because Mr. McCarthy and Abigail would arrive any day. Colin had received a telegram from Mr. McCarthy stating he would be there two weeks ago. Colin thought they had probably missed the ship or train connections somewhere along the line. Colin was praying they wouldn't all be on the same train. He had nightmares of Abigail meeting Edith and Rose.

The train pulled in and he saw Rose and Mia waving from the Pullman car. God had answered his prayers because the McCarthys didn't get off. Rose and her party departed the train. Colin approached Rose expecting at most she might kiss him on the cheek. Instead, she kissed him on the lips—a long kiss.

She pulled back. "I have missed you so."

Colin smiled broadly. "I missed you too."

Mia was standing next to him and she looked at him. "What about me?"

He hugged her and kissed her on the forehead. "My little angel, you are back! I have missed so much."

"I'm so happy to be here!"

"I have some fun things planned for you!" he replied.

Mia smiled and hugged him tight.

"Colin, I would like to introduce you to my mother, Countess Louise Winston."

Colin did a proper bow. "Lady Winston, it's a pleasure to meet you,"

Countess Winston was stern and cold. "I was hoping you wouldn't kiss me in public."

Colin smiled. "You're so lovely I considered it."

Surprised by his nice compliment, the countess smiled and replied, "I can see your Scottish charm already."

He returned her smile and inquired, "How was your journey?"

She replied, "Long and tiring. I had forgotten how far apart things are here in America."

"Yes, and you only came across a part of the country. Now your accommodations are ready. Let me make sure your luggage is all gathered. My dear ladies, I'll be back in a minute."

Colin stepped away and Rose whispered to her mother, "He is handsome, isn't he?"

"Yes, and charming too," replied the countess.

Colin got everyone together and with the aid of several carriages, he ferried them and their luggage to the hotel. After they checked in,

Colin said, "Tonight, I have dinner planned at my home. I'll return here at six o'clock."

He kissed Rose and Mia, said goodbye and left.

Soon everyone was in their rooms resting. A porter brought a telegram for Countess Winston. She opened it.

Countess Winston: Abigail McCarthy does not have the locket. Her deceased sister owned it. A Colin Stuart in America has it now. She would be willing to obtain it from him. Please advise. R. Compton.

She sent a telegram back:

Do nothing at this point. You may return home. Countess Winston.

Abigail never had the locket, the countess concluded. That meant the letter was to Colin's wife, not to the sister-in-law. Somehow Abigail had gotten one of Colin's letters.

It was a lovely day outside and the countess wanted to take a walk and think about what she should do. The town of Lake Geneva was scenic and the lake was nearby. She strolled around the town then sat on a bench that looked out over the lake.

Nearby, a young woman was finishing an oil painting. The countess could see the picture from where she was sitting.

"My dear, what a lovely painting! You have captured the scene so well."

The young woman turned to her. "Thank you! I love it here. This spot, with the sun reflecting on the water and the majestic swans, is a peaceful place for me."

"Yes, it's beautiful here."

The girl inquired, "I noticed your accent. Are you English?"

"Yes, I'm from London. I arrived today."

"Welcome to you."

"Thank you."

"There is a terrific story about our swans and an English lady who visited here last year. Would you like to hear it?"

The countess nodded. "I would."

The young woman put down her brush. "This is one of my favorite stories. A Scotsman moved into the town some time back. He met an English woman on his voyage to America and he made her an origami swan on the ship. He told her there was a real swan trapped in the paper and if she put the origami swan on a lake, it would turn into a live, beautiful swan. During the trip, he fell in love with the woman and he asked her to visit him here. When she arrived, she reminded him of his story about the swan. Secretly, he had men scour the countryside to find a perfect swan so he didn't disappoint her. The next morning after putting the paper swan on the lake, a mating pair of swans appeared. The swans you see are because of the love of a man for a woman he didn't want to disappoint."

"Young lady, what a romantic story. Is it true?"

"It's a true story. When I'm ready for marriage, I want a man like that."

The countess nodded. "My dear, in your story, do you know the English woman's name?"

"Oh yes, her name is Lady Rose. I'm not sure if Rose is a first or last name."

"It's her first name."

"Do you know her?"

"I do." Countess Winston smiled then asked. "What is your name?"

"Roberta Gentry."

"Roberta, I'm Louise Winston. Is your painting for sale?"

"Yes."

"How much are you asking?"

"Generally, my paintings sell for $25."

"Roberta, I'm willing to pay you two hundred dollars for it."

Roberta put her hand over her heart. "Madam, thank you! You are so generous. I will have it done later this week."

"That's fine. Please bring it to the hotel and I will have the money for you." The countess handed her a card.

The young lady's story about Colin made her heart melt. She began to love Colin as well.

CHAPTER 48

———

UPON RETURNING TO THE HOTEL, the countess had a plan in mind to resolve the mystery of the locket. She sent a note to Colin asking if Edith could attend dinner. He replied she would be welcome. The countess sent a note to Rose asking if Edith could attend dinner and one to Mia asking if she could wear her locket but keep it hidden.

Colin arrived at the hotel to pick up everyone. Countess Winston surprised him with a warm greeting and a kiss on the cheek. Rose noticed and thought it was unusual for her mother. Edith was surly as usual.

When they arrived at Colin's home, Mia wanted to see Supper and the swans. Colin took them down to the lake. Mia did not see the duck there. "Where's Supper?" she asked.

"I have a surprise for you." Colin took them to a small pen and Supper was there with her nine ducklings.

Mia squealed with joy. "Colin, you didn't tell me Supper is a mummy!"

"Yes, I was surprised. I wanted to wait and let her out once you were here so you could see her babies."

"May I let her out now?"

"Yes, the ducklings are big enough now."

Mia opened the gate and they all headed for the water.

The countess said, "Mr. Stuart, I heard a fabulous story today about the swans here."

Colin winced and said, "You can't believe all the stories you hear around here. Wisconsin people are known to stretch their stories a bit."

"Are they worse than Scots?" asked the countess with a chuckle.

Colin laughed. "No, we Scots are the best storytellers there are."

Rose laughed. "You're right about that."

"Is the swan story true?" asked the countess, smiling.

Colin examined her face carefully. "If you mean the story of the origami swan turning into a mating pair of swans, yes, that story is true."

"Is the rest of the story true?"

Colin looked at the countess. "If you heard a Scotsman loved an English baroness so much he would do anything for her, the story is true." He winked at Rose who winked back.

The countess said, "You must make me an origami animal."

"Of course," Colin agreed. "Do you have anything in mind?"

"I have always wanted a giraffe. I assume if you make me an origami giraffe, one will magically appear at my farm in England."

Colin laughed. "Maybe we should start smaller. How about a duck or swan? I'm good at making those appear." Everyone laughed except for Edith, who was solemn.

They walked to the house and prepared for dinner. The countess had Edith sit directly across from her. Once dinner started, the countess started the conversation. "Colin, the locket you gave to Mia is lovely. Please tell us about it."

Edith asked, "What locket?"

"This one. Colin gave it to me at Christmas." Mia pulled it out from under the collar of her dress.

Edith was shocked and grew pale.

Colin said, "My grandfather made it for my grandmother. He was a watchmaker."

"It looks like a rather common locket," commented Edith, trying to help her position.

Colin disagreed, "No, it's one of a kind."

The countess asked, "Colin, you owned only one of these?"

Colin nodded. "Yes."

The countess stared at Edith. "Mia, please show everyone the butterfly."

Mia opened the locket and showed off the hidden compartment. "You may not be able to see it, but there is a jeweled butterfly inside."

Edith asked sharply, "How can you be sure there is only one locket?"

Colin started to reply, but the countess interrupted, "I checked with a woman in Scotland who might have a second one. She doesn't have one and never did. There is only one and Mia has it. Anyone who says otherwise is lying. Any letter saying so is a fraud."

Mia knew what she meant and so did Edith. Mia smiled and Edith frowned.

Colin said, "I'm missing something. Who is the woman in Scotland?"

The countess waved her hand. "She isn't important. Your gift to Mia is so endearing. It's one of a kind and I love it. I also love the swan necklaces. After hearing about the swans and how they got here, I think I'll get a swan necklace."

Colin nodded his head. "I'll have one made for you."

"That would be wonderful! Edith, don't you love the swan necklaces and the locket?"

Edith frowned. "Yes madam, I do."

"Now Mr. Stuart—would you mind if I called you Colin?" asked the countess.

"Please do."

"Colin, I must tour your distillery. I want to taste your whisky. What does Rose call it? Let me think, the angel's nectar. Is that correct?"

Colin said, "Some people call it that. I would love for you to visit."

That evening when Edith returned to the hotel, there was a letter for her. It was from Abigail.

Edith was hopeful she could still salvage something. She prayed Abigail was somewhere in town.

Dear Edith,

I will not be coming to America. I decided to change my life. I took the money from the ship ticket to America plus my savings and moved to London. I have a small part in a play here and I am making ends meet, barely. I have met several gentlemen and I am making progress on that front.

I decided Colin was never going to be with me. He was always frank with me about it. I never wanted to accept it but I do now. I apologize to you for making you believe something different.

I also must admit to you the letter I gave to you from Colin was not mine but my sister's. I'm so sorry for deceiving you. I feel so guilty about it. At that time, I felt desperate to do whatever I could to try to keep Colin. I hope the letter has not caused you any trouble.

I pray you can forgive me for everything I did.

Sincerely, Abigail

P.S. My father went on to America without me. I would not be surprised if he never shows up. He gets lost walking to work.

Edith felt defeated and if the countess told Rose about their conversation and the letter, her career was over. The only thing now was to try to put on a happy face and suffer through her stay in America even though she knew it would be difficult.

EPILOGUE

——◆——

THE DAY AFTER THE DINNER, the countess told Rose she thought Colin was a perfect gentleman and he would be right for Rose and Mia. Rose immediately told Colin.

After receiving the permission of the countess and Mia, Colin took Rose down by the lake with the swans in the background and he asked her to marry him which she readily said yes. They agreed to return to England for the wedding.

Countess Winston returned to England to make the wedding arrangements and she asked Rose if Edith could go with her to help. The countess left one of her lady's maids for Rose. Edith went second-class and didn't interact with the countess or her staff till the end of the voyage.

The day before they arrived in England, Countess Winston summoned Edith to her stateroom where she told Edith she was to resign immediately. The countess told her to send a telegram to Lady Rose telling her she wanted to stay in England and was resigning. Only if Edith resigned, would she get a much-needed reference for another position. Edith had no choice so she resigned. The countess recommended Edith to a no titled acquaintance of hers who she didn't like but deserved someone like Edith. Edith accepted the position at lower pay.

A day after the countess left for England, Mr. McCarthy finally arrived. He said Abigail had moved to London and didn't want to come. He explained he was late because he had decided to go out west first. He had traveled to several states and the west wasn't at all like he had read in his cheap novels. The towns in the novels were vibrant and colorful, however, in real life they were either dusty or terribly muddy. The cowboys were rough and not overly friendly to an English tourist. He stayed in Wisconsin two days. He borrowed money from Colin to get home and didn't pay the hotel bill, which Colin had to cover.

Rose and Mia stayed in Wisconsin with Elizabeth until six weeks before the wedding. Rose and Colin married in London in October and it was breathtaking in its splendor. Soon afterward, Rose and Mia returned to America along with Elizabeth and a new lady's maid.

Countess Winston put the painting of the swans in her bedroom. She often thought about the swans on that beautiful lake and how they were there because of the love Colin had for Rose and how he couldn't disappoint her. She loved Colin and never thought about him being a commoner.

Rose, Colin, and Mia returned to England every year to check on her business and to visit the countess and Colin's family. Colin and Rose purchased Mr. Jones share of the business. The whiskey business continued to grow and prosper.

Mia loved America and developed several friends there. She prayed every night she would soon have a sister, but she also said in her prayers that she would tolerate a brother.

Every Sunday afternoon when the weather was good, Rose, Mia, and Colin flew kites on the large hill nearby and had a picnic. Mia always chose a butterfly kite and Colin chased hers with his dragon kite. The ladies expected Colin to entertain them with a new story each week and he always did. No dragons showed up in Wisconsin, however, Colin told Mia to expect one at any time.

The end of Volume 1.

The story continues in Volume 2 of the **Real Whisky Has No "E"** series.